FIRE ANGELS

FIRE ANGELS

Christine Green

This first world edition published in Great Britain 2001 by
SEVERN HOUSE PUBLISHERS LTD of
9–15 High Street, Sutton, Surrey SM1 1DF.
This first world edition published in the USA 2001 by
SEVERN HOUSE PUBLISHERS INC of
595 Madison Avenue, New York, NY 10022.

British Library Cataloguing in Publication Data

Green, Christine, 1944–
    Fire angels
    1. Serial murders
    2. Detective and mystery stories
    I. Title
    823.9'14 [F]

ISBN 0–7278–5733–9

Typeset by Palimpsest Book Production Limited,
Polmont, Stirlingshire, Scotland.
Printed and bound in Great Britain by
MPG Books Ltd, Bodmin, Cornwall.

Prologue

*H*e stared at his handiwork; soon the bright flames would lick at her feet, slowly at first then bursting into bright orange, as if she were being kissed by the sun. Death would become life and just for that moment they would be together in heaven with God.

He made a final adjustment to the faggots of newspaper that lay at her feet. He could feel sweat on his forehead, hear his own heart drumming in his ears, hear the wind and the rain outside.

He took the box of matches from his pocket and continued to stare at her. Even now with her skin so mottled her body looked wonderful: her breasts proud and erect, her belly soft and round, her hair tumbling to her smooth shoulders – she was magnificent.

He struck the match. He had forgiven her now. She would soon be another of his fire angels. Waiting for him.

One

A country road, past midnight, no moon, rain as noisy as a riveter's gun battering and filling every dip in the tarmac, every gutter and gully, puddles becoming ponds, roads overcome by rivers. It had rained all day. Earlier, gales had torn down the oldest trees and now hefty branches seemed as fragile as match sticks, except that is, when they lay in the path of drivers.

Detective Sergeant Denise Caldecote, known as Denni, manoeuvred and swore as she negotiated either flooded roads or parts of trees. She tested her brakes after water reached the hubcaps and was grateful that no other drivers seemed to be braving the storm. As she drove on she began to feel slightly disorientated due to the noise of wind and rain, the lack of white lines and cat's eyes and, worst of all, the lack of street lighting.

Somewhere nearby was derelict Haddon's Farm, situated between the villages of Marston and Merridale. It was reported to be on fire. She'd been off duty when DCI Fenton had rung and asked her to attend. She'd been awake, but curled up in bed under her duvet with a mug of cocoa, a mere four pages away from a happy ending. She only read novels that delivered escapism and she resented this intrusion into her fantasies. Everyone else, she presumed, was either busy or had been drinking. Alec Fenton, pot-bellied, near retirement and obnoxious, had designated arson attacks, even a dustbin fire as being zero-tolerance rated. Consequently, CID had to attend each one. Denni's job was to interview all bystanders and witnesses, file a report and in Fenton's words 'before the little sods go too far' get the proverbial 'result'. 'The little sods' were thought by the fire brigade to be young boys under twelve from the local town of Harrowford's council estate. Denni reasoned that with no public transport, and a major storm in progress, young lads would hardly be the culprits this time. Equally, it seemed an odd time for any arsonist to choose, young or old.

Denni eventually found the turn-off point for Haddon's Farm, she saw the sign a little late and had to swerve in sharply. In the narrow lane the car headlights caught the churned-up wet mud and the overhanging half-torn-down hedgerows, showing that at least one fire appliance had fought its way through. After the dark lane the view at the top was almost a relief. She wasn't wasting her time, this was a proper fire.

From the car, with the engine still running and the windscreen wipers running at top speed, Denni watched as the fire-fighters directed their hoses towards the orange spouts of flames which emerged from the smashed windows of the stone farmhouse like demented snakes. Smoke drifted slowly upwards, no worse than a chimney fire. About twenty yards away a stone barn with a tiled roof and double doors held the attention of the second fire team. Neither flames nor smoke emerged from there.

It was then that she saw in the wet shimmering light two figures standing to the left of the farmhouse. Fires always attracted onlookers but they made a strange duo or trio, if the dog was included. One appeared to be a young boy wearing a black anorak and jeans. The other, an older man, holding a tan-coloured mongrel on a lead, wore a hooded mac so that she couldn't see his face.

Reluctantly leaving the warmth of the car to brave the wind and rain Denni had almost reached the 'spectators' when one of the fire-fighters intercepted her.

'Are you the DS?' he asked. His tone suggesting surprise. She nodded, the rain hitting her face as she looked up at him.

'Your gaffer is on his way . . . there's a body in the barn,' he said, then added, almost as an afterthought, 'Could be murder.'

Glancing over towards the barn she saw three fire-fighters in a huddle just outside the barn door. If there were any good tyre tracks or footprints either the rain or the fire-fighters' boots had long since obliterated them. 'I'll talk to the "audience" first . . . thanks.'

The fireman nodded, murmured something into his chin about paraffin then, heavy footed, returned to his crew who were now 'damping down' and doing final checks on the remains of the farmhouse.

Denni knew her first priority was to speak to the onlookers who may have witnessed more than a fire. They still stood in the same position side by side, as if mesmerised either by the now dying fire or by the activities of the fire-fighters. What the hell were they doing there anyway? It was after midnight, in pouring rain . . . even the dog looked wretched.

Detective Inspector Thomas Rydell was alone and asleep when the phone rang. He found the noise as irritating as a wasp, but once he'd picked up the receiver he was immediately wide awake and dressing himself with his free hand as he listened to vague details of a woman's body being found at Haddon's Farm.

Rydell shook his pillows, pulled up the duvet, walked the short distance to his kitchen, made himself half a cup of instant coffee, drank it quickly, washed and rinsed the cup, dried it carefully on a paper towel, then returned the cup to the tray. In the bathroom he thought for a moment about having a shave, felt his face and chin, decided he hadn't got the time to spare and contented himself with combing his hair. It never failed to surprise him that he was going

grey, he was only thirty-six after all. At least he wasn't
going bald he told himself, if anything his thick dark hair
seemed to grow faster than ever.

He'd lived, since his divorce, in a one-bedroom flat on
the second of four floors and he never left his small
home without performing the little rituals that made his
mind easier. Partly it was a sense of responsibility to the
other residents but mostly it was because he couldn't help
himself. He simply had to check and recheck that the oven
and hob was switched off, that all plugs were out, that the
taps didn't drip and that all windows were closed. As he
left by the back door he set the burglar alarm then locked
the door and walked down the fire escape. He looked up
at the security lights, a new addition to the flats, his idea,
and felt well pleased that the other residents had willingly
agreed they were necessary.

Rydell had no specific fears, no one was after him, or
not that he knew of, he simply feared disorder. If he had
his environment under control, he had control.

Once in his car he began to relax, he drove too fast but
he was aware that his rituals were time consuming and he
didn't want to be thought slow. The scant details he'd been
given sounded like murder. If it was, this would be his first
case in West Mercia. He'd recently transferred from the
Met following post-divorce depression treated with Prozac.
He wasn't sure if the Prozac had worked wonders or if his
resuming cross-country running had done the trick but now
he was feeling fit and looking forward to proving himself.
His only misgivings were how he would cope with his DS.
He supposed she was in her late twenties or early thirties,
she was attractive, even pretty, had eyes the colour of pale
sultanas, bottle-blonde hair and was easy going and friendly.
But she wasn't his type. He liked tall slender brunettes with
dark eyes and pale skin. Your trouble, old son, he told
himself, is that you're still in love with your ex-wife and
the idea of getting involved with any woman, right type

or not, frightens you shitless. In fact he was beginning to wonder if his sex drive hadn't sunk without trace in a sea of Prozac. Not that Denise Caldecote had shown any interest in him at all. He found that reassuring because prior to joining the police force she'd been a psychiatric nurse, although she couldn't, he'd decided, recognise an ex-depressive, just by looking. And, if she had noticed some of his little . . . eccentricities, she'd never made any comment or even lifted an eyebrow.

By the time he arrived at Haddon's Farm there was only one fire appliance remaining and the fire crew of that were obviously ready to leave. It was also obvious that any clues, such as tyre tracks, would have long since been lost so he parked midway between the shell of the farmhouse and the barn. He could see Denni sheltering from the rain just inside the open double doors of the barn. She had her hands in her pockets trying to look nonchalant but not succeeding. Denni was less than average height for a police officer and he'd heard on the grapevine that she'd been turned down by several forces on those grounds. Now, soaking wet with windswept hair clinging round her face and wearing a purple skirt, black boots and a black jacket it crossed his mind that in the six months he'd known her she'd never worn trousers. Maybe, he thought, she had a bum complex. His wife, spindle thin, had been phobic about her rear. Ex-wife he corrected himself once again.

'What have we got?' he asked.

'Female, Guv. I haven't ventured inside yet. The fireman who found her says it could be murder.'

The barn, constructed of local red stone, had a tiled roof and a quick glance inside showed a high ceiling with no tiers. Rydell shone his torch upwards. He could see a light bulb high up, but there appeared to be no switch. There was a smell of paraffin, wood smoke and something pungent he didn't recognise. The floor was wet and sodden: mud mixed with bits of straw. He swung the beam of the torch to inspect the high ceiling, a criss-cross of wooden beams hung with the webs of countless spiders.

Alongside him Denni used her own torch to gaze into the murky interior. They moved further into the barn being systematic, taking it slowly, trying not to miss a detail or an oddity but all the time expecting to see a body. There was a spade in one corner, a coil of rope and a wooden ladder propped against the farthest wall.

The realisation that they had walked too far into the barn occurred simultaneously. The body had to be behind them. Spinning round they saw in the right-hand corner pierced by their torchlight, the naked, upright body of a young woman with a hangman's noose round her neck. Her arms were outstretched, secured by rope to wall hooks. Her bare feet were supported on an upturned wooden box. The rope round her neck had been thrown over a beam and then secured around another hook in the wall. At her feet were faggots of newspapers tied into bundles, some had singed slightly, some had not.

Neither of them spoke. Rydell had never before seen a body so ritually arranged in death. Her head was pulled taut, somehow giving her whole frame an almost proud appearance. Her long thick red hair obscured most of her face; a slight gust of wind raised a few strands giving a sudden image of animation. But in the bluish white of her skin there was only the cold stillness of death.

For a few moments they listened to the rain drumming on the slate roof and to the wind that now seemed louder than ever. Then with a slight pinging noise Denni slipped on a pair of rubber gloves and moved nearer to the body. She didn't plan to touch the body but she might touch *something*. With her torch beam she lingered on the woman's neck. With a glance at Rydell she placed one foot on the box. He nodded his permission. Once on the box, Denni regretted her act of bravado. In such close proximity to the body she could smell decomposition. She wanted to throw up. But if this was some

7

weird suicide she needed to know. With one finger she lifted
the rope slightly. At first she'd thought the rope was black, now
close up she could see it was purple. There were no rope marks
around the neck. Another inconsistency struck her. The hair,
unlike most other corpses she'd seen, was not dishevelled and
matted; this was fresh looking and bouncy . . . and neat. As
if the murderer had groomed her hair after death.

Denni shivered and became aware that the hand that held
the torch was shaking slightly. Rydell helped her down from
the box. 'Rather you than me,' he muttered.

She paused to take several deep breaths. 'No rope marks,'
she said.

The sound of cars arriving came as a welcome relief.

The arrival of the scene-of-crime team and the police
surgeon meant that she and Rydell could vacate the dark
barn. She began shivering again; a chill seemed to have crept
into her body that had nothing to do with the weather.

The two spectators, having stood around for a little longer,
left together by the bridle path. The man with the dog,
Vernon Greenly, carried a torch and murmured occasional
words of encouragement to his tan mongrel. 'Soon be home,
Rusty' or 'not long now'. Vernon was forty-two years old,
divorced and had returned to the village of Marston to live
with his widowed mother, bringing with him the remnants
of a ten-year marriage: the dog, a hundred or so books, his
clothes and his computer.

The fellow fire watcher, Liam King, was eighteen years
old, looked sixteen and lived in a rented room in a house
occupied by five other men because he had nowhere else to
go. He spent his days aimlessly, and his nights drinking and
playing bar billiards or merely wandering around. He rarely
went back to his room before one a.m.

'Will the Old Bill pay us a visit tonight?' asked Liam
without looking at Vernon.

There was a pause as Vernon wiped rain from his thin

face. 'Let me put it like this, if someone rings your doorbell in the early hours it will be them.' Then he added as an afterthought, 'I suppose we could be suspects.'

'What for?'

'Arson . . . murder.'

Liam stopped in his tracks. 'Shit,' he murmured.

'Just think before you speak,' said Vernon quietly.

'Yeah, I'll do that.'

At the end of the bridle path they walked off in different directions. Liam knew his way in the dark and Vernon hardly needed his torch because Rusty knew the way. As Vernon approached his mother's cottage he was disappointed to see her bedroom light was on. He held Rusty back and waited at the gate hoping she would return to bed. After several minutes, during which the dog began to whine piteously, Vernon could wait no longer. He unlatched the gate to a loud creak and, with Rusty pulling excitedly on the lead, took a deep breath and inserted his key in the lock.

Outside the barn in the warmth of a car with the engine running Rydell and Denni sat, waiting. The police surgeon had arrived and left within ten minutes, cameras were flashing and the white boiler-suited SOC team were bagging samples of the environment.

The yellow and black plastic tape now sealed off the bridle path, the farmhouse and the barn to all comers. It fluttered noisily in the still strong wind. A proper inch by inch search would have to wait until daylight. Rydell felt uneasy doing nothing and he tapped his fingers on the steering wheel. Denni found it irritating but said nothing.

'She fits the description,' he said.

'Who of?'

'Local missing woman – in her twenties, medium build, red hair, five six.'

Denni had heard talk in the canteen of a local woman being missing, which wasn't that unusual. Thousands of adults countrywide left home every year and they rarely rated a major investigation. Most returned after a few weeks. Some, of course, never returned, alive.

'Where's she from?'

'Gaddine's Bridge – wife of the head teacher of Harrowford Comprehensive.'

'How long has she been missing?'

'This is the eighth day.'

Denni said sharply, 'But the doc said—'

'I know,' said Rydell. 'He thinks she's been dead three days max. So our murderer kept her for some time or she met up with him three days ago. Judging by the preparations and the ritual, she wasn't killed on a whim – it was well planned.' He paused. 'I think he could well be a complete nutter.'

Denni didn't comment on that, she merely asked, 'Where to next, boss?'

'We'll go and see our fire watchers,' he said with a smile. 'Wake them up – if they can sleep of course.' The smile transformed his face. Unsmiling, his thin face, aquiline nose and rather cold blue eyes could be rather intimidating. Denni remained faintly in awe of him and his reputation, he was six foot two in height and it was known that he was a keen cross-country runner and even belonged to a gym. Not that he seemed overly muscular as a result. First impressions were of the lean and hungry type. She was usually unprejudiced, but she did hold major reservations about people who enjoyed any sort of suffering or discomfort. Denni liked warmth and comfort, hot perfumed baths, soft floaty clothes and the nearest she got to physical exercise was the occasional line dance. Even that was tinged with an ulterior motive. She'd once read a novel where the hero was a cowboy, so she'd gone line dancing in the hope of meeting her own personal hero. Mostly she'd just met cranks with plaid shirts over pot bellies, wearing large stetsons. Her pastimes formed part of her secret life, a buffer against the rawness of police work and criminal lowlife. Reading novels and line dancing had about as much kudos as nude gardening and, like an alcoholic, Denni jealously guarded the evidence. After all, she was a nineties' woman who was supposed to down a pint with the blokes, have one-night stands and develop a good physique or at least worry about it. Unlike the thirty-something women of novels Denni was more preoccupied with the care of her mother than her calorie intake. Her mother Jean had been widowed at fifty-six when Denni was twenty and in the middle of her nurse's training. Twelve years on Jean had become elderly and depressed. In fact, she had become a cross that Denni resented bearing.

All in all, she thought, she and Rydell had little in common other than a desire to escape as often as possible from the real world.

As they drove into the village Rydell asked, 'Do you know anything about knots?' Denni shook her head. 'I wore a tie at school and I can do a Windsor knot.'

'You'd better find out then, because chummy used a noose and two other types of knot to bind her feet and hands.'

'A sailor?'

'Tinker, tailor, soldier or bloody sailor, we're going to find him.'

'Come to think of it, Guv, all those could probably tie knots.'

He didn't reply. He knew, both by instinct and experience, they were hunting a 'sicko' and a deep uneasiness settled on him.

Two

Three a.m. chimed from a grandfather clock inside Vernon Greenly's cottage. He opened the door promptly, wearing a black terry bathrobe and a wide-awake expression. Now Denni could see his face properly she saw it was thin and sharp featured, his greyish complexion reddened slightly by broken veins on his cheeks. He seemed flustered but offered them tea which they accepted and, as they waited for Vernon to reappear from the kitchen, took the opportunity to be a little nosy.

The cottage living room was cramped and busy with chintz, brassware, potted plants, ornaments ranged along the mantelpiece above an open fire and a variety of china plates on every wall. There were antimacassars and lace doilies and Denni thought she could smell lavender. It was an old lady's home and there was no sign of the dog.

When Vernon returned he carried a tray of cups and saucers and used a tea strainer when he poured the tea. 'I've lived here with my mother,' he explained in a quiet voice, 'since my divorce.'

'What do you do for a living, Mr Greenly?' asked Rydell.

'I'm a contract worker – computer programmer – between contracts at the moment.'

Rydell nodded and stared at him as he sipped his tea.

'What made you go to the farm in such weather?' asked Denni.

Vernon shrugged. 'Nothing *made* me. I always walk the dog very late, whatever the weather.'

'And do you always walk to the farm?'

'Yes. At least once a day.'

'Why?'

He didn't seem surprised by the question or its bluntness.

'Rusty likes it. Lots of interesting smells and I can let him off the lead. Otherwise I'd have to keep to the road.'

Rydell, having finished his tea, placed his cup and saucer carefully back on the tray and said, 'So, the dog found the fire?'

'Not exactly. Rusty got a bit excited so I kept him on the lead. He smelt the fire before I did, but then he would . . . being a dog.'

'Tell me exactly what happened from the time you left here,' urged Rydell, 'all the details. Don't leave anything out.'

Vernon's hand trembled as he settled the cup back in its saucer. 'I haven't got anything to hide,' he said. 'I left here with Rusty about twenty past eleven – that was later than usual but I was hoping the rain might stop, but it didn't, so off we went. I walked through the village and started up the bridle path. As I said, Rusty was excited and at the end of the path I saw the farm was on fire. So I rang nine nine nine on my mobile. It was about fifteen minutes before the fire brigade arrived. The sergeant turned up a little later.'

Rydell stared at him. 'That's your statement, is it?'

'I didn't know I was making one,' he said.

'Not technically perhaps,' agreed Rydell, 'but if you were, that would be near as dammit – would it?'

Greenly nodded. 'Yes. I can't think of anything else.'

'What about the boy?' asked Denni.

A momentary expression of puzzlement crossed Greenly's face. 'Oh yes . . . I don't know him. I've seen him walking around. That's all.'

'When did he turn up?' asked Rydell.

'Just after me. We just stood there watching the fire. That's not a criminal offence, is it?'

'Certainly isn't, Mr Greenly. I just wondered why you didn't mention him.'

'We didn't talk to each other.'

'Why not?'

'We just watched.'

'Did you find it exciting?'

Greenly coloured slightly. 'Sort of,' he said with a shrug.

'What precisely did you find exciting?' asked Rydell. 'The men in big boots or the fire itself?'

'The fire of course. I'd never been so near to a fire before.'

'And when did you realise there was a body inside the barn?'

'When I heard the fire-fighters talking about it.'

'And what did you think?'

Greenly looked puzzled. 'What do you mean?'

Rydell stared at him silently while Vernon looked increasingly uncomfortable. 'I thought . . .' he said eventually, 'I thought it might be the missing woman.'

'Why should it have been her?'

He shrugged. 'Why not? It seemed a logical deduction to make.'

'How did you know she was missing?'

'I heard people talking about it in the post office.'

'What people?'

Greenly looked irritated. 'I don't know their names. Mothers with children. I heard them saying the head teacher's wife had walked out a week ago in the middle of the night. So I assumed it was her.'

'You assumed she was already dead and just happened to be in the barn?'

'Yes. I suppose so.'

'Wouldn't your first assumption be that she died in the fire?'

'No,' he replied swiftly. 'The fire in the barn hadn't really got going. There wasn't even much smoke.'

'But you thought the dead body was the missing wife?'

Greenly's hands clenched and unclenched. 'I don't know why you are labouring the point, Detective Inspector.'

'I'm trying to get to the truth,' said Rydell softly. 'A body is found and you seem sure that it's the missing woman. Is that because you knew her?'

'No, I didn't know her! I've only just moved back here. I don't really know anyone locally.'

'Except Liam King.'

'Who?'

'The lad you were watching the fire with.'

'I didn't know that was his name.'

There was a long pause and in the silence Greenly began to look increasingly uncomfortable. 'There isn't any more I can tell you. I was merely walking my dog. I just guessed it was the missing woman. I'd be grateful if you could leave now. My mother's elderly and not in good health.'

Rydell nodded. 'It doesn't end here, Mr Greenly. We'd like to take away the clothes you wore last night.'

'Why?'

'For forensic to take a look at.'

'Don't you need a warrant for that?'

'No. Do you have something to hide?'

'I do not,' he snapped. 'I've done nothing wrong. You can have the clothes with pleasure.'

He presented a black plastic bag of damp clothes to Rydell moments later. 'There's everything in that bag. I'd like to have them back as soon as possible.'

At the front door Rydell said, 'There were one or two things missing from your account of events.'

'What?'

'That's for both you and me to think about, Mr Greenly. We'll call back later sometime to see if you've remembered.'

Vernon Greenly sighed audibly.

'By the way,' asked Denni, 'where do you keep the dog?'

For the first time he managed a tight smile. 'Rusty sleeps on my bed. My mother won't have him downstairs. She says it affects her asthma.'

Outside, before they drove to Liam King's residence, Rydell asked, 'Well, what do you think of him?'

'Devious little sod.'

Rydell laughed. 'Cut the jargon,' he said with a grin, 'tell me what you really think.'

Liam King lived in a large, grim Edwardian house that was an eyesore in town or country. The paint peeled. The stone steps to the front door were deeply cracked and the stained glass above the front door was half boarded up with plywood. Even the phone entry system had been partly yanked away and to make it work it had to be pressed back against the wall.

King didn't even bother to ask who it was, he simply opened the front door. By the time Rydell and Denni had walked up three, dimly lit, flights of threadbare carpet they had encompassed the varying smells of male communal living – stale tobacco, BO, damp of uncertain origin, curry, cooking fat and beer – possibly vomited.

Liam stood at the open door of his room in a pair of blue boxer shorts, bare footed, smoking a roll-up. Here there was no chintz – no knick-knacks – just a basic bed, wardrobe, wooden table and chair, roaring gas fire and a two-seater sofa with foam, as bulbous as boils, peeping through holes in the material. In one corner was a plastic curtain, opened to reveal a sink, a Belling cooker and assorted unwashed plates and saucepans.

'It's a bit of a mess,' he said, waving his cigarette at the room. 'Do you want to sit down?'

Rydell and Denni shook their heads in unison. 'We've

just been to see Vernon Greenly,' began Rydell. 'He's been telling us about the fire. He was out walking his dog. What's your excuse?'

'I don't need one, do I? I only went for a walk.'

'Why?' asked Rydell.

Liam shrugged his narrow shoulders and then took a deep drag of his cigarette. 'I like walking. I don't sleep well . . . you wouldn't sleep well in this fucking dump. Some right morons live 'ere. I get out as much as I can.'

Rydell nodded. 'How often do you meet your friend?'

'What friend?'

'Vernon Greenly.'

''E's not a friend.'

Rydell stared at him and King grew uncomfortable. He stubbed out his cigarette clumsily into a saucer. 'I don't know why you think 'e's a friend. 'E's a posh git and 'e's old.'

Rydell smiled. 'Don't get upset, Liam. He just gave me the impression you two were quite friendly.'

'Well we're not,' he said sulkily.

'Tell me about your day – before you went walkabout.'

Liam perched on the edge of his bed. 'Same as usual on a Sunday. I got up late. Went to see my gran. She gave me a dinner and a tenner. I went to the pub, the Goat in the village – it stays open all day. I 'ad four pints of cider then I came back 'ere – 'ad a kip, watched TV downstairs with two of the other blokes, then someone came in pissed so I went out for a walk.'

'Why did you go to Haddon's Farm?'

He paused for a moment, then said with a sly smile, 'I like it there. It's creepy. The farmer there shot 'imself.'

'Why should that interest you?'

'I dunno. Perhaps I'm warped.'

'Have you ever been inside the farmhouse?'

Liam paled slightly. 'It's not a crime . . . Yeah. I've bin

17

inside. I got in round the back . . . just 'ad a look round and came out again.'

'What about the barn?'

'Never bothered . . . nothing in there.'

'Until tonight.'

'Yeah well . . . we 'eard from the firemen there was a body in there.'

'And what did you think?'

'What was I supposed to think?' he asked, small jaw jutting, trying to look aggressive.

'Now, Liam,' said Rydell softly, 'I ask the questions because I'm the Bill. You answer them because you're a suspect . . . sorry . . . witness.'

'I went for a walk . . . I haven't done nothing.'

'I haven't said you've done anything wrong . . . yet,' said Rydell slowly. 'I just have a deeply suspicious nature. That's why I put it to good use and joined the police force. Now tell me exactly when you met up with Vernon Greenly.'

Liam folded his arms protectively across his white hairless chest. 'I 'eard his dog barking first. Then I saw him at the top of the lane. I walked up and saw the farmhouse was on fire.'

'What were your feelings when you saw the fire?'

Liam looked puzzled. Rydell guessed he wasn't used to discussing his feelings – feeling 'pissed off' was probably the nearest he got to verbalising how he felt and now he had to struggle to find an answer. 'Well . . . er . . .' he stumbled '. . . I was sorry it was burning. I told you I liked the place.'

'Did you enjoy watching the fire?'

There was a long pause. 'Yeah . . . it was sort of exciting. But I didn't start it . . . I didn't.'

'Who do you think did?'

'I dunno.'

'Did you hear anything or see anyone?'

'No, only the bloke and his dog. I keep telling you.'

Rydell shrugged. 'How strange. If someone else started the fire and the barn fire didn't fully take hold it seems funny you missed the arsonist. Because he must have been there.'

Liam by now looked thoroughly miserable. Rydell signalled with a slight movement of his head that Denni should take over. 'Don't look so worried, Liam,' said Denni. 'We have to ask these questions. The fire isn't our main concern – the body is. What do you know about that?'

'I don't know sod all.'

'You knew it was a woman?'

'Yeah . . . I 'eard that.'

'Young or old?'

'I don't know,' he snapped. 'I didn't see 'er.'

'Do you think she died in the fire?'

'There weren't no flames.'

'You got near enough to see, did you?'

'No . . . you're trying to fucking trap me.'

'No I'm not, Liam. Just tell me what you saw.'

'Just a bit of smoke—' He broke off. 'Look I'm fed up with this. I just went for a walk. I often go up there. I've never been in trouble. Just because I'm not working don't mean I'm a criminal.'

'Don't get upset, Liam. I only want to ask you one more question. Have you heard there's a woman missing from Gaddine's Bridge?'

'No. It's posh there, init? Never been there.'

Denni smiled. 'I see. So you haven't heard anyone talking about her?'

He shook his head. 'No. I go to the pub and talk football and cars. I don't know what goes on round 'ere. I'm not interested.'

'Fair enough. Just one more thing – we'd like the clothes you wore tonight.'

Liam's mouth dropped open in shock and he paled slightly. 'No . . . you can't 'ave 'em. I 'aven't got many clothes.'

Denni, at this point, felt genuinely sorry for him and looked to Rydell for guidance. Any clothes taken could be gone for weeks. Rydell thought for a moment and then said, 'Let me look at your shoes.'

Liam made his way miserably to the kitchen area and returned with a pair of trainers stuffed with newspaper. They were soaking wet and caked with mud. Rydell looked carefully at the soles. Liam still seemed to be in a vague state of shock. Then he said, almost in tears, 'They're the only pair I've got.'

Any bravado he may have shown was now gone. He looked like a bullied child awaiting the next blow.

'OK,' said Rydell. 'I've clocked them. Don't get rid of them. If you've been telling the truth, there won't be a problem, will there?'

'No, mate,' agreed Liam, visibly relieved.

'Detective Inspector to you.'

'Yeah . . . yeah.' His cockiness reviving, he turned to Denni. 'Are you really a detective?'

She nodded. 'Don't ever doubt it.'

Outside, Rydell said, 'What was all that about?'

Denni smiled. 'Call yourself a detective, boss? Think about it.'

Rydell did, but he was none the wiser.

Three

At just after eight a.m. at 4 Gaddine's Bridge, David Bolten was already pacing the kitchen floor, dressed and wearing a grey suit and a blue shirt. He hadn't been sure what to wear but whatever the news he needed to be at school today. The Humanities department had arranged a meeting for four thirty, an architect's visit had been booked for two, and worse, new post interviews had been booked for ten a.m. He certainly didn't want to miss those. It was vital he should be there, he didn't trust anyone else's judgement. But at the moment all he could do was wait for the detective inspector to visit.

DI Thomas Rydell had telephoned at seven thirty to say he had some news and would be at the house by nine. From the tone of his voice Bolten guessed it was fairly inconclusive, but nonetheless it was news.

The past week had been a real trial, his emotions had see-sawed between anger and despair and back to anger. Their baby, Benjamin, had screamed incessantly and only the arrival of Sara's mother had made a slight difference. He could hear her now, in the nursery via the intercom, trying to sing him to sleep. It seemed to be working. Rhoda had a sweet, clear voice.

A few minutes later she came downstairs. 'He's finally asleep,' she said. He glanced at Rhoda's face, she was in her early fifties and the last week had taken its toll. He wondered how much longer she would be prepared to stay. She'd taken time off from her secretarial job and as a divorcee of two years she'd just acquired a new boyfriend.

'Do sit down, David,' she urged him. 'They'll be here soon.'

He finally sat down but even then he didn't *feel* still. The need to keep moving was as strong as ever.

'Shall I make a large pot of coffee?' she asked.

'No, don't do that,' he said. 'We don't want to encourage them to stay any longer than necessary.'

Rhoda patted him on the shoulder. 'We both need coffee,' she said firmly. He didn't bother to argue. He was happy enough to go along with what Rhoda wanted. He remained very grateful that his mother-in-law had moved in the day after Sara left. He couldn't have coped with Ben on his own.

Once the coffee was started Rhoda went upstairs to wash and dress. When she returned she'd scooped her long hair into a pleat, wore a blue jumper and black cords and with make-up on he thought she looked young enough to be Sara's sister.

'I feel more ready to face them now,' she said as she poured the coffee. Then she added softly, 'Who am I kidding?' She glanced at the kitchen clock. It was five to nine.

'Not long to wait now,' she murmured.

He noticed her eyes were full of tears. He felt anger in his chest, wedged like a large stone. When he heard the car draw up and then the sharp sound of the door knocker echoing through the house Bolten swallowed the saliva that surged to his throat, took several deep breaths and finally opened the front door.

Rydell was aware that David Bolten searched their eyes and mouths for an indication of the news with a desperate intensity. And Rydell knew, from bitter experience, that although there was no easy way to give bad news it should never be rushed or so drawn out that anxiety itself became overwhelming. Here, he thought, is a man lurching towards middle age, minus most of his hair, his young wife had left him literally holding the baby and now he sensed the police had come to take away any remaining hope.

'Do you mind if we sit down, Mr Bolten?' asked Rydell. Bolten shook his head and showed them through to the kitchen. Rhoda half-stood and then sat down again, nervously unsure. 'This is Sara's mother, Rhoda Lydney. She's been staying here to look after Benjamin,' he explained.

'Last night,' began Rydell as he sat down, 'last night a young woman's body, fitting the description of your wife, was found in a farm building not far from here.'

'Oh God . . . no,' murmured Rhoda as she began rocking backwards and forwards. Denni, who sat beside her at the refectory style table, put an arm round her.

Bolten said nothing at first but he seemed to shrink visibly, his head sagging into his chest. After a few moments he lifted his head and managed to ask in a hoarse whisper, 'Was it exposure?'

Rydell shook his head. 'The post-mortem hasn't been done yet but it does look like murder.'

There was a long pause before Bolten muttered, 'I can't quite grasp this. Oh Christ. Murder? Why would anyone . . . kill Sara?'

'She may simply have been in the wrong place at the wrong time,' said Rydell as though it were some sort of consolation. 'As I explained,' he continued, 'until the PM we're all in the dark.' He waited for the question, 'How did she die?' but it never came. He wasn't surprised, many people simply didn't want to know. For some the manner of death was as hard to bear as the shock of loss.

Bolten eventually managed to ask in a voice barely above a whisper, 'What happens now?'

'We need you to come with us to . . . view the body.'

'I can't . . . I just can't,' he muttered. Rydell thought he looked close to fainting, his complexion having taken on the sickly colour of wet cement.

It was Rhoda who spoke then in a shaky but clear voice, 'If it's my daughter I want to see her. I'll see her.'

Rydell nodded. 'Of course. If you get your coat we'll drive you there now.'

'Where do we have to go?' she asked flatly.

'The mortuary at the hospital.'

She shuddered as she rested her trembling hands on her son-in-law's shoulders. 'Will you come with me, David?'

He shook his head. 'I can't face it. I know I should, but I feel sick.'

There was a long pause, while Rydell gave him a chance to change his mind. He didn't. 'Fair enough, Mr Bolten, but I think it better if my sergeant stays with you . . . just in case the baby wakes.'

Bolten didn't argue. He loosened his tie and stared miserably at the quarry tiles of the kitchen floor.

As Rydell left with Rhoda, he thought that, although in these sorts of situations women cried more, it was usually the men who fainted or vomited – the price of repressed emotions, he supposed. He was almost an expert on that score if personal experience could be counted.

In the kitchen Denni poured more coffee and sat beside her charge. She remembered the one or two head teachers she'd known at school. They'd had charisma and strong personalities and, having been in trouble on a few occasions, she'd got to know them better than most. Bolten, with his roundish face, sparse hair and slightly mincing walk, seemed to have few attractive attributes, but then she was meeting him in the worst of circumstances.

On the pretext of using the bathroom Denni checked on the baby, who lay, pudgy hands clasped together, eyes closed, pink cheeked with thick black hair that made him look older than six months. She didn't pause too long at the cot side. Sleeping babies seemed to trigger broodiness that lasted for weeks. She peered into the master bedroom and caught sight of a wedding photograph. Sara looked young and lovely. Bolten looked more like the bride's father than the groom. A watercolour painting of Benjamin hung above the bed. He was smiling down cherubically.

As she came back into the kitchen, Denni noticed Bolten's mood had changed. He was poised tensely on the chair, rubbing his hands together in agitation. 'Maybe I shouldn't say this,' he said, 'but I feel really pissed off and bitter towards the police. She's been missing more than a week. A pet dog would have caused more concern and action.'

Denni sat down beside him. 'I'm sorry to admit it but only children get the highest priority, I'm afraid.'

He shrugged. 'Well that's no bloody consolation to me. She's my wife and she's dead.'

'Tell me about the night Sara left home.'

He stared down again as if he could focus all his emotions on the quarry tiles. 'We hadn't had a row. I've been asked about that. She wasn't depressed either. I was out late. I got home about midnight. I assumed she was in bed. I fell asleep on the sofa . . . Ben crying woke me up. There was no sign of Sara.'

'And no note?'

'No.' He'd paused before answering, a pause that was slightly too long. She knew then that he was lying.

'Tell me about the note,' she said firmly.

He looked up at her quizzically. 'How did you know I was lying?'

She shrugged. 'A guess. It's common. When an adult goes missing the family think the police will respond more quickly if there is no explanation for their "disappearance".'

'When I say a note,' he explained, 'I mean the start of a note. She did sometimes do that when I was out for the evening.'

'A sort of love note?' queried Denni.

He nodded. 'I wasn't out that often – work-related meetings and the like. She'd jot a few words down . . . Anyway, the Saturday evening she went the note began, "Darling, Ben has screamed all evening. Feeling shattered. Couldn't wait up . . ." That was all.'

'She didn't sign it?'

'No. And that *was* unlike her – no kisses either. I got the impression it was unfinished.'

Denni watched his expression carefully as she asked, 'Was your wife in any way upset? Had you had an argument about you going out?'

He stared back at her and answered confidently, 'No, there wasn't any row or bad feeling. She often said she enjoyed her evenings on her own. She always coped well with the baby. She did get very tired at times but she managed the home very well . . .' He paused. 'Does that answer your questions?'

'You still sound angry, Mr Bolten.'

'I am bloody angry. Angry with her for going and with the police for doing nothing. And, strange as it may seem, I think I could still be angry if she's dead.'

Denni showed no surprise. 'Have you tried all her friends?'

'Yes,' he said irritably. 'Friends past and present, and neighbours. I've contacted minicab firms, the missing persons helpline and hospitals. All with no result. Either she was whisked away by aliens or she simply walked off into the night. Which is why I assumed the body . . . is Sara . . . and that she died of exposure. The night she left it was bitterly cold.'

'What did she take with her?'

He shrugged. 'Nothing really . . . A jacket – one of those quilted things, that's all.'

'What about her handbag, her purse?'

He paused. 'Yes. Yes. She took her handbag and her purse. She would have had some cash but not much.'

'Credit cards?'

'Yes and a cheque book but she hasn't used them.' He stared at Denni miserably for a moment and then added, 'I don't think there are any clothes missing but I can't be sure. I do know that one of her nighties is missing.'

'Did you tell this to the duty officer at the station?'

He frowned. 'I think so,' he said uneasily. 'I've just realised something else. She left wearing bedroom slippers. I feel a complete idiot for not thinking of that. She had two pairs of slippers . . . one pair I haven't seen . . . since—' he broke off, his voice thick with emotion.

Denni stayed silent for a while. Then she said softly, 'Just one more question – would she have answered the door if you weren't here?'

He stared at her, eyes watery with tears. 'Yes,' he said. 'Sara wouldn't have given it a thought. She seemed to think this was the safest place in the world.'

Rydell stood with Rhoda in the mortuary. The smell pervaded their nostrils, a smell reminiscent of infection and body odour overlaid with a strong disinfectant. It was a smell never to be forgotten.

When the sheet was drawn back, Rhoda gasped. She swayed slightly and murmured in a hardly audible voice, 'So young . . .' Then she turned away, tears falling silently down her cheeks.

'I'm so sorry,' said Rydell, holding on to her arm. She pulled away sharply.

'No . . . no, you don't understand. It's not her . . . it's not Sara. She's like her but it's not her.'

Later in the police canteen Rydell and Denni ate lunch almost in silence. All Rydell's plans had been thrown into disarray. Now they had a Jane Doe and no PM report until later in the afternoon. Once they had that they could contact the media. So far there had been no reports of a missing woman of quite the right description, although there were some leads they could follow. Denni had already contacted the National Missing Person's Helpline and the depressing news was that there were 16,000 cases on their books, younger men being far more likely to go missing than women. Sara Bolten was already on their books.

Rydell's uneasiness always manifested itself in his inability to eat. He stared at his salad and then pushed it away hardly touched. Denni looked up. 'You should eat more, boss.'

'Don't get motherly with me,' he said, half smiling. 'I'm pissed off because we've got double the problem now. A missing woman and a dead one.'

'Having talked to Bolten,' said Denni, 'I think there's real cause for concern over Sara Bolten, but I don't suppose we can do much about it until we've made headway with this one.' Then she added hopefully . . . 'Can we?'

Rydell shrugged. 'I think we'll try to do them in tandem. Ramesh can take an interest in the farm. Whoever killed our Jane Doe must have known of the existence of the farm, so Ram can follow up that aspect. He's keen.'

Denni smiled. She and DS Ramesh Patel, known as Ram, shared minority status within the force. He was British born and Asian – she was British born and female. They both had nicknames, hers was Knockers, the more polite calling her Shorty because she was shorter than the average female police officer. Ram was known as Sabu. 'I don't give a burnt chapati' was one of Ramesh's less graphic reactions to any banter or teasing. The word was he'd once worked undercover with the drug squad in Moss Side in Manchester. The reasons for his transfer were the cause of much rumour and speculation. Only Ram and the Chief Superintendent knew the truth and neither of them was telling. Secrets never lasted long in the force. Someone was always being transferred and personal details travelled with them. The latest was that in the Met Rydell was known as 'Runner'. Denni realised that before long

her previous nickname would also come back to haunt
her – 'Mars Bar' because of her habit of offering Mars
bars to stroppy or violent cell occupants. She'd worked
on behaviour therapy wards and Mars bars were given as
rewards and withdrawn as punishment. She'd noticed they
did have a calming effect.

'Denni – you're dreaming. Ram!'

'Oh yes . . . I'll let him know now, boss,' said Denni,
'he'll think I'm winding him up.'

'You cruel bitch,' said Rydell with a smile.

Denni found Ramesh in the offices now in use as the major
incident unit. He sat in front of a computer, his desk strewn
with files and papers on which sat a large bag of sweets. He
had a round face, close-cropped hair, gold-rimmed glasses
and women described him as 'cuddly'.

'Hi, Denni. Want a humbug?' he asked, smiling.

She shook her head. 'Ram, by the time you're forty you'll
have a waistline to match your age.'

He nodded. 'Yeah, yeah. I hardly drink, don't smoke,
have no sex life and you begrudge me a mint humbug.'

'You're a paragon of virtue.'

He shook his head. 'No, I'm just a sad bastard.'

Four

*H**e was convinced he had made a good choice. She was the right one: quiet, no screaming, no pleading. She'd done exactly as he wanted. Somehow the cock-up at the barn didn't seem to matter so much since he'd had her safe with him. When he could trust her, she would have sole charge of the baby. Until then he would take Angela to the baby whenever she needed feeding. She'd balked at the first feed and he'd had to slap her twice, but after that she'd got the message.*

Maria had been a mistake, no maternal instinct. Hadn't wanted to breastfeed. The bitch had given him trouble at every turn. This one had proved herself already. With a little luck she might stay for a while. Until he was ready.

The cellar had been a bonus when he bought the house. The estate agent hadn't known it existed and it was only when he moved in and took the original carpet up that he'd found the trap door. It had been dodgy at first getting down the near vertical ladder and when he'd reached the bottom it was flooded with four inches of water. It had taken him a year to transform the cellar into a decent room. He'd drained the water, soundproofed the walls, then painted it a soft green. There was no room for a bath but he had plumbed in a sink and a toilet. He'd put up shelves, for toys and books, and with the addition of a single bed, bedside table, lamp and a radiator, it was a warm cosy room. Maria had complained about the lack of a window but she was a complaining cow anyway and when he'd relented and allowed her upstairs for a while she'd tried to escape. He'd made her as comfortable as possible, cooked her wonderful meals, seen to her every need, protected her. What else did she want?

The snooty bitch in the cellar was trying to get clever with him, talking to him, asking him questions. So far he hadn't told her about Maria. He didn't plan to at the moment. He'd already vowed he wouldn't make the same mistake with this one. She'd have to adapt. All she had to do was be a good mother. That wasn't too much to ask, was it?

Five

In his office, Rydell waited impatiently for the post-mortem report. The weather was calm now, no rain, no wind, just a wet gloss and the debris of the storm in the roads.

Most of the team had been allocated their various tasks and were busy either doing an inch-by-inch search of Haddon's Farm or house-to-house enquiries. Rydell seemed to be merely waiting. It was six o'clock and dark outside and he'd stared at the photographs of the dead woman for far too long. Mere images on paper pinned to a notice board wouldn't yield up her name, and media involvement would have to wait for both the post-mortem report and budget details. Rydell knew that if there was no result in the investigation after six weeks, they'd be lucky to have a single DC left on the case. Speed was essential and impatience gave him indigestion.

He tidied his desk, moved his keyboard half an inch to the right, put the cover on his terminal, checked the office generally for any sign of disorder then, satisfied, he switched off the light and made his way out of the building. He hoped not to be accosted by anyone with a problem, he wasn't, and within fifteen minutes he was sitting in the pathologist's office. Still waiting. As he sat, he began to think of other times he'd waited in institutions. He tried to push those memories to some far compartment in his mind but hard seats, corridors and waiting brought them to the surface. The worst of those memories were of being led from the labour room when his then wife's delivery began to go horribly wrong. He'd felt so bloody helpless. He'd actually struggled with the midwife and the doctor, but in the end he'd had to give in and wait outside. The baby had been born eventually. A boy, Paul, weighing seven pounds, a full head of dark hair with soft rounded limbs. He was perfect. Or he would have been if he could have breathed. The staff didn't give up on him though but the minutes ticked past, vital minutes that lacked oxygen. If he had known what the future held at that moment for his son he would have said: 'Enough – let him go.' But he'd wanted him to live so badly.

Footsteps and the door opening brought him back sharply to the present. Bertram Howellson's head poked round the door as he boomed, 'I haven't got many windows of time, Inspector. Come through while I wash up.'

In the changing room Dr Howellson peeled off his green working garb and began scrubbing his hands and forearms. 'Out, out damn spot,' he said cheerfully as he carried on his ablutions. 'Fit young woman . . . or rather she was. No evidence of any disease. Death was caused . . .' he paused, smiling at Rydell, 'that's what interests you, old man, it was by drowning. I think she hit her head on the side of the bath. Not accidental of course. There was some bruising on her ankles, fingertip bruising indicative of her ankles being raised to tip her back hence the minor bump to her head.' He began drying his hands. 'I don't think she struggled much, no evidence of clawing or torn fingernails. She'd eaten a big meal, steak, et cetera. I don't know yet about alcohol or drugs, the blood tests will, of course, take a few days.'

'Any idea when she died, Doc?'

Howellson shook his head. 'Rigor mortis has come and gone so three days at least . . . Thursday evening sometime post evening meal . . . good teeth by the way, no fillings but she needed one or two. I don't think a dentist will be able to help you with identification.'

Rydell sighed inwardly, why should it be easy – murder investigations were like life – subject to obstacles and cock-ups at any time.

He watched with interest as Howellson went to his locker and began donning leather biking gear. He didn't seem the type. Small and dapper, he would have looked more at home at the opera or the ballet, but then Rydell was constantly surprised at appearances being deceptive. Never make assumptions, he told himself.

'I've got a brand new Harley Davidson,' said Howellson proudly. 'So far it's given me less trouble than any woman in my life.'

'Might be the answer for me,' said Rydell, hoping Howellson might offer him a ride. He didn't.

'One more thing before I forget – your Jane Doe recently had a baby, her uterus is still a bit bulky, not her first, and she was still lactating. She was between twenty-two and twenty-five and I think she's got gonorrhoea – don't know yet for sure.'

'I didn't know that was still around.'

'The clap is forever with us,' pronounced Howellson as he placed a black helmet with visor on his head.

'Cheers, Doc, I'll remember that.'

Rydell went back to his office and jotted down some notes on the post-mortem by hand, after which he contacted the NMPH via the Internet. Their Identification and Reconstruction Department could enhance her photos in death to make her look more as she did in life. Jane Doe would be with Sara Bolten somewhere on the database. He wondered idly what else the two women might have in common apart from similar ages, both breastfeeding, both good-looking.

After a while, he reasoned that all he could do now was to wait until tomorrow and then revisit the fire-watching duo. He'd ask the same questions in different ways, get a different perspective, a little more background. In his mind Rydell had already started a criminal profile. The murderer was male, physically strong (he'd had to handle the body), mobile, local or with past local connections. Not for him the anonymous woodland grave or body in the lake. The perpetrator liked ritual and order and a certain showiness. Rydell also sensed that the murderer was either very intelligent or very cunning, perhaps insane. He'd been disturbed, or, for some reason, the fire didn't take hold – damp matches, the fuel ran out, the faggots of newspaper were too damp, almost any bloody reason – he'd had to leave in a hurry, but his plan had been to see her burn. Not for the purposes of destroying the evidence but simply for the spectacle.

The briefing the next morning formally allocated Ram Patel to investigating any possible farm connection. Denni was to re-interview Greenly and King. And Rydell was told without a satisfactory explanation by DCI Fenton to 'find Sara'. Why he'd been allocated a missing person instead of a murder he didn't know. Not until he heard the rumour in the canteen. He knew then why it was worth going to the canteen: gossip and rumour flourished there in a rich compost of soggy chips and stewed tea, and the current rumour was that Bolten was a Mason. Rydell wondered if the Masonic Lodge called when you reached a certain age, or promotion passed you by, whichever came the soonest. At a mere thirty-six but feeling older, all he could see of his senior officers were bald heads, vast paunches and a tendency to justify their existence by acting like accountants.

Rydell drove to Gaddine's Bridge, which was not aptly named because there was neither bridge nor river. The sun had reappeared and a watery light filtered over still wet roads and fields.

Gaddine's Bridge had once been a hamlet of three farmworkers' cottages belonging to the local grand estate of Gaddine's Park. Now the estate was no longer farmed but the house and grounds were open to the public. Stone walls and trees bounded the whole estate and it was impossible to see the stately home from the main road. New detached houses had been built next to the row of cottages on land that was an adjunct to the estate. What had once been a woodland dell at the end of a short track was now a mini housing estate. The houses had been styled to look traditional in local stone with sash windows and stone porches. Only the double garages looked out of place and canteen talk was that the turn of the century, two up, two down cottages were as expensive as the new houses.

The Boltens' neighbours to their right was Rydell's first call. There was no reply. At the house on the left he struck lucky. A young woman, ponytailed, wearing trainers and a red jogging suit, answered the door with a black and white cat tucked under her arm. At first glimpse of Rydell the cat made an immediate bid for freedom, leaping from her arms as if stuck by a pin.

'Never mind, he'll be back,' she said with a grin which exposed protruding but ultra-white teeth. Rydell found himself watching her wide mobile mouth much as he would observe someone's eyes.

'I guess you're a policeman, come about Sara,' she said, still smiling. 'No one just passes through this place.'

He showed her his warrant card and she nodded. 'It's not every day an inspector calls. Come on in, we'll have coffee.'

Over coffee, seated at a breakfast table overlooking the back garden, it was hard to stop Lee Ann Parsons talking. She was American by birth, had lived in various parts of the USA and had met and married David Parsons in the States. She gave a fairly brief résumé of their romance and then concluded with, 'And so I landed up here in this virtual graveyard.'

Just for a moment Rydell thought she was serious. She laughed at his expression. 'I only meant it's so quiet and now that Sara . . . has gone, escaped . . . whatever . . . it really is dire.'

'Escaped is a strange word to use. I take it she wasn't happy?'

Lee Ann gazed at him steadily from eyes the colour of tree bark, brownish with traces of green. 'I guess she wouldn't have left if she was ecstatically happy, would she?'

'Her husband seemed to think that she was neither depressed nor stressed.'

'Gee . . . if her husband said that it must be so.' Her words dripped sarcasm. 'I'm not saying she was weeping all the time or not eating or not sleeping—'

'I'm just an ordinary cop and a mere man,' interrupted Rydell. 'Explain it to me.'

Lee Ann stared out of the window for a few moments then said thoughtfully, 'She hated it here. They'd lived here for two years, before that they lived in town and she was a townie at heart. She was delighted when Ben was born but once she got into a routine she was bored – bored rigid.'

'How often did you see her?' asked Rydell, wondering just how well Lee Ann did know Sara.

'Most days,' she answered. 'Sometimes she spent nearly all day here – I'm not working at the moment – other times it was a couple of hours. Once a week we went to the gym for an exercise class or to the pool. Ben loved water.'

'You didn't go to her house?'

Lee Ann shook her head. 'Rarely. She cleaned and tidied her house and then came to me. I guess she needed a change of scene more than I did.'

'In more ways than one,' observed Rydell dryly. Then he added to get everything straight in his mind because here was someone who spent more time with Sara than either her husband or her mother, 'I've heard that Sara was a devoted mother and that she wasn't career minded.'

'Did you, indeed?' Lee Ann paused to pull her ponytail tighter. Judging by her expression she wished that it were someone's neck. Then she stared at him closely and Rydell had the impression she was about to say something significant. He was wrong. 'What's your first name?' she asked.

'Thomas, but I prefer Tom.'

'Do you mind if I call you Tom?'

Rydell smiled. 'Call me what you like, just talk to me.'

Lee Ann shrugged. 'OK. Sara loves Ben dearly but she hadn't wanted him at this point in her life.'

'What point do you mean?'

'David's biological clock was running out or he thought it was, Sara wanted to do other things before she started a family.'

'What things?'

'Travel, maybe make some sort of career plans. She used to enjoy amateur dramatics before the baby was born. She was very good, quite talented. Did you know that?'

Rydell shook his head. 'No. But I'm learning.'

'Teaching school wasn't her idea . . .' she paused staring at him. 'You don't know how she met David, do you?'

'I'm a blank sheet – fill me in.'

Lee Ann smiled her toothy grin. 'Sara met him first when she was just sixteen at school. She fell for him in a big way but it wasn't until she was eighteen that they became an item. Sara still planned to go to Oxford University but her dear parents, especially her father, thought that in view of her relationship, marriage was her best life option. And teacher's training a perfect career option.'

Rydell wasn't totally sure what point Lee Ann was trying to make. He grasped the idea that Sara had given the impression of being a dutiful wife and daughter. But in reality what had she been?

'I see,' said Rydell. 'So are you saying Sara was dissatisfied rather than depressed?'

'Yep. Exactly that.'

Rydell frowned. 'So why then she did leave without any sort of preparation? After all it seems she left wearing her nightdress and in her slippers. That says to me – desperation rather than dissatisfaction. Or that she wasn't planning to go far.'

A flicker of annoyance crossed Lee Ann's face momentarily. 'Am I missing something here, Inspector? Are you saying that I helped her? That she came here . . . to me.'

It hadn't crossed Rydell's mind until that moment and suddenly it made sense. Perhaps the baby had been crying, Sara had needed help or a shoulder to cry on.

'Who else,' he asked, 'would she turn to but her best friend?'

Lee Ann's teeth hid behind tight lips. 'She didn't come here. My husband was at home that night. Perhaps you'd like to come back later this evening and ask him to verify that we had no callers that Saturday night.'

Rydell knew there came a point in any interview when little is gained by pursuing the same line of questioning. Gone now was the grin, the 'may I call you Tom' attitude. He needed to soothe her, take her off guard. 'Thanks for your help Mrs Parsons. Just one more question before I go.'

She relaxed her shoulders and managed a half smile. 'Go ahead.'

'What are your feelings about David Bolten – do you like him?'

She didn't need to pause for thought. 'No,' she said abruptly. 'I think he's a sonofabitch and Sara is far too good for him.'

Rydell hid his surprise. 'Perhaps you'd explain why you hold him in such low esteem?'

Lee Ann stared at him. 'I really don't want to say anymore. All I will say, is that if Sara contacts anyone it will be me.'

'You said "if" as though it's unlikely.'

'She'll hardly ring me from the grave.'

Again Rydell tried to show no surprise. 'Why do you think she's dead?'

Shrugging her shoulders, she murmured, 'I've been in denial I suppose thinking she'd just left on a whim. Now I've had time to think and be realistic I know that Sara may have been unhappy enough to leave both husband and son, but, and it's a big but, she would never ever have left Ben alone in the house.'

Six

At Lowland Farm Ram Patel looked down at his mud-splattered feet and wondered why he hadn't remained an accountant. As he did so, a tethered collie barked at him ferociously. Ram walked on fast. Muggers, pimps and run-of-the-mill criminals were nowhere near as worrying to him as animals, either loose or tethered.

This was the third local farm he'd visited today and so far he'd found farmers and their wives cagier than the average drug dealer's runner. They had told him nothing he didn't already know. The Haddon family or what was left of them seemed to have disappeared.

The dog, still barking, had obviously alerted the occupant of the house because she was waiting for him on the porch.

'Yes?' she said. Her one word was in such a tone that Ram was left in no doubt as to its meaning. It conveyed: 'What the hell do you want?' or even, 'What the hell do you want – stranger?'

She was tall and thin, wearing the ubiquitous mud splatters on her jeans and black jumper. Ram supposed she was somewhere between forty and fifty but her skin was weather-worn so it was hard to tell. Her greying hair straggled over her forehead and she flicked it away from her eyes to peer at him suspiciously.

He introduced himself and explained his mission. 'I'm Madge Davies,' she said as she examined his warrant card with thoroughness bordering on paranoia. 'You don't look much like a policeman.'

'I'm incognito.'

He could see she really didn't understand but she did at least ask him in. In the kitchen something foul smelling simmered on an ancient Aga.

'You'd better sit down,' Mrs Davies said. As he sat down at the kitchen table, she stood, arms akimbo, with her back to the cooker. 'Well?' she said. Ram could immediately interpret that as, 'Well – don't just sit there. Get on with it.' He'd also sussed that it would be wise to ask her only open-ended questions.

'I'd like you to tell me all you know about Haddon's Farm and the suicide of the farmer.'

She stared at him for several seconds with her hands behind her back warming them on the Aga door. Then she shrugged, and gave a half smile. 'I don't see how a farmer topping himself years ago could have any connection with that woman in the barn—' she broke off looked quizzically at Ram and obviously decided he did have a genuine reason for asking footling questions. 'No backbone,' she said briskly. 'His wife ran that place. The herd went down in 1986. He shot himself.'

'Where did he shoot himself?' asked Ram, who already knew that much.

'In the head of course.'

Ram tried not to smile. 'I meant the location, Mrs Davies. Outside or inside?'

'In his bedroom. He did that on purpose so his wife would have to clear up the mess. His brains went everywhere.'

Ram didn't want to visualise the scene but the image was already there. 'What happened to his wife?'

Madge Davies frowned. 'She stayed on for about three months and then left.'

'Have you any idea where she went?'

'Derbyshire I think.'

'Just her?'

She shook her head. 'No. Her and the three kids. They

were in their early teens then. Two boys and a girl. Grown up now of course.'

'Can you remember their names?'

'Of course I can,' she said. 'They went to the same school as my kids.'

'Which was?'

Frowning again, she turned her back on him and began stirring whatever was cooking in her big saucepan. 'God this stinks,' she said. 'It's for the dog.' She turned back to face him. 'Why are the police so interested in the farm?'

'The body that was found there hasn't been identified yet,' Ram explained, 'and whoever put the body in the barn must have known of the existence of a derelict farm.'

'It was in the papers,' she said, slightly more animated now. 'Big headlines. They called it "the farm that died". No one went near it for years and I don't think anyone in the Haddon family would ever want to see the place again.'

'You're probably right,' agreed Ram. 'But we do have to check all avenues when dealing with a murder.'

She half smiled as if in recognition that here was a man merely doing his job. 'You don't think the murderer's local, do you?'

Ram sensed the answer she wanted. 'Yes, Mrs Davies,' he said gravely. 'We do.'

'Do you drink tea?' she asked.

'I'm addicted to it.'

'I'll make us a cup then.' As she filled the kettle she called out above the noise of running water and noisy taps, 'Being a Pakistani I thought you might not drink tea.'

Ram was used to this sort of ignorance especially in remote districts where he was a minority of one. 'I'm Indian,' said Ram. 'Where the tea comes from.'

'Oh, yes,' she replied. 'What part?'

'Manchester. I was born here.'

'Oh. I see,' she said. 'What's your accent then?'

He smiled. 'I thought it was Mancunian.'

She nodded sagely. 'Anyway, you were asking about the Haddon kids. Their dad killing himself caused a lot of trouble. The eldest boy was fourteen at the time. He went off the rails. Thieving, truanting from school, that sort of thing. It was best that Liz took them away. Gave them a fresh start. Much the best.'

It dawned on Ram as she spoke that she knew where they were. Perhaps it was just that she was giving him more information, perhaps it was her tone. Either way he was determined to find out.

'Did the kids keep in touch?' he asked casually.

'Oh yes—' she broke off, realising she had been caught. Slightly flustered, she looked towards the Aga. 'The kettle's nearly boiling.'

It didn't look nearly boiling to him. 'You were saying, Mrs Davies, that the Haddon children kept in touch with yours.'

'Was I?' She sounded defensive now, almost sullen.

Ram changed tack. 'What about your husband? I expect he knew the Haddon family quite well.'

'He knew Bill. He didn't rate him much. Bill Haddon was the sort who always looked for short cuts. Dying was a short cut for him. Leave the worries to every-one else.'

'Perhaps I could have a word with your husband,' suggested Ram.

She stared at him. 'Only if you're a medium. He's been dead three years. Accident with a tractor.'

'I'm sorry.'

'No need. He was a nasty piece of work. I've got two big sons. They work the farm.'

'Could I have a word with them?'

'I don't suppose we've got much choice, you being police.'

'It is a murder investigation, Mrs Davies.'

She nodded. 'We've got nothing to hide. My boys have never been any trouble to their father or me. Other lads might have taken against someone like Ivor but they . . . put up and shut up.'

'Would you like to explain that, Mrs Davies?'

'No,' she snapped. 'I wouldn't.'

Ram was stumped now. He longed for a cup of tea but doubted the Aga would boil in the foreseeable.

'Where can I find your sons?' he asked.

She inclined her head towards the kitchen window. 'There're fixing fences in the fields. They'll be in soon. Kettle will be boiled by then.' She began opening tins of cake and biscuits and buttering bread.

Ram, meanwhile, stared around the kitchen. He supposed it was 'basic farmhouse' with its quarry-tiled floor, gingham curtains at the window and matching gingham tablecloth. The walls had once been painted cream but had long since lost any lustre. On one wall was a painting of a collie dog. It could have been the one outside but he'd only seen that one with bared teeth and hackles rising. The one in the painting was calm. If a dog could be smiling this one was.

The 'big boys' came in a few minutes later. And they *were* big. Both were over six foot, and once they'd taken their jackets off he could see they had muscles he hardly knew existed. They eyed him with suspicion but said nothing. They didn't even speak when their mother introduced him. They sat down after washing their hands at the sink and began eating bread and butter.

'Tuck in,' she urged Ram. Mrs Davies didn't sit down herself, she hovered around the table, ready to fulfil the needs of her 'boys'. Ram joined in the eating. It was four o'clock and he was starving. The Aga had eventually produced boiling water, and a squat teapot now took pride of place on the table.

'This is Morgan,' she said proudly as she patted the slightly taller one on the head. 'My eldest.' Then repeating the gesture, 'And this is Trefor.' Her silent sons nodded vaguely in his direction. Ram was about to ask them about the Haddon family when Mrs Davies enquired, 'Are you married, Sergeant Patel?'

He shook his head. 'I can't find anyone to have me.' This was true in part. He was in love but his girlfriend wouldn't discuss marriage. It was on her list of dirty words.

'Well fancy that,' she said. 'I would have thought your mother would have fixed you up with an arranged marriage.'

He laughed. 'She keeps trying, but no respectable Indian family seems to want a police sergeant in the family.'

'Strange,' she murmured.

Ram turned to Morgan who had grey eyes like his mother and a slightly flattened nose quite unlike his mother's. His black hair, although short, stuck out at odd angles and a blob of jam had wedged itself in the corner of his mouth. 'I believe you knew the Haddon children – that you went to the same school?'

'I did, yeah,' he mumbled.

'Speak properly, Morgan,' ordered his mother. 'You sound retarded.'

Morgan glanced resentfully at his mother and then at Ram. 'It was Lynsey I knew best.'

Ram noticed the surprise on Madge Davies's face. 'I thought it was Richard you were friendly with?' she said.

Morgan shook his head. 'Trefor was Richard's friend.' Then he smirked, and Ram noticed Trefor growing red faced.

'Well!' said Madge. Again a world of meaning was encapsulated in that one word.

Trefor slammed his piece of fruit cake on the plate. 'Morgan, why don't you keep your big mouth shut.'

Morgan glared at his brother. 'I only said you were *friendly* with Richard Haddon.'

Trefor, the less pugnacious-looking of the two, thrust himself from his chair with such force that the chair crashed onto the kitchen floor. Then he offered his brother a one-fingered salute and stormed out.

Meanwhile, Morgan continued eating and drinking unconcernedly as his mother replaced the chair and at long last sat down.

Ram felt he had outstayed this family drama. It was time to be assertive. 'Right, Morgan,' he said firmly. 'Just give me a forwarding address of the Haddons and I'll be off.'

Without looking up, Morgan said flatly, 'Ten Highcroft Road, Buxton, Derbyshire.'

'Thanks.'

Ram stood up to leave. Madge sat staring at her son with a puzzled, shocked expression on her face.

'They're not Haddon any more,' Morgan announced. 'They call themselves Harris now.'

On the drive back to town, Ram thought that he could have found out their address without leaving his office, but he also knew that in a murder investigation emotional nuances made a difference, sometimes a big difference. It was just possible, although perhaps unlikely, that the young woman in the barn was Lynsey Haddon, now Harris. *That* was something he wouldn't have suspected from a computer printout.

'Good hunting, Sabu?' asked the uniformed sergeant in reception as Ram walked through. 'Very very good, Sahib,' answered Ram in his best Indian accent. The banter and teasing was hardly ever malicious – it was part of the police force. Fat, thin, Welsh, Scots, Irish, hairy, bespectacled, flash, intellectual, female – the jokes and nicknames were ever present, as solid as crime. Ram's police colleagues were, more and more, the only people he associated with socially. His links with his London-based mother, brother and cousins were now severed for a while. It was safer that way.

He found Rydell and Denni manning busy phones so he waved and mouthed, 'See you later,' and went back to his office and logged on to his computer terminal. The Home Office Computer, PNC11, would quickly supply him with the criminal records, if any, of both the Davieses and the Haddons (now Harrises). They did. Morgan Davies had one conviction for ABH – Actual Bodily Harm. He'd been in a pub brawl and broken someone's jaw. As it was his first offence he had been fined and given a suspended sentence of three months. He'd been eighteen at the time. There were no other convictions. Ram made notes and went back to Rydell's office.

Rydell looked up as he entered. 'Are we currying favour, Ram?'

Ram smiled. 'Not exactly. Just wondered if anyone was fit for a few bottles of Cobra and the delights of a tandoori.'

It was Denni who answered first. 'Does the invite include me?'

'It wouldn't be the same without you.'

'You're a smooth talker, Ram,' said Rydell. 'I'm game. Give us five minutes to get someone to man the phones.'

'Any luck?'

Rydell shook his head. 'So far, three nutters, four women missing who bear no resemblance to our Jane Doe and two sightings of someone who *could* be Sara – one in London, one in Cornwall – the local police are investigating those.' He paused to place a pen beside a neat stack of notes. 'How about you?'

Ram stroked his balding head thoughtfully. 'Probably nothing. But I have traced the Haddon family. They call themselves Harris now.'

'Well done.'

Later, in the plush warmth of Mother India, second home of many of the force, especially those living alone, Rydell and Ram drank bottles of Cobra and chose a variety of dishes. Denni drank white wine and ate the house speciality, a chicken korma with slices of fresh strawberries. They talked about little else but the case. Ram appreciated the fact that Rydell always listened carefully to any ideas. For those suggestions he didn't agree with, he said, 'We'll shelve that one.' Often they would remain shelved.

Finally it was agreed that a very real interest should be taken into arsonists past and present. A nationwide check on mental hospitals might yield up a few suspects and criminal records would give details of convicted arsonists.

Denni, who had listened intently, suddenly said, 'Let's not lose sight of the fact that Sara Bolten is still missing and NOT presumed dead. We can't just forget about her.'

Rydell frowned. 'Want to swap jobs, Denni? See how far you get asking Bolten about the Masons.'

'What's that got to do with Sara going missing?'

'Nothing as far as I can see but it carries weight in terms of a more senior cop being involved.'

She paused to wipe her hands on the hot flannels the waitress had just brought to the table. 'I think we need to know far more about Sara. Was she having an affair? Or was she being stalked by someone?'

'There's been no suggestion of that,' said Rydell, folding his white flannel cloth and then absentmindedly folding and positioning the other two so that the three sat neatly on the silver tray. 'Her neighbour Mrs Parsons seemed to know her well.'

There was a short pause before Denni said, 'We all have our secrets.'

Ram laughed, a response a little too quick and nervous for Denni not to notice.

Seven

An unidentified body made Rydell irritable. A missing wife and mother made him even more irritable. He'd woken up feeling heavy-eyed and weary and now he felt a definite unease. He lay in bed staring at a tiny crack in the ceiling that would bother him now until he found time to fix it. He told himself a tiny crack in the plaster wasn't important, that a blind man would be glad to see it, but it made no difference to his mood and he knew the only thing to improve it was to run. Two days without running meant he needed a fix. It was five a.m.

He slipped on a tracksuit and trainers, drank a small glass of milk, ate a banana, did all his last-minute checks and left the flat at five twenty. Although he drove in slight drizzle the roads were quiet and in a few minutes he was at Baborough Country Park. He liked to run there because it was a mix of woods and open spaces and he knew all the pathways even in the dark. As he left the heat of the car the cold air hit him. He began running immediately and within minutes felt warm. The first few miles were always the best: he felt wide awake and alive and his thoughts seemed clearer than at any other time. Gradually, though, his heightened senses seemed to dull, his legs grew heavy and his chest tightened, but he knew he could run well beyond that stage.

By six thirty it was growing lighter, the birds began to sing and he began the run back towards his car. The drizzle mixing with his sweat had soaked him but he hardly noticed. He was on a high. It was only when he was back in the car driving home he got the post-run low. Fleeting but intense. It was then he remembered his son: the son who would never run with him.

After a quick shower and breakfast his mood had lifted and he jotted down a few reminders for the day. By eight thirty he was at his computer checking e-mails. There were possible IDs to investigate, but he was puzzled and surprised that no one had come forward with a positive on the dead woman. After all, the woman had given birth – so where was the baby? GPs, health visitors, midwives, social workers – someone must know her. No one could be that isolated – could they?

There were no e-mails but there were various handwritten notes. Mostly run-of-the-mill memos that he tried to ignore, usually by filing them neatly and getting Denni or Ram to remind him of their contents. Today was the first showing of the video made by the SOC team. *That* he obviously couldn't ignore. The filming of murder scenes was a real advance in murder investigations. No matter how observant a detective, the presence of a body always had an emotional effect and little details got missed among the drama of a lost life: the eyes could play tricks, the light could be poor, a smell could be overwhelming, the victim's injuries horrific. In the arena of murder the victim held everyone in its sway. A video gave the surroundings a chance to have their say.

'Morning.' Denni's voice broke into his reverie. 'Did you get my note?'

He swung round on his chair to face her. 'What note was that?'

'About the phone call – from a woman saying she knew our victim.'

'Great. Who is she?'

Denni frowned at him. 'You didn't see the note, did you?'

'You should have stuck it on my computer. There was a pile of memos on my desk this morning – internal politics as usual. So . . . speak to me.'

'A PC at the desk took the call. The woman sounded worried, said she was calling from London and she was pretty sure she knew the dead woman . . .' Denni paused. 'Only one fly in the ointment, Guv. She rang from a phone box and ran out of change. She gave her first name only, Sonia, and her line of work.'

'Which is?'

'She works for an escort agency.'

'Did she say which one?'

Denni shook her head. 'Somewhere in north London but she didn't give the agency name. It seems she promised to ring back today.'

'That's promising in itself,' said Rydell cheerfully. 'It could even mean a trip to London.'

Later that morning Chief Superintendent John Norman – in West Mercia parlance, the Gaffer – chaired a brief introductory meeting.

'Money is tight,' he said in his loud booming voice. 'Overtime payments will be minimal. And help from other forces will be so sparse you'll just have to work your . . . proverbials off. Keep me informed of what's going on and . . .' he paused to look in Rydell's direction, 'I want to know how far you've got towards finding the missing woman.'

Rydell nodded. 'We're pulling out all the stops, sir, with media coverage on both women. Plus talking to friends and associates of Mrs Bolten. So far, no leads.'

John Norman pulled on one ear and raised an eyebrow. 'Just get on with it. Our force might be half in the sticks but for God's sake let's show the other forces we know how to conduct an efficient, economical investigation.'

This raised polite nods all round. As a 'gaffer' he was well regarded, not for his crime busting abilities but for allowing everyone to get on with their work without too much interference. His job was a mixture of man management and accountancy and it seemed to work. One and all, in contrast, perceived DCI Alec Fenton as a TOW, a Tired Old Wanker, whose ability and even his honesty was sometimes in question. Rydell and Ram avoided him whenever possible but for some reason she'd never explained Denni seemed quite sympathetic towards him.

It was Fenton now who inserted the film into the VCR. Someone at the back of the room switched the light off and everyone sat back to watch. Those who had good eyesight were poised to take notes. Nothing happened.

'Switch the bloody lights on,' shouted Fenton. In better light Fenton's round face could be seen to grow puce to the top of his ears, his bald head didn't colour though but remained a virginal white. Unwilling for any further humiliation his eyes scoured the room to find Denni. 'DS Caldecote,' he said, tight-lipped. 'Come and fix this.'

Denni walked to the front of the room, glanced momentarily at the machine and then switched on the plug at the mains. The VCR whirred into life. Fenton sat down at the side of the video screen and said, 'That just proves women *can* cope with machines.'

No one laughed.

The film of the barn emphasised again the theatrical positioning of the body. Occasionally Fenton paused the video to highlight items, the pile of rope, the faggots of newspaper. 'We don't need a fire report to tell us the cause of the fire,' he said. 'Paraffin was the accelerant used but obviously chummy took the container with him.' He paused, patted his large stomach and announced, 'Forensic has informed me that the newspapers used around the body were all copies of the *Daily Telegraph*, last year's. I'll leave you to draw your own conclusions on that one.'

Someone at the back muttered something about a Tory nutter but Fenton let it pass.

'Right then everyone. That's it. Any questions?'

Arms akimbo over his fat gut, Fenton surveyed the room.

There never were any questions when Fenton gave a briefing and he certainly didn't ask twice.

Once he and the Chief Superintendent had left the room everyone relaxed and began talking, airing their own pet theories. Rydell and Denni went back to their shared office where their phones were ringing simultaneously. Denni's phone call produced the short straw. She mouthed to Rydell that she was listening to an obscene call – a 'kinky'. After a few moments she said coldly, 'I know your name and I know where you live. If you ever call again two very unpleasant officers will pay you a visit.' It worked every time. The shock of supposed recognition always made them put the phone down as if it were the proverbial red-hot poker.

Rydell's call was from the Norfolk police about another sighting of Sara. This time she'd been seen walking a dog along a beach. He was disappointed it hadn't been Sonia from London. The impulsive caller rarely rang back, and Sonia may have thought too long and too hard about her good intentions.

He checked the Internet for north-London-based escort agencies and found four listed. He rang all of them as though he were a client asking for Sonia. Strangely they all had a Sonia on their books. No doubt if he'd asked for a Brigitte they could all have supplied one.

He decided visiting in person was the only way of finding the caller.

'Denni, do you fancy a trip to London tomorrow?'

'By train?' she asked eagerly.

He shook his head. 'Norman will never sanction that expense. We'll have to go by car.'

Denni tried to hide her feelings. Car trips to London invariably meant hours of traffic jams on the motorway and then the struggle of trying to find a parking space.

'What time do you want to start out?'

'We'll start out early to avoid the rush hour. I'll collect you at six a.m.'

Denni's heart sank, that would mean getting up at five. She'd planned to go out this evening, and possibly have a late night with a short-standing boyfriend. He was going to be well impressed because she would have to cancel their date – all that heavy breathing and his rather haphazard fumblings wouldn't enhance her mood for a long drive. Somehow only other women found dishy, competent men. She found mother's boys, virgins and the type that sang off key in your ear and who, if asked, would have described themselves as caring and considerate. For God's sake she had girlfriends who were caring and considerate. She needed a man for other reasons. She wanted a hero, someone sane but slightly mysterious. But deep down she knew that she was the one at fault. She'd missed out during her teenage years nursing her father. She'd had no boyfriends at all until she was twenty then a slightly spotty boy called Brian had seduced her with cider and a Chinese takeaway. Having lost her virginity to someone so unprepossessing she was mortified to pass him often in the street and although she pretended not to recognise him she always had the strange urge to shout: give it back! She didn't of course, but given one wish she would have wished to succumb to love rather than curiosity.

She arrived home at eight; outside was damp and cold. Inside was her warm haven. Although small, her two-bedroom end-of-terrace house was heavily mortgaged partly because she'd had to fund having central heating installed and partly because she'd spent a small fortune on decorations and furnishings She'd wanted it pretty and cosy and now she just hoped it wasn't twee. She'd once harboured romantic notions of a four-poster bed but her bedroom wasn't large enough, so she had settled for a white lace bed cover, pale lavender walls and dark-purple cushions. Once, very briefly, it had almost been a marital home. Soon after she'd finished her nurse's training she'd lived with Gordon for a while. He'd seemed the *one*. Ten years older that her, intelligent, strong, good at putting up shelves and decorating, lusty, but easily bored. Bored with her long shifts and irritated that she read in bed, he had left one day after a blazing row. When she'd got over the shock she'd been grateful – and at least the shelves were still up.

The new man in her life, Malcolm, of two dates, two lingering kisses tinged with garlic and a neat line in boots and plaid shirts was meant to be picking her up at nine. She drank a glass of wine before ringing him.

'Hi, Malcolm. I'm really sorry. I can't make tonight, I have to work.'

Although he was silent she could sense his irritation. Eventually he said, 'You could have let me know earlier in the day.'

'I didn't know myself till after seven—'

He didn't let her finish. 'In that case we'll make it tomorrow night.'

She hadn't been expecting such assertiveness, so she said, 'Fine. But I've got to go to London tomorrow so I might not be back in time.'

'Are you giving me the brush-off?'

'No. I'm on a major case.'

'I'll ring you tomorrow to check your availability.'

'Sarky sod,' she said aloud as she put the phone down.

Later, just as she'd settled down on the sofa with a Wilbur Smith novel the phone rang. It was Malcolm. He only said a few furious words before slamming the phone down. 'You could do with a good seeing to – bitch!'

She felt upset partly because it was probably true, partly because he hadn't given her time to make a suitable response. So she said, 'And bollocks to you,' and drank another glass of wine. She was soon lost in chapter five and thankfully the real world and Malcolm receded.

At six a.m. precisely Rydell was waiting outside for her. The journey took four hours during which Denni sucked boiled sweets and tried to chat but Rydell either stayed silent or talked about the 'job'. Denni found this disconcerting, she liked to understand people, to judge their motivation, sometimes even their sanity. Rydell she'd observed *was* slightly neurotic. He couldn't fail to hide his little compulsions. She wondered if they had started before or after his wife left him.

London traffic was as she'd expected – frenetic. Rydell drove well, he'd worked in the Metropolitan force so he knew his way around, but he drove too fast and Denni was a twitchy passenger. Every so often after a close encounter he would mutter, 'Don't panic.' She resented those words when her survival seemed at stake.

The first escort agency was in Camden Town. One room, at the top of a narrow staircase in a tall terraced house above a financial consultancy and a chiropodist. On one side was a kebab house and on the other a Chinese restaurant. The smells of perpetual cooking seemed to have permeated the walls and made Denni feel slightly queasy.

A cardboard sign hanging on the doorknob announced: INTERVIEW IN PROGRESS. The small silver plaque to the left of the door said: Jo Jo Escort Agency. Prop. Joanne Woods. There were two wooden chairs in the corridor so they sat down and waited.

Eventually a middle-aged man emerged. He wore blue jeans and a denim jacket. His thinning grey hair was worn in a long thin straggle of a ponytail. Without looking at them he muttered, 'She's free. You can go in.'

Joanne Woods didn't fit the image Denni had of a high-class madam. She was short, plump, grey haired and motherly looking. She sat behind a large desk in front of a computer with a phone to each side of her. She wore a grey pinstripe suit and a white blouse. Her hair cut in a short bob rested well above her collar. The only jarring feature of her appearance were her bright red talons. She took one glance at them and said disconcertingly, 'Police?'

Denni smiled. 'Is it that obvious?'

Joanne failed to smile back. 'Vice squad?'

Rydell shook his head. 'We're from the West Mercia police investigating murder.'

'Fuck!' Her veneer of respectable motherliness was suddenly shattered. The red nails were obviously more *her*.

'How can I help you?' she said, smiling, her composure restored.

'We are trying to locate a woman called Sonia,' explained Rydell, 'who rang us yesterday with information about a murder victim. She said that she worked for a north-London escort agency. Yesterday when I contacted you you did say you had a Sonia on your books.'

'Perfectly true but then I thought you were a client. We do have a Sonia Kay on our books but I doubt that's her real name.'

'It'll do,' said Rydell. 'Let me have her name and address.'

From a filing cabinet Joanne produced two sheets of paper. 'This is her "promo" which we send out to clients. Home addresses we keep on computer.' She wrote the address down and handed him the sheets. 'You could ring her from here.'

He did. There was no reply.

Outside the air of Camden Town smelt strongly of chips and curry mixed with petrol fumes. Chill gusts of wind wafted litter over two homeless youths who sat begging outside the tube station The traffic and the noise and the variety of people who were milling about surprised Denni. There seemed to be every nationality on the streets: Africans in bright robes, Asian women in shalwars or saris, Japanese, Chinese, Turkish, plus a real assortment of drunks and eccentrics. Denni had only ever seen the tourist attractions in London, Camden Town seemed to her a different country.

'I know a few people at the station here,' said Rydell. 'We'll get something in the canteen. Are you hungry?'

'Starving.' Denni sighed inwardly. London with all its variety of eateries had so much to offer but Rydell's culinary imagination went only as far as a police canteen.

In the reception area of Wood Green Police Station Rydell disappeared for half an hour leaving her sitting on a plastic seat that was bolted to the floor next to a mumbling drunk who had come to report he'd been mugged.

On his return Rydell looked more cheerful. 'I've got some info. Next stop Stoke Newington.' Then he added, 'I haven't forgotten your stomach. Here –' From his coat pocket he produced a squashed packet of sandwiches.

'I bet you're a real ladies' man, boss.'

'What's that supposed to mean?' he asked as he strode to the car.

'Just an observation.'

He gave her a mystified glance and changed the subject. 'We've got a lead. Our Sonia isn't an escort. She runs an agency, called Class Act, from her own home.' Then he added as a proviso, 'It's not a sure thing that it's our caller, but the vibes are good.'

The house in Stoke Newington was four storeys high, grey and crumbling. Inside though it was rather impressive, with high moulded ceilings, large windows and subtle colours of cream and pale green. Tall stately plants graced corners of the large hall and the furniture if not antique certainly looked it. A tall slim woman with Cleopatra eyes wearing a silky black short skirt and frilly white apron opened the door. Observing their warrant cards she said, 'I'm Grace the housekeeper. Please wait in the lounge and I'll fetch Miss Langley.'

Rydell perched on a silver striped sofa and Denni sat opposite him on a rose pink armchair. A glass coffee table as big as a pond separated them. After about ten minutes Miss Langley swept in on cloud Chanel. Denni supposed she was in her early forties, glamorous rather than beautiful, with long black hair piled in a soft coil on top of her head which, together with her high heels, gave her artificial height and elegance. She wore an obviously cashmere cardigan in cream with a slim-fitting cream skirt. Not the type, thought Denni, to get herself messy.

Rydell certainly didn't seem fazed by her looks. 'Were you the Sonia who called yesterday?' he asked bluntly. Before answering she sat down gracefully next to him. Her voice was as warm as syrup on waffles. 'Yes, Inspector. I did. I was out shopping when I remembered. The battery on my mobile was flat so I rang from a phone box. Change was a problem. I'm so glad you're following it up.'

'It is a murder inquiry.'

'Quite,' she said evenly with a half smile on cherry coloured lips.

'You didn't ring back,' he said.

Denni thought he sounded definitely peeved.

'I tried,' said Sonia. 'Several times. The lines were engaged.'

Rydell didn't look convinced. 'What information do you have?'

Sonia crossed her shapely legs. 'I'm not sure but I think I know the dead girl – she worked from home.'

'Did she work for you?' asked Rydell, his eyes flickering momentarily on her ankles.

'Occasionally. If I found someone right for her.'

Rydell looked puzzled. 'Could you explain that to me?'

'It's a fairly long story. Would you like a drink?'

Denni couldn't help herself. 'Yes please.'

'We'll have tea if that's OK,' she said, pulling a cord by the side of the cream drapes. A few minutes later Grace entered with a tray of tea. Either she was psychic, thought Denni, or this was normal teatime. It was by now just after four.

Grace poured tea into fine bone-china cups and handed them round and Denni tried not to smile at Rydell who struggled to seem at ease with a delicate cup and saucer.

'Carry on, Miss Langley – you had begun to tell us about your first meeting with . . . ?'

'Maria Seaton. I don't know if that was her real name. Sometimes she called herself Marie, sometimes Maria. I met her first in the red light district of King's Cross. She was fifteen but looked twelve.'

Rydell spoke before Denni got a chance. 'You just happened to see her there purely by chance?'

'No,' said Sonia. 'I went looking for her deliberately. A friend of mine told me about her, said she looked well under age. So I drove to King's Cross at midnight and picked her up.'

Rydell's mouth tightened. 'You didn't think to inform the police or social services?'

Sonia stared at Rydell. 'No. It never crossed my mind. If a girl is out on the streets at fifteen she has *big* problems.'

'What sort of problems did Maria have?' asked Rydell.

She shrugged. 'She never told me much about her past. She didn't need to. She just had the nightmares . . .' she paused. 'I just knew she was escaping from something even *worse*. Worse than walking up and down half dressed, perished with cold, waiting for punters to breathe their bad breath or alcohol fumes all over her. Haggling about money and then watching some prat getting his little dick out and expecting admiration.'

Rydell, feeling uncomfortable, murmured, 'Put that way it doesn't sound much of a career option.'

Sonia's answering glance was icy. 'I suppose you think that's funny. Some of your cop friends treat kids like Maria as criminals instead of victims.'

There was a long awkward silence before Denni said, 'Tell us more about Maria – we do *want* to catch her killer.'

Rydell interrupted her. 'You were telling us why you didn't ring social services about Maria.'

'I thought I'd explained that.' She glanced at Denni, her expression conveying her contempt for men in general and at that moment Rydell in particular. 'Maria was already supposed to be in care and had nearly as many foster parents as punters. She had, or thought she had, a boyfriend. Even with that slimeball taking most of the money she earned, she still had more money than before. Anyway, I picked her up, took her home and more or less kept her indoors for a few weeks.'

'Did she want to leave?' asked Denni.

Sonia nodded. 'Yes. She thought her pimp loved her. She also thought she loved him. He'd brainwashed her of course. Anyway, she was sickly, underweight, verging on anorexia . . . I didn't recognise her at first when I saw her face on television.' She broke off and walked over to a small mahogany cabinet, opened the drawer and took out a photograph. She stared at it for a moment and then handed it to Denni. 'That's how she looked when I first met her.'

The skinny girl in the photo had a gaunt and haunted look. Denni couldn't help a slight shudder. She was barely recognisable but the photo somehow seemed a portent of doom as though at fifteen she'd been marked for an early death.

Sonia sat down again. 'Maria decided to stay with me after her pimp beat her up and found a new girl.'

'Why would you put yourself out for a girl you'd only just met?' asked Rydell.

Sonia sighed. 'I don't want to go into details, but I was once in Maria's position and someone helped me. Maria lived with me for three years, she did a little housework and I arranged some private tuition and she got some GCSEs. I'm not sure what she expected a few exams to do for her but she wanted a glamorous job and a fat salary. When she couldn't get that she moved into a flat with another girl and built up a more up-market client base.'

'What does that mean exactly?' asked Rydell.

'She could pick and choose. The punters she looked for had unusual tastes. If she didn't like the sound of them she turned them down.'

'It sounds only slightly better than King's Cross,' ventured Denni.

'Of course it was better,' snapped Sonia. 'Maria had power. She was her own boss and that's what most of her punters wanted. For her to be the boss. She hated sex anyway.'

Rydell managed a smile. 'Perhaps I'm being dim but how could she be on the game and not have sex?'

Sonia laughed. 'Men who go to the trouble of phoning and booking in advance don't just want straight sex, they want a fantasy. Maria provided that. She made it quite clear that her own body was inviolate: if she allowed a foot massage they paid extra. Some wanted a good whipping, some to be trodden on, some had unusual tastes like wanting smoke blown in their face and being punched. Some of course wanted to be tied up. Either way she became the ultimate dominatrix.'

Denni *could* see that was preferable to walking the streets. In fact a few of her ex-boyfriends she would have enjoyed trampling on.

'When did you last hear from her?' asked Denni.

Sonia thought for a moment, looking vaguely distracted. 'About five months ago. She had short hair then—' she broke off. 'I'm very puzzled.'

'Why?' queried Denni.

Sonia's eyes flicked from Rydell to Denni as if seeking answers from *them*. 'Because . . . five months ago I reported her missing to the police. I was sure *then* that she'd been murdered. Two days ago I see her face on TV and hear she's been murdered not months earlier but only a few days ago. So . . . where was she for that time?'

'Why were you so sure she was dead and not just finding herself a new life?' asked Rydell.

Sonia shrugged. 'Maria always kept in touch. She told me I was the only family she'd ever had. She either wrote to me or rang me. Every week. Sometimes she rang every day. Then when she told me she was pregnant she wanted me to be at the birth.'

'Was she pleased to be pregnant?'

Although Denni had asked the question, Sonia addressed her answer to Rydell. 'Before you say anything, inspector . . . if Maria became pregnant it would have been through choice. She rang to tell me of the pregnancy and we met once or twice for lunch. She seemed happy enough. Then when she was about six or seven months pregnant we arranged to meet but she failed to turn up. I never heard from her again.'

'Did she mention the man involved?' asked Rydell.

'No.'

'And you didn't ask?'

'No. If she'd wanted me to know anything about him she would have told me.'

'What efforts did the police make to find her?' asked Denni.

Sonia sighed loudly. 'Fuck all. Just another tom doing a disappearing act according to them. Some girls do manage to get away from pimps or they meet respectable men and they don't leave forwarding addresses. But I'm sure if she had been able to, Maria would have contacted me.'

Rydell asked, 'What about her friends and clients – did you contact them?'

'Of course I did,' said Sonia. 'Her housemate, known as Sabine, had been away for a week. When she got back Maria was gone.'

'And she took nothing with her,' murmured Denni.

'How the hell did you know that?'

There was a pause before Rydell asked, 'What exactly did she take?'

Sonia stared at Rydell for a moment. 'It was what she didn't take that worried me more.'

'Such as?' queried Rydell.

'For Christ's sake, according to Sabine she didn't even take a toothbrush. I knew then that she hadn't left of her own accord. She'd been taken.'

'You were very fond of her,' observed Denni. Sonia smiled sadly and shrugged her shoulders. 'She was the daughter I never had. But to the police her disappearance was run of the mill. "Prostitutes go missing every day," I was told. And every day for weeks I expected to hear her body had been found. Then I thought maybe she was living an ultra respectable life and had been forced to cut all ties with her past. Some men do make those sorts of demands.' She paused and spread her hands. 'And then I saw her on TV and I knew the bastard who took her away had finally killed her.'

Rydell cast a glance at Denni and indicated by a slight head movement that it was time to go. Sonia noticed and her words came in a rush, 'I know you lot don't give a damn about the murder of a working girl but somewhere out there –' she jabbed a thumb towards the window '– is Maria's baby. Dead or alive? And what are you going to do about that?'

In Palmer's Green, Rydell and Denni visited the end-of-terrace house which had once been the home of Maria Seaton. Sabine answered the door. Tall, with close-cropped dark hair, she wore jeans and a sloppy black jumper.

'Sonia phoned me,' she said. Denni thought she sounded Roedean at the very least.

In the living room a coal fire roared and an array of cushions and books were strewn in front of it on an oriental carpet. Wind chimes clinked eerily in a draught somewhere out of sight. Thick black curtains decorated with silver moons encased a bay window and two blue shaded lamps cast a dark glow. The room had a muggy, warm airlessness.

'Do park yourselves somewhere,' said Sabine. As Rydell and Denni looked round for chairs they realised there were none. There was a table and bookshelves and African masks on the walls and various artefacts mostly of naked black women, but no chairs.

'I don't have a television, as you can see. If I'd seen Maria on television, I would have contacted you.'

Rydell sat on the floor, half on half off a cushion, looking very uncomfortable.

'We've come,' he said, 'hoping you could name the man Maria became involved with.'

Sabine smiled, her wide mouth showing perfect white teeth. 'No you haven't, Inspector. Sonia and I would have traced Maria if we could have given him a name. You came here hoping we would have a little black book with names and addresses in. We didn't work like that.'

'How did you work?' asked Rydell.

'Discreetly. We advertised. The punters phoned us and we discussed their requirements and our fees. If we didn't like their attitude or their accent or if we merely found them creepy we would say we were fully booked and they should ring again – in a month or so. They usually got the message. We gradually built up a regular clientele of men. A few, of course, came just once.'

'And you never kept any records?' queried Denni.

Sabine laughed. 'You sound like a tax inspector. No, we kept times and occasionally we used our own codes – to remind ourselves of their particular penchant.'

'But no names or addresses?' persisted Denni.

Sabine shook her head. 'If they called themselves Mickey Mouse that was fine by us.'

'Was Maria . . . attached to any particular man?' asked Rydell.

'You mean a client?'

He nodded.

'No.'

'Did she have a boyfriend?'

'Not in the way you mean.'

'You'll have to explain it to me,' said Rydell, growing irritated.

'I should have thought it was pretty obvious,' said Sabine. 'Maria and I were lovers. The baby was planned and the father targeted.'

'Targeted?' asked Rydell.

'Chosen. A young man, healthy, high IQ, well balanced, good-looking with a good pedigree and the right colour eyes.'

Rydell looked across at Denni and flashed her a glance, which expressed his general feeling of being out of touch. Denni was far less surprised than Rydell. She read women's magazines. 'Did you tell him about the pregnancy?' she asked.

Sabine shook her head. 'No, that would have complicated things.'

'Was he a client?'

'Certainly not.'

'So, let me get this straight,' said Denni. 'Maria starts a relationship with this man, gets to know him quite well, gets pregnant and then dumps him.'

'That sums it up.'

'When Maria disappeared didn't you suspect he might be involved?'

'No.'

Denni, by now getting slightly scorched by the fire, began to feel fidgety. 'Sabine, we are trying to find Maria's murderer. This isn't a game. We would appreciate a bit of help.'

'I know this isn't a game, Sergeant. How do you think I've felt this past year? She was my lover, my business partner and my best friend. I've alternated between hope and despair and now I find I can't even cry—' she broke off. Denni swallowed her apology as Sabine continued. 'The man involved,' she said, 'went to Australia before Maria disappeared.' There was a short silence, broken only by the crackle of the fire and Rydell murmuring something about the French Foreign Legion.

He eased his position on the floor before asking, 'I believe you were on holiday when Maria left.'

'Yes. I was away for a week. When I came back there was no sign of her. I got in touch with Sonia. Everywhere we looked we drew a blank.'

'Do you have any suspicions about any of your clients?' asked Rydell.

'No. None of our clients have violent or aggressive tendencies, just the opposite in fact.'

Rydell by now had pins and needles in his bum. As far as he was concerned the interview was going nowhere. He stood up relieved to feel his legs again. 'Just one more question,' he said. 'Who else knew Maria was pregnant?'

Sabine was on her feet now, stretching herself, flexing her long legs. 'Only Sonia and me.'

'What about her doctor?'

Sabine shook her head. 'She didn't have one. She distrusted doctors, especially male doctors . . . we had one or two as clients.'

'We'd like to look at her room,' announced Rydell.

'Our room,' corrected Sabine. 'What exactly are you looking for?'

'Her diary,' said Rydell.

'She kept her diary in her handbag – that was all she took with her.'

The bedroom revealed very little. Expensive clothes hung in Maria's wardrobe plus a selection of working clothes in leather and PVC. Several pairs of boots and stiletto heeled shoes were stacked in boxes. In a drawer, Denni found chains and whips, a long length of purple rope and a few photographs.

'Do you mind if we take these with us?' she asked

Sabine who stood in the doorway. 'We will return them of course.'

Sabine nodded. 'The time's right for me to clear away her things . . . now that I know she's not coming back.'

Denni was closing a drawer when she glanced out of the bedroom window. The night was dark and murky and under a street lamp opposite a lone man stood. She called Sabine over to have a look.

'He's a client,' she explained. 'He's early. He's always early. He'll wait there until the appointed time.'

'I thought he was a stalker,' said Denni. 'Did Maria ever mention being followed or anyone taking an *unusual* interest in her?'

Sabine perched herself on the edge of the bed. 'I don't suppose it's got anything to do with her death, but some months before she disappeared she was raped in the local park.'

'Was he caught?'

'No, she didn't report it.'

'For Christ's sake, why not?' snapped Rydell.

'It's all so simple for you cops,' said Sabine in head-girl tones. 'Get raped then have to be undressed, examined, touched, swabs taken, blood tests, give evidence.' She paused. 'Tell me, Inspector, what would *you* do if someone spat in your face?' He didn't answer. 'It's a genuine question. What would you do?'

Rydell stared at her. The prospect of being spat on was almost a phobia. There was no way she could have known that but the mere thought made him want to throw up.

'You know damn well what I'd do,' he said. 'I'd wipe my face and wash it off as quickly as possible.'

'Yes,' she said. 'That's a normal reaction. So too is to strip off and burn your clothes, then jump straight into a hot bath – which is what Maria did.'

He did, of course, take her point.

Denni then asked, 'Did she see his face?'

'No, the bastard took her from behind. She said she scored

down his shin with the heel of her shoe but he didn't let go of his grip around her neck. He had a knife and he threatened to kill her.'

'Did she say anything else about him?'

Sabine's eyes had filled with tears. 'She said he was tall and strong and she thought she was going to die. She stayed calm thinking of the baby.'

'She was pregnant at the time?'

'Yes. But only a couple of weeks. After she was attacked she wouldn't go out alone after dark, and occasionally she'd say that he was still out there. And that she'd blame herself if he raped again.'

'Do you think she may have left here because she was depressed about the rape?'

'No way,' answered Sabine sharply. 'She was a tough cookie. She'd been raped before. She always said she felt safe with me. We'd even bought the cot.' Tears flowed silently down Sabine's cheeks. 'Just go now,' she said. 'I'll ring you if I think of anything.'

As they were leaving Denni asked, 'Was there any sign of a forced entry or any sort of struggle?'

'No,' said Sabine dully. 'Nothing. And although it may seem a strange thing to say, I'm sure she wouldn't have opened the door to someone she didn't know or at least expect.'

'Not even during daylight?'

Sabine shrugged. 'Before the rape maybe,' she said slowly. 'But I can't help wondering why, if that happened, she didn't put up a fight. I have a feeling she knew him and for some reason went with him willingly.' She paused. 'There's still the other questions.'

'Which are?'

'Where the hell was she for the weeks before she died? And what about the baby?'

Sabine's question hung in the air; unanswerable.

'I promise you,' said Denni. 'We'll do our very best to

answer both questions and as soon as we know anything we'll let you know.'

The client in waiting still stood patiently beneath the light of the street lamp. Rydell felt a lumpen depression settle on him.

Denni muttered, 'I hope she gives him hell.'

Eight

*H*e'd been chopping onions when the knife slipped. The fine blade caught the tip of his little finger. He watched fascinated as the blood dripped on to the diced onions turning them a bright pink. Surprising, he thought, how much blood could drip from a small cut. After a while he ran his finger under the cold tap, applied a wodge of kitchen paper, raised his fisted hand and waited for the bleeding to stop. After five minutes he applied a plaster and then added the pink onions to the hot extra virgin olive oil. He savoured those words – extra virgin. Could anything be extra virgin?

He was making chicken casserole and he prided himself on being a good cook. I'm a bloody good cook, he thought as he added pieces of skinned chicken to the pan. He always cooked from scratch, disapproving of anything ready-made. His daughter would always have the best.

The cellar ladder was proving to be a nuisance. It was the expandable aluminium type that could be lowered whenever needed. Once he'd decided to go down to the cellar, he shouted at her to stand behind the bed where he could see her feet. But with Angela in his arms it was always difficult.

She was still scared enough of him to do as she was told but it was only a question of time before she made a bid for freedom. She'd been crying on and off for days now. And he'd caught her flushing food down the lavatory. So now he had yet another chore – watching her eat. The lazy bitch only *had to feed the baby. He wasn't going to take any nonsense from her. If she didn't eat, her milk would dry up.*

He loved watching Angela at the breast, seeing her tiny mouth fixed firmly on the nipple. Her chubby hands would touch the white breast softly, her eyes closed. After being winded, sometimes a trickle of milk would appear at the corner of her mouth. As soon as she'd been fed he would snatch her away so that the satisfied smiles would be his and his alone.

Yesterday he'd had to go out so he'd left the baby with her for several hours. He had taken his van to the car wash for the third time. This time he had the inside cleaned by a young, dim-looking lad in a green uniform with a Best Valet badge on his chest. He had watched the boy at work and he had been meticulous. Well pleased, he had given the boy a large tip.

When he had returned home and looked down into the cellar they were lying in each other's arms, fast asleep. Jealousy had caught him in the stomach, hard as a fist. Then anger mixed with desire. He needed a woman. Not the one in his cellar. She had a purpose. He needed a woman or a girl who was useless. Expendable. Not missed. Easy.

Soon it would be dark. Then he would go out again. Hunting bitch.

Nine

D avid Bolten hardly noticed the grey looming clouds as
he drove to Harrowford School. He used the time to
clear his mind, to focus on work. Sara, he compartmentalised
into a section of his mind and marked it, *pending*.

He'd noticed the staff treated him differently, as if he
were ill or delicate in some way. He found it unnerving.
He wanted everything in his working day to be normal.
Work, in his opinion, was not only his salvation but also
everyone else's.

The winter term was always particularly long and difficult, especially in bad weather. Storm and winds seemed to
unsettle the students and the staff too seemed edgy but he
did his best to appear calm and unruffled at all times.

David's deputy, Jackie South, although a worrier had
coped reasonably well. Last week's interviews had been
cancelled on his instructions and would take place today.
The most senior position which needed to be filled after
Easter was for the head of the English department, but he had
two junior posts available which he felt were equally important. After all, he reasoned, today's probationary teacher was
tomorrow's head of department.

Just before morning break, as he was casting a watch-
ful eye over the school grounds from his office window,
wondering if the rain would hold off, he saw Inspector
Rydell talking to the school caretaker. For a moment he
wondered if the most sensible thing to do was intercept
him before he began talking to members of staff. But

then he realised if he *did*, it might be thought that he had something to hide. If Rydell had any bad news then he would have come straight to his office. Bolten sat down at his desk and waited.

When Rydell did arrive, half an hour later, he said, 'There is no news, Mr Bolten. Just one or two sightings which we're following up.'

'I see,' said Bolten. 'Then you'd better sit down and explain what you want.'

Rydell, refusing a seat, stared out of the window. 'I wanted to find out if any of the staff knew Sara.'

Bolten didn't comment, but he did feel disconcerted that Rydell wasn't sitting down. In his office people sat down.

Rydell turned abruptly, keeping his back to the window. 'It seems, according to sixth-form gossip, that Sara did know someone on the staff.'

'Really?' said Bolten. 'Sixth-form gossip is hardly to be relied upon.'

'True,' agreed Rydell. 'But in this case it may well have an element of truth.'

Bolten fixed his eyes stonily at Rydell. 'Tell me then, Inspector. There is really no need to prolong this.'

'The word is,' began Rydell, 'that Sara was seen with one of your teachers at the gym on several occasions.'

'Harrowford's gym is hardly private,' said Bolten, deliberately keeping his voice even and level. 'It would be very surprising if she didn't meet other locals there.'

'True.'

'Well?'

Rydell shrugged. 'I'm waiting for you to ask who this teacher is but you obviously know.'

Bolten felt an uncomfortable warmth creep upwards towards his face. Should he lie or brazen it out? 'Very well,' he said. 'I had a feeling she was – flirting – with someone and I was tipped off it was Chas Trinity, our head of English.'

'Only flirting?'

Bolten stared at Rydell. 'Yes. If you must know, even before the tip-off, I knew she liked him. Sara told me she chatted to him at the gym. She told me she thought he fancied her.'

'So you decided to sack him?'

'No. He resigned.'

'Just like that, no argument, no denial?'

Bolten shrugged. 'He's a married man with children. The rumours would have eventually got back to his wife. He assured me he and Sara only chatted and not much was likely to go on with them side by side on rowing machines. It wasn't exactly conducive to a full-blown affair.'

Rydell didn't answer but he did agree. Romance amongst the pedal pushers at the gym wasn't something he'd ever noticed.

'Anyway,' said Bolten, 'what has all this got to do with Sara's disappearance?'

'If Sara had been taken by force and it's only "if" at the moment, then she could have been targeted.'

'You mean stalked?'

Rydell nodded. 'Someone knew you were out that evening. Perhaps he was watching the house. Had, in fact, been watching the movements of you both.' He paused to observe Bolten's reaction. His face remained bland. 'Was it usual for you to go out on Saturday evening alone?'

Bolten shook his head. 'Occasionally for Lodge meetings, that's all. That Saturday was a university reunion. I organise one every year. We meet in a pub, have a meal, talk about old times.'

'You didn't tell me that before.'

'You didn't ask.'

'How long have you been a Mason?' asked Rydell.

Bolten paused before answering. 'I sense the disapproval in your tone, Inspector. It's nearly five years since I joined. And I'm proud to be a Lodge member. It's a welcome change from my job.'

'You find being a head teacher stressful?'

'Very. Although I try not to show it.'

'What about at home?'

'What about it?'

'Some men take their work stresses home.'

'That's personal experience, is it, Inspector?'

'A common experience I would suggest,' said Rydell, beginning to dislike Bolten intensely. '*Were* you stressed at home?'

Bolten shrugged. 'I was tetchy and irritable at times. Especially since Ben was born. Continually broken nights can be wearing.'

'I'm sure they are,' agreed Rydell. 'Very wearing too for Sara.'

'At least she didn't have to work,' snapped Bolten.

Rydell smiled wryly. He was beginning to break through. Bolten now looked a little agitated. 'Although of course,' he blustered, 'I do realise that looking after a baby *is* work.' He glanced at his watch. 'I do have several appointments today, Inspector.'

'Just one more question, Mr Bolten.'

'Fire away.'

'We know from your account that Sara wasn't depressed, but was she happy?'

Bolten frowned in irritation. 'Of course she was happy.'

'How did she show her happiness?'

'I don't know what you want me to say. Are you trying to say I didn't know my wife?'

'Not at all, but how many men really understand their wives?'

'I wouldn't know. Let me repeat that as far as it is possible to know, Sara was happy – both with me and Ben.'

'Fair enough,' said Rydell, 'but I shall have to seek other opinions.'

'Mine is the only one that counts,' said Bolten.

He sounded sure, too sure.

*   *   *

It was fifteen minutes later that Rydell found Chas Trinity in a near-empty staff room.

'We can talk in my office,' he said. 'In here, even the pencils have ears.'

Trinity was tall and athletic-looking, with slightly greying hair and solemn brown eyes.

Rydell noticed that Trinity's desk was a mess: essays vied with memos and paper cups and open textbooks. He resisted the urge to tidy up and, although he sat down, he angled his chair so that he didn't face the clutter. Trinity was now willing to talk freely behind closed doors. 'Yes, I did know Sara, before you ask, and yes, I did fancy her, but that's as far as it went.'

Rydell nodded. 'If nothing happened why are you leaving?'

Trinity smiled. 'I haven't got a great deal of choice. The rumours have made an innocent friendship into a passionate affair, especially since her disappearance. The latest gossip is that she is waiting at some unspecified place for me to join her.'

'And is she?'

He laughed, an easy good-natured laugh. 'Sometimes I wish she was, but only from a safety angle – her safety.'

'You don't think then she left of her own free will?'

Trinity shook his head slowly. 'I didn't know her very well. You can't actually have intimate chats as you work up a sweat but sometimes we had coffee together afterwards and she did open up then.'

'About what?'

'Mostly about the relationship with her husband.'

'And how would you describe that?'

'Rather troubled, but no more so than many marriages.'

'Troubled in what way?' asked Rydell.

Trinity thought for a moment. 'Bolten is mill-pond calm at work but, according to Sara, a stormy sea at home.'

'Violent?'

78

Trinity shrugged. 'Hard to say. All Sara did say was that it had been weeks since they'd made love and occasionally they went for days without speaking.'

'Hardly sufficient cause,' said Rydell, 'to abandon both husband and child.' He paused and looked directly at Trinity. 'Where were you on the Saturday before last – the night Sara disappeared?'

'I was at home with my wife and teenage daughter.'

'You stayed in the whole evening?'

'Yes.'

Rydell stood up to go. 'Do you find it easy to work in chaos?' he asked.

Trinity stared at him, puzzled. Rydell glanced meaningfully at the desk. 'Oh.' He smiled. 'That's tidier than usual.'

As Rydell left the school it occurred to him that even chaos was only relative.

Ten

'Don't be late, Steph,' shouted Janice Upton to her daughter from the bathroom, 'be back by ten or there'll be trouble. And don't forget your coat.'

'Yeah. Yeah.'

Stephanie Upton walked out into the night wearing a black miniskirt, a grey cropped top and a black cardigan. Her white trainers had the laces tucked in but not secured into a bow. 'That's how everybody wears them,' she'd told her mum.

It was freezing cold and she walked fast. She was supposed to be going to her friend Katie's house but she wasn't, she was going to the precinct to meet a boy she'd fancied for ages.

On Harrowford's Kestrel Estate the precinct consisted of a row of six shops, two boarded up, one chippy, one newsagent's, a charity shop and a mini-mart. She was meeting Daniel at the chippy.

Steph hurried on, pulling her cardigan round her, shivering, wondering if he'd be there. She rounded the corner and saw the chippy lights and two lads she didn't know standing around. There was no sign of anyone else. She hung back

'Steph – Steph.'

Stephanie turned. Katie was screeching her name and hurrying towards her in huge platform shoes.'

'I like your shoes,' said Stephanie. 'They're great.'

'Yeah. Me mum got them from the market.' She raised a slim leg under the light from a street lamp so that her friend could see them more clearly. 'Only nine ninety-nine.'

'I've got to be back by ten.'

'Yeah, so have I. Have you seen him?'

Stephanie shook her head. 'Shall we walk round a bit?'

They linked arms and walked towards the chippy. A few more of their mates had ventured out, and some huddled together on the wooden benches outside the shops. One of them, standing alone, had cigarettes.

'Can I buy a fag off you?' asked Katie.

'You talking to me?' He was tall with a nose stud and three earrings in one ear. Katie knew his name was Michael Downs and that he was a mate of Daniel's. 'Yeah,' she said. 'How much?'

'Fifty pence.'

She laughed. 'I'll give you twenty. For fifty I'd want spliff.'

'You've got a fucking cheek,' he said but he handed her a cigarette and waved her money away. Then he took her hand and held it as he flicked his disposable lighter into life. She took a deep drag and said, 'Have you seen Daniel?'

'Why?'

'My friend Steph was seeing him here tonight.'

He looked towards Steph. 'He's busy. He'll be here later.'

Steph, hearing that, felt a stab of disappointment. It was perishing cold, she hadn't done her homework, and she hadn't got any money with her. She knew Katie really fancied Michael Downs. He was older than the rest and he didn't hang around the precinct for long. Steph hung back. Michael and Katie were sharing a cigarette and whispering. After a while Katie came over and linked arms. 'Look, Steph, Michael says I can go with him. Do you want to come?'

'Where to?'

'His place. His mum's out.'

Steph shook her head. 'No, my mum'll kill me if I'm late. And his place is too far away.'

'Please yourself. What are you going to do?'

'I'll wait around for a while, see if Daniel turns up.'

'All right then, see you tomorrow.'

'Yeah. See you at school.'

Steph watched the two of them walk away. A few of the others followed them. She paced up and down outside the chippy for some time. By nine forty-five she was on her own. The chip shop stayed open till twelve but from now its customers were mostly men who'd been to the pub. That's why Mum wanted her home by ten. She took one last look. 'Sod you, Danny boy,' she muttered aloud and began walking home.

She'd only walked a few yards when it began to drizzle. Then the drizzle changed to sleet. There was no one about. She walked on, head down, arms wrapped round her body. The mean council-house windows didn't shed much light, but Steph wasn't too worried: she would soon be home in the warm. And she'd be there on time.

There was even a short cut, a footpath that saved a few hundred yards. When she came to the gap in the bushes she paused. It wasn't pitch dark, and there was no one lurking about, she could see that. She walked faster; almost ran. As she got to the end she breathed a sigh of relief as she reached the cul-de-sac and saw the lights of houses.

She'd taken only two steps when the arm came round her throat. She was aware of being lifted upwards and backwards. Her feet moved but seemed to kick at nothing. She knew she was being dragged back along the footpath. The pressure around her neck was choking her.

'Keep still, bitch,' he whispered in her ear. 'I'll kill you if you don't.'

She went limp. Trying to think. What do I do? *Mum! Mum!* She wanted to scream but she couldn't. He was forcing her down on to her knees. One hand hard on her neck Her face against gravel. She couldn't breathe. He pressed something cold into her neck.

'One sound and you're dead, bitch.' Then, he was pulling

and ripping at her skirt, yanking at her tights and knickers, pulling her knees up and scraping them against the ground. She could hear his harsh breathing. As he relaxed his grip slightly on her neck she gulped for air, suddenly a knife-like pain tore between her legs but she could only scream on the inside. The pain went on and on, then stopped. His breathing altered and he lifted his hand from her neck. 'Don't move and don't speak,' he said. She felt dizzy, black speckles danced in front of her eyes. Then she heard his footsteps going away slowly; he wasn't hurrying. She didn't move for a long time.

The sleet changed to snow and the wet and the cold began to seep into her. She knew she would die if she didn't move. She tried to shout for help but the sound she made was soft and croaky, not like her voice at all, although in her head it sounded loud. Using her hands she managed to kneel upright. She still felt dizzy and now she was beginning to shake. Once on her feet, she staggered towards the end of the footpath and lights but fear got the better of her. He could be waiting for her in the same place. Steph turned and began going back to the precinct. She tried to run, but couldn't. Her tights and knickers were round her ankles and she'd lost a trainer. Her mum would be furious. She pulled up her tights and knickers as best she could. Her heart was pounding in her chest and she felt sick, she couldn't breathe. By now she could see the precinct lights and two men coming towards her. She saw the look on their faces and looked down: blood was pouring down her legs. One of them took off his jacket, then picked her up and carried her to the chip shop. Her mum arrived before the ambulance or the police.

Even though she was wrapped in blankets she couldn't stop shaking. 'I told you to wear your coat,' said her mum. Then when the ambulance came she said to the driver, 'She's only fourteen,' and then she started to cry.

Steph would have liked to cry too but she felt numb and lifeless. The ambulance man kept telling her she was safe now. But was she? He was still out there. He could still come after her.

Eleven

R hoda Lydney struggled to get out of bed. She peered at her travelling clock – it was two thirty a.m. How long Ben had been crying for she didn't know, but she resented David expecting her to get up every night. The more she got to know her son-in-law the less she liked him. She loved her grandson, but after a few broken nights in a row she felt utterly exhausted.

Ben, red-faced and distressed, stopped crying once she'd picked him up, but by the time she'd walked down to the kitchen he'd started again. He quietened when she eventually produced a bottle.

Rhoda had been away from work for more than two weeks now and she desperately wanted to get back to her desk, not because her job at Crossley and Palmer was in jeopardy, but because she was in love with the junior partner, Philip Palmer. Before Sara disappeared Rhoda had spent every weekend at his place and at least twice during the week they would spend the night together, and of course they saw each other at work. Everyone in the office knew they were an item and as soon as their respective houses were sold they planned to buy a small house together. Philip had been very supportive at first but his phone calls over the last two days had verged on the peevish. He'd never been married before and was ten years younger than Rhoda: he wasn't used to sharing her.

Once Ben was changed and back in his cot he did gradually settle but Rhoda, although heavy-eyed and weary, found that she couldn't sleep. Sara kept coming into her mind. Had life become so intolerable for her daughter that the only escape had been to disappear? Had she fallen in love with someone else? Had she become exhausted and no one had noticed? Rhoda could now see that she should have offered Sara more support, because the way she felt at the moment she wanted her freedom too. Was that how Sara had felt? The idea that Sara may not have left of her own free will she pushed firmly to the back of her mind. She had to believe Sara was alive.

Rhoda had already made the breakfast coffee and toast when David appeared, dressed, at seven a.m.

'You're up early,' he said as he sat down, expecting to be waited on.

'I've been up since two thirty.'

'Oh. Not feeling well?'

'Your son woke me.'

'I didn't hear a thing. Was he awake long?'

'Long enough.'

David glanced up at her. 'Do I sense a certain frostiness?'

At that moment Rhoda could have easily walked out wearing her slippers. She had come to realise that her son-in-law behaved towards *her* as he must have done towards Sara.

'I can't stay on here,' she said. 'You'll have to make other arrangements for Ben . . . I love him dearly but I'm past my mothering date. I want to go back to my own home and life.'

David frowned, but he didn't seem surprised. 'I knew you wouldn't be a permanent fixture, Rhoda, and I am grateful. I'll get something fixed up as soon as I can.'

'I'm going tomorrow, David. You'll have to take time off from your job.' Somehow his shocked expression pleased her.

He continued to stare at her. 'Couldn't you just give me a couple of days?' he said. 'I'll have to interview prospective nannies.'

'Ben could go to a nursery in the day.'

'Is that what you want for your grandson?'

'Of course it isn't. I want my daughter back but we don't know when that will be – do we?'

He leant across and touched her hand. 'Are you leaving because I didn't hear Ben crying last night?'

She moved her hand away. 'You never hear him cry – any night. I can't help wondering what else you didn't hear or didn't notice. Or simply ignored.'

'What's that supposed to mean?'

'Do I have to spell it out?'

He nodded and she realised he genuinely didn't know what she meant. 'I'm talking about your wife,' she said. 'At first I couldn't believe Sara would just walk out, but now I'm not so sure. Who knows how desperate she felt that night. During this past two weeks I've begun to imagine how she might have felt. You took her for granted. You—'

'That's enough, Rhoda,' he snapped. 'I don't want us to have a row. I do the best I can. I just want to hold my job down and care for Ben until Sara comes home.'

'*If* she comes home,' muttered Rhoda.

Twelve

*I*t wasn't the first time he'd raped. The first time, he'd waited to read about it in the papers, but there had been no report. It had taken a while for the penny to drop – the silly bitch hadn't reported it. The idea that the police would be looking for him had given him a buzz.

Strange, he thought, how raping had made him feel extra-special, in control, powerful. Raping a bitch he'd hunted calmed him. No drug could compare with that. He felt able to cope now with the bitch in the cellar. He wasn't going to let her get to him. She'd been trying to befriend him, trying out her amateur psychology. It was all I want, I want, with her: she wanted fresh air; she wanted to write to her husband; she wanted a bath. Bossy cow. She'd never get the better of him.

He couldn't resist telling her how he'd raped the girl. That shut her up. He told her everything, in detail. She trembled and said she felt sick. He said when it was in the paper he'd let her read all about it.

He'd have to think seriously about letting her write a letter. He'd dictate what she said of course, but at least then the police would stop looking for her. He'd have to be careful about fingerprints, only hers could be on the letter and the envelope: fingerprints could be lifted from paper.

He still hadn't told her about Maria. She wouldn't be asking for a bath if she'd known.

The police were likely to draw a blank on Maria. There was nothing to connect him with her. Absolutely nothing.

88

Thirteen

Denni was late for work the next day. DCI Fenton's belly seemed all of a quiver as he harangued both her and an absent Rydell. When Fenton was in full flow she fixed her eyes on his stomach and somehow his words failed to wound.

'Well – where the hell is he?' he demanded finally.

'I'm not sure, sir,' said Denni calmly. 'Although he did mention toothache to me yesterday.' She guessed Rydell had gone running, but the less Fenton knew about the personal lives of staff the better. Fenton's expression suggested he had heard teeth used as an excuse before. 'Well, find him quickly. I want words with the organ grinder not his monkey.'

Now that Fenton had poured out some his venom his face became less puce and he allowed himself a pause to take breath.

'We do have a name now for the unidentified body, sir.'

'I'm glad your day in London wasn't completely wasted. Pity you haven't come up with the perpetrator.'

'We will, sir.'

He eyed her with distaste, handed her a report sheet and said, 'Rape case, last night. I don't like rapists on my patch. The girl wasn't fit to be questioned last night. You deal with it and make sure you check the personal descriptive forms – the uniformed branch knock on a lot of doors for those. Get them on computer today.'

Rydell turned up just as Denni was getting into her car.

He didn't offer an explanation and Denni didn't ask. She merely said, 'You had toothache and Fenton's bursting a blood vessel about our trip to London.'

'I'll cope. Where are you off to?'

'The Kestrel Estate, there's been a rape.'

He sighed. 'That place is a cesspit. Don't be too long. I want you back here.'

As Denni approached the estate a sliver of sun broke through the greyness. It did nothing to lift the bleakly dismal sight of boarded-up houses and gardens that seemed to grow discarded television sets and old mattresses. Even the play area had been vandalised, the remaining swing hanging by only one chain.

The rape victim, Stephanie Upton, lived in one of the neater cul-de-sacs. The garden was a patch of yellowed grass, but flouncy white nets brightened up the small windows. Stephanie's mother answered the door. She was of average height but small-boned, almost fragile-looking. Her red eyes and pale face reflected a long, sleepless night.

Denni introduced herself.

'Come in, love. She's still in bed but she's awake.'

Janice Upton paused at the bottom of the stairs and yelled, 'Steph. Rouse yourself. Someone here to see you.'

There was no response. 'I'll take her up some tea. Do you want some, love?'

'I would, thanks.'

Denni followed Janice into the poky kitchen which was clean and tidy but obviously damp as black mould was spread over the walls like a disease.

'I've been on the transfer list for bloody years,' said Janice as she dunked tea bags into three mugs. 'When I complain about the mould the council says it's my fault for not having enough ventilation. We'll never get out of here. There's hundreds like me.'

'Are you on your own?'

'Yeah. Her dad took off before Steph's first nappy change.'

Janice directed Denni into the narrow damp-smelling living room while she took tea to Stephanie. Denni sat down to wait on a worn blue Dralon sofa. The room was tidy to the point of sparseness but a gas fire roared and both the central light and the lamp had lampshades. Denni had been in some homes on the estate where bare lightbulbs were a sign of unrelenting poverty.

'Poor little cow,' said Janice when she came back. 'Do you think she'll ever get over it?'

'In my experience,' said Denni cagily, 'catching the man really helps.' Denni also knew some women, especially young girls with no previous loving sexual experiences to remember, who were mentally scarred for life.

Janice slumped in an armchair in a corner of the room and wiped a hand wearily over her face. 'If I had a chance, I'd gut the bastard . . . But then I keep blaming myself. I should have kept her in.'

'You couldn't keep her a prisoner.'

'She's a good kid,' Janice murmured. Then she stared at Denni, her eyes filling with tears. 'I don't know what to say to her. She won't talk to me and we used to talk about everything. I think she thinks it was her fault.'

'It might be better,' said Denni, 'if I talked to her alone. She might open up to me and remember something significant.'

'Yeah. OK. If you lot catch him will she have to give evidence?'

'Let's say *when* we catch him – yes, she might have to appear in court but they will be very sympathetic towards her. And with any luck he'll plead guilty.'

Soft footsteps on the stairs signalled Stephanie's arrival. Somehow Denni expected a leggy, verging on womanhood fourteen-year-old. Instead a slight girl, no more than five foot tall, entered the room dressed in blue pyjamas. Straight dark hair framed an elfin face. She looked no more than twelve. Only her eyes looked aged.

'Have you caught him?' she asked. Denni caught the edge of hope in her voice.

She smiled and patted the sofa beside her. 'Not yet – but we will – with your help.'

'I didn't even see him. How can I help?' Her voice was a strange mixture of childish petulance and fear.

'I'm here to help you remember things you probably noticed but haven't realised yet.'

Stephanie sat down and began rubbing her knees.

'I'll make us some more tea,' said Janice.

Denni noticed Stephanie hadn't acknowledged her mother's presence and she didn't look up as Janice left the room.

'Your mum says I can speak to you on your own – is that all right with you?'

'Yeah. Suppose so.'

'What time did you go out last night?'

'About eight.'

'Where did you go?'

'The precinct.'

'Did you go to meet anyone there?'

'My friend Katie.'

'Was there anyone else there?'

'Yeah. A few of my mates.'

'What did you do?'

'Just hung around.'

'Who did you talk to?'

Stephanie shrugged and fell silent.

'Did you go out to meet a boy?'

There was no response. Stephanie's small mouth was pursed and she began picking at her fingernails. 'A doctor cut my nails,' she said, staring intently at her bluntly cut nails. 'I was trying to grow them.'

'They'll soon grow,' said Denni. 'Do you know why they had to be cut?'

She shook her head. 'He never said.'

'You may have scratched the man who attacked you or caught a fibre from his clothes. That could help to catch him.'

'I don't think I scratched him. I can't remember.'

'Don't worry about it. Tell me about this boy you were meeting.'

'He didn't turn up,' she said. Then, giving Denni a quick glance, she muttered, 'Caught me there, didn't you?'

'You haven't done anything wrong, Stephanie. Your mum doesn't need to know anything you don't want her to.' Denni noticed that the girl's shoulders relaxed a little. 'What's his name?'

'Daniel.'

'What about Katie? Did she like him too?'

Stephanie smiled fleetingly. 'No. She fancies Michael. He turned up but he never hangs around for long. Katie went to his place . . .' she paused, looking worried. 'Don't tell my mum, will you? She'll think Katie's a little slag. And she isn't. My mum will stop me seeing her.'

'I won't say a word,' said Denni. 'When Katie went, what did you do?'

'I just hung around, I had to be in by ten.'

Denni could hear the tremor in her voice now and she reached out to hold the girl's hand. 'I know this is difficult, Stephanie, but you're a brave girl. I want you to try and remember every little detail from now on. Can you do that?'

'Yeah. I'll try.'

'Good girl. Close your eyes if it helps.'

She shivered slightly but closed her eyes.

'You've just decided to leave the precinct,' said Denni softly. 'Was there anyone around?'

Stephanie, eyes still closed, shook her head. 'No. The chippy was empty.'

'You saw no one? And you didn't hear anyone follow-ing you?'

A small voice answered, 'No.'

'Were you walking fast?'

'Yeah. It was cold.'

'Was it raining?'

'Not then.'

'You kept walking. Did you hear anything?'

'Not really. Just somebody shouting, but no one was following me.' She broke off, eyes still closed, small hand gripping Denni's.

'I got to the footpath – it's a short cut. I looked down it to make sure there was no one hanging about.'

'Tell me about the footpath.'

'It's got high fences both sides and sort of gravel on the ground.'

'Then what –'

Stephanie trembled slightly and spoke in a rush. 'I got to the end of the path, I'd taken a couple of steps into Wren Avenue and then there was an arm around my neck and he was dragging me backwards and –'

'Slow down. Take it easy,' murmured Denni. 'Try to remember the arm – *just* his arm. Was he wearing gloves?'

There was a short pause. 'No. No, I felt the skin of his hand against my ear.'

'Good. Now try to remember his sleeve. He had his arm around your neck – you probably felt the material and saw the colour.'

She thought for a while. 'It felt soft – padded.'

'Good. Good. And the colour?'

'Black. Black. It was definitely black.'

Denni felt that now they were on a roll. 'Did he seem tall? Did he tower above you?'

'He was a lot taller than me.'

'Was he wide or skinny?'

'Wide.'

'Was he a man or a boy?'

'A man.'

'You seem very sure, Stephanie. Why don't you think it was a boy?'

This time she hesitated. Eventually, still with her eyes tight shut, she said, 'He smelt like a man.'

'How does a man smell?'

'I dunno – just different.'

'What sort of smell did he have? Was it alcohol? Or tobacco?'

She shook her head. 'He smelt clean but there was another smell . . .'

'Was it aftershave?'

'No.'

'A chemical smell? Like petrol?'

'Maybe. I can't think. I've never smelt it before.'

'That's fine . . . you're doing well. Tell me about his face.'

'I didn't see his face. I told you,' she murmured, tears only just at bay.

'Remember this, Stephanie,' said Denni. 'He didn't *want* you to see his face.'

She brightened a little. 'Yeah, I suppose so.' It was a grudging acknowledgement, but Stephanie was proving to be a good witness. Denni had interviewed young rape victims before who were so shocked by their experience that they had blanked out the memory completely. Stephanie, although frail-looking, was courageous and Denni felt sure she would remember even more, given time.

'Although you didn't see his face,' began Denni, 'did you feel it?'

There was a short pause and then, 'Yeah, I did. He didn't have a beard, his face was smooth. I felt it when he spoke.' She shuddered at the memory.

'What did he say?'

'He . . . he . . .'

'Take a deep breath, Stephanie. You're doing great.'

She gulped rather than breathed. 'He called me a bitch and said he would kill me.'

'Can you remember his *exact* words?'

She thought for a moment with her eyes tight shut. 'He said – "Keep still, bitch. I'll kill you if you don't." Then he pressed a knife in my neck. I think it was a knife. I didn't see it. He said, "One sound and you're dead, bitch."'

'Was he loud-spoken or soft?'

Stephanie shivered and opened her eyes. 'He whispered it.'

'Do you think he had a local accent?'

'I'm not sure. He didn't sound *common* if you know what I mean.'

'Would you know his voice again?'

'I think so,' she said uncertainly.

'You're doing brilliantly,' said Denni. 'Only a few more questions now.'

'He hurt me,' she said suddenly. 'He really hurt me.'

'I know.'

'Does it always hurt?'

'Being raped is not like having normal sex, Stephanie,' Denni tried to reassure her. 'Having sex is about making love. Rape is just violence. It's an attack.'

Stephanie's tears overflowed now, with racking sobs that made Denni feel powerless. 'Do you want your mum?' she asked.

Stephanie nodded, unable to speak.

'Janice,' Denni called loudly and Janice was beside her daughter in seconds enveloping her, making soft soothing noises until at last her sobs quietened.

'She's doing really well, Janice.'

'I think she's had enough, poor kid,' she said, stroking her daughter's hair.

'I'm all right, Mum, honest. I'm helping. I want him to be caught.'

'OK, pet. If you're sure.'

'We don't have to talk about the actual attack,' said Denni. 'Tell me about when he left you. What did you do?'

'I just stayed still on the ground.'

'What did you think about?'

'Nothing. I just listened.'

'What for?'

'To make sure he was going away.'

'And what did you hear?'

She thought for a moment and then managed a brief smile. 'I think he was wearing trainers. It was that sort of sound.'

'Good. And when his footsteps finished?'

Another pause. 'A car. I heard a car.'

Denni felt a sense of elation. She wanted to punch the air. Instead she gave Stephanie a big hug. 'We know so much about him now and it's all down to you being so brave.' She paused and touched Stephanie's face. 'Do you want to know what you've just told me?'

The girl nodded, and tried to smile but failed.

'Here goes,' said Denni. 'He's a grown man, tall, well built, clean shaven, wearing a black padded jacket and trainers. He drives a car and he talks quietly, maybe has a local accent. He smells of a substance that might be chemical.'

Stephanie gave a loud sniff and looked relieved but not overly impressed. 'Did they find my trainer, Mum?'

'No, love,' said Janice.

'I think police funds might run to a new pair,' said Denni.

'Great.' For the first time Stephanie managed a proper smile. A happy teenage smile that Denni hoped was a sign that she would resume her life without having to constantly look over her shoulder. Somehow, though, she had the feeling that would take a long time.

Fourteen

R am Patel, living temporarily in a five-bedroom guest-house, surveyed his breakfast with suspicion and won-dered why the superintendent had ever suggested it was a 'safe house'. There was nothing safe about it, except that trees enclosed the building itself, it had a long drive and the elderly Irish owner, known as 'Bridie Mac', verged on paranoia. Ram's fellow male guests worked away from home and stayed there from Monday to Thursday. Ram conceded it was respectable – but *safe* he wasn't convinced. He knew as well as anyone that once a detective's cover had been blown you took your chance, altered your appearance a bit and carried on in another patch. He supposed then this place was some sort of *reward* because it was a damn sight better than the run-down hostel they called a section house. Changing his appearance wasn't an option, even losing weight and wearing a wig he'd still be the 'Paki cop' to Manchester villains.

The Emerald Isle Guesthouse was situated on the outer reaches of Harrowford in the middle of a gaunt row of once splendid Victorian houses. All were now either hotels or flats or bed and breakfast establishments. Bridie Mac's place boasted no bar, Bridie herself didn't need one. She was pickled as a herring at most times of the day or night; and yet she functioned – Ram admired that. Bridie was a tall bony woman with huge hands and feet, coal-black hair lacquered into complete stillness and a pale complexion rarely found in the still living. Bridie, or maybe her apparition, seemed to be everywhere in the house. Ram found her at every corner he turned. Merely opening his door – she was there. And yet somehow she also managed, seconds later, to be in the kitchen cooking and serving breakfast.

He'd been sitting in the dining room, staring at his breakfast in the subdued light of a forty-watt bulb that forced its way from beneath a pink tasselled lampshade. He'd chosen the vegetarian option, which, he thought, would be less fattening, when Bridie approached the table where he sat alone.

'And what's wrong with it?' she demanded.

'Nothing,' he said, staring down at two veggie sausages, two fried eggs, mushrooms, tomatoes and baked beans plus fried bread and toast on the side. 'I'm just wondering if I was man enough for it.'

She shrugged her wide shoulders. 'I can't abide a man who's fussy. What did you expect – vegetable biriani?'

Ram smiled. A biriani he could have managed. 'I'll do the best I can, Bridie.'

'You do that, Mr Patel,' she said as she walked away fast but heavy footed. He began to eat. Ferocious dogs and Bridie had a lot in common and he was wary of both.

He'd been staying at the Emerald Isle for two months now and before the murder inquiry had started his girlfriend had stayed for two weekends. Now weekends no longer existed and he'd have to tell her tonight that he couldn't go to Manchester on the super's express orders. 'A blown cover is a blown cover,' he'd said, and there was no arguing with that.

Manfully enough he managed to eat breakfast and promised himself he would go on a diet. On Monday. Strange how motivated he could be on the calorie-restricted front when he had a full stomach. Monday was a few days away so he stopped on the way to pick up Denni to buy boiled sweets to last till then.

The plan was to drive to Derbyshire to see the Haddon/

Harris family. Rydell was spending all his time trying to find Sara Bolten and Fenton had decided he would organise the Maria Seaton investigation. Word had it that he was making progress as fast as sifting sand through a tea strainer. Neither colleagues, nor witnesses, nor criminals warmed to Fenton. Ram, among others, often wondered how he'd managed to make chief inspector. Rydell held the view that the interview board had been impressed by his tough, uncompromising attitude towards 'incompetent' staff. So convincing was he at the time that a DI was transferred and then another. Rydell had only just found out he was the token 'sicko'. Ram supposed he was the token 'ethnic'.

Denni was not waiting in the car park. She was already at her desk working, trying to collate names and addresses of all known local sex offenders.

'You're keen, Denni,' said Ram from the doorway.

She opened her mouth in surprise as her memory re-located.

'Don't apologise,' said Ram. 'Just get your coat, it's bloody freezing outside.'

Harrowford had a traffic problem: it hardly moved until about nine thirty and even then Ram crawled along in second gear.

'Are you an expert on arsonists now?' asked Denni.

Ram shrugged. 'It's like religions – many different branches. There's fire worshippers – fire turns them on – ecstasy on wings of fire. They get hot pants from just watching. Then you have –' he paused to go past a car turning right, 'the heroes. They start a fire with the intention of saving someone. Then there are the worshippers of money. They do it for the compensation –' Ram paused again to offer her a humbug.

'Is that it then?'

'If only,' he said. 'Wanker!' admonished Ram calmly as a silver BMW cut him up. 'Some arsonists concentrate on burning certain buildings – strangely enough, barns are a hot favourite.'

'I've nursed a couple of arsonists,' said Denni.

'Why didn't you tell me before?'

'I like the sound of your voice.'

'Tell me about them, Denni. This could be useful.'

'One was a teenager, a paranoid schizophrenic, and his *voices* told him to rid the world of evil red cars. He'd burnt out five and then he was hospitalised. With medication he was fine.'

'And the other?'

'A depressive. He'd made two attempts to set fire to his own home.'

Ram crunched his sweet for a while and then said, 'Some arsonists don't seem to fall into the mad or the bad category. They're fascinated by fire itself. It doesn't turn them on sexually. It's more a childhood ambition like . . .'

'Like becoming a detective.'

Ram didn't comment on that. It embarrassed him to think he'd always wanted to be a cop and even more to admit to having been side-tracked into accountancy. 'It doesn't help our case,' he said, 'just knowing that most arsonists are young, male and nuts. And a high percentage are banged up anyway.'

He sounded despondent and Denni was beginning to feel the same way. 'I'm supposed to have re-interviewed Greenly and King,' she said. 'But the rape case has got in the way.'

'Tell Uncle Ram all about it.'

She did at length and it helped.

Derbyshire's fields and dry-stone walls were covered in a fine damp mist. A journey that should have taken less than an hour had taken two, due to various, so-called, traffic improvement schemes. Buxton was larger and more hilly than Ram had expected. The local police directed them to

Highcroft Road and he found the council estate built of grey stone easily enough. Number ten, one of a small number of bungalows, looked dull but solid in the gloomy mist. A thin-faced, grey-haired woman eventually opened the door. Denni's opening spiel received an, 'I've got nothing to say to the police.' Then, suddenly, came a grudging, 'You can come in if you want.'

In a cramped sitting room, four cats slept on the available chairs. The room was hot and humid and smelt of cat. A coal fire glowed and Mrs Haddon/Harris poked it for no reason at all. Then she picked up her knitting which lay as if reserving her chair against marauding cats, sat down, covered her knees with a blanket and continued knitting. Denni and Ram stood awkwardly. Ram began to sneeze and Denni realised he was allergic to cats. He looked in no condition to speak.

'I believe, Mrs . . .' she paused.

On cue, sharp eyes looked up from her knitting. 'Harris. I changed my name. I didn't want that old bastard's name.'

Denni, a little surprised by the sharp retort, said bluntly, 'A murdered woman was placed in your old barn and someone set your farmhouse on fire.'

'Nothing to do with me,' Mrs Harris said, eyes firmly on her knitting.

Denni tried again. 'The murderer must have known about the farm. Maybe he had a grudge, perhaps he once worked for you.'

There was a short pause, the silence broken only by clicking needles. 'We did have a farmhand once – he bore everyone a grudge. Worked with us for years. We couldn't get anyone else so we had to make the best of him. Sidney Beaver, known as Sly.'

'Could you give us his address?'

With a slight twitch of her thin lips, Mrs Harris said, 'He's in Harrowford. Marsh Road.'

'And the number?'

She thought for a moment. 'Third on the left.'

Denni knew Marsh Road; it was long and twisting. 'Is that from the Harrowford side?'

Mrs Harris's mouth seemed to want to smile but merely twitched again slightly, then she nodded. Denni decided it was a nervous tic.

'I did wonder if your children Richard and Lynsey might be able to help with our enquiries.'

'I don't know how,' Mrs Harris snapped. 'We left Harrowford when they were teenagers.'

At this point Ram began another round of sneezing, which disturbed the cats. As the cats moved so did Ram. 'I'll wait for you in the car,' he said, making a quick exit to the door with one black cat in hot pursuit.

'He'd be no good on a farm,' declared Mrs Harris. 'As for my kids: Richard lives in London; Lynsey's got a job in Spain.'

'So you don't see much of them?'

'Enough.'

By now Denni felt this visit had been a complete waste of time. She tried one more time. 'Is there anyone you know, Mrs Harris, perhaps connected with the farm, or at least local, who you suspect could be capable of murder and arson?'

She finished a row of knitting and stuck the silver needles into her ball of blue wool. 'There's only one person I can think of.'

'Who's that?'

'Richard.'

'Your own son?'

'He's a shirt lifter.'

'Just because he's gay doesn't mean—'

'Don't you lecture me, my girl. I know him. He's odd. He always liked making bonfires.'

'Have you got his address?'

'No. I'm not interested.'

'What does he do for a living?'

'Some sort of poofter's job – a social worker I think.'

'And that's all you know?' asked Denni, trying to keep her irritation and dislike from being too obvious.

'What did you expect?'

Denni was beginning to wonder.

'Close the door on your way out, won't you,' said Mrs Harris.

As Denni stood up to leave the room a grey and white cat rubbed herself slowly against her legs. For some reason it set her teeth on edge.

Rydell parked his car on the narrow approach road outside Gaddine's Bridge. Thin sunlight struggled through a pale-grey sky. The trees barely moved. The only sound he could hear was the rumbling of his own stomach. He'd had a run earlier and stupidly no breakfast. A letter from his ex-wife had ruined his appetite. She was getting married in the spring. He'd thought he wouldn't care but he did. Although the memories of the bitterness and wrangles of the divorce had almost faded, strangely, vivid happy memories of their first year together remained. The year before Paul was born.

He stared out towards the enclave of neat houses and wondered if he would find anyone in. These were mostly the homes of two-income couples, thirty-somethings who left home at seven a.m. and were lucky to return twelve hours later. Both then too tired to cook, but needing alcohol to unwind. Too tired even for the news at eleven. Bed was a solace rather than a place of rampant passion. Or was that just his own experience?

At the first two doors he knocked on there was no reply, but Lee Ann Parsons was in.

'Come in, Inspector,' she said. 'Another visit so soon. I feel like a cross between neighbourhood watch and neighbourhood grass.'

Her coffee percolator was full, so he accepted her offer of coffee. 'Is there any news of Sara?' she asked as she settled herself at the breakfast bar.

'Nothing on her whereabouts,' he said. 'A little gossip, that's all. Gossip you didn't tell me about.'

'I guess *gossip* isn't what it was,' she said in a mock drawl. 'A few chats with a co-worker of Sara's husband doesn't even rate a mention in my gossip arsenal.'

'What does?'

She raised her coffee cup to her lips and gazed at him thoughtfully. The gaze made him uncomfortable. She was trying to fathom *him*. 'I repeat,' he said evenly, 'what *does*?'

He thought he might have made her uncomfortable but her gaze was as even and level as he'd tried to make his voice. 'Are you married?' she asked

'Shall we keep to the point?'

'That is the point,' she said as she lowered her cup into the saucer. 'At least as much the point as saying that the information I have is mere gossip.'

Rydell couldn't keep the irritation from his voice. 'Stop the games, Mrs Parsons, and tell me what you know or think you know.'

'My, my. You're not such a cold fish after all.'

'Oh, yes I am,' he snapped.

She smiled irritatingly. 'I've not told you this before because I felt that if Sara was alive it would reduce your efforts . . . would concentrate them closer to home.'

'I can guess, but tell me anyway.'

'No one heard a car that night, no one saw anything. Strangely, I didn't see her the day before. She did miss a day now and again so I wasn't worried but David was potentially violent—'

'Would you like to explain "potentially" to me,' interrupted Rydell. 'In my opinion every human being has the *potential* to be violent.'

Lee Ann shrugged. 'I'll be blunt. He had slapped her a couple of times, but if all men who occasionally did that were capable of *murder* there wouldn't be many women left. It was his tightly controlled anger that was more scary. The white knuckles, the flashing eyes, his whole body language.'

'So now you think he killed her?'

'Don't tell me it hasn't crossed your mind.'

'Have you seen him angry?' asked Rydell. 'Or is his body language just hearsay?'

'Only once,' said Lee Ann tersely. 'They came for supper. Sara got tipsy and got rather flirtatious with my husband. It was perfectly harmless, funny even, but David was white with fury and stormed out.'

'That sounds fairly normal to me. Most men hate their wives drunk.' He paused thoughtfully. 'Drunk and flirtatious, she was asking for trouble.'

For once, Lee Ann was lost for words and Rydell was delighted. 'If I assume Bolten has murdered his wife in a fit of pique, he still had to dispose of the body. You seem the likely person to have an idea on that score.'

'I am *trying* to help, Inspector. Sarcasm isn't necessary.'

'Well?'

'I haven't seen him digging up the patio, if that's what you mean. Or cremating her in the back garden, or shoving the body in the boot of his car.'

Rydell managed a brief smile. 'Well, that covers most methods of disposal. Any other ideas?'

'No.' Suddenly she looked crestfallen. 'I don't *want to* think ill of David. He is my best friend's husband after all. I just pray that she has simply walked out. But in view of what happened yesterday my suspicions have increased.'

She really is the most irritating woman, thought Rydell, but he took a deep breath. 'Fill me in. What did happen yesterday?'

'Sara's mother left and has been replaced by a young, very attractive girl.'

'Has he explained why?'

'No, not a word. In fact he's hardly spoken to either of us since Sara disappeared.'

'And you put that down to guilt?'

'Well it could be, Inspector. Couldn't it?'

Rydell left the house feeling a bleak sense of failure. He hadn't been suspicious enough, although it had crossed his mind that Rhoda and Bolten might have been a little closer than normal for mere in-laws but he'd dismissed that idea. Bolten had already proved himself susceptible to young girls, so he shouldn't have been surprised that another young girl had entered Bolten's life. What really worried him was whether he had allowed his senior officer to influence him. The fact that Bolten was a Mason made him neither saint nor sinner. It just meant he had friends in high places.

Denni and Ram found the third on the left in Marsh Road easily enough.

'A small residence,' said Ram dourly.

'Rent free and stone built,' commented Denni. 'Cosy and needs minimal maintenance.'

'What an old crow.'

'She didn't exactly lie,' said Denni.

They stood for a few minutes staring down at the plot third on the left with its stone cross inscribed: Sydney Beaver R.I.P. 1920–1992.

'I wonder if Richard Harris will offer us any surprises.'

They checked him out later: he had no criminal record, worked as a social worker in Tower Hamlets and, for the past year, had been on an exchange placement in New York.

'It's strange she didn't even know he was working abroad,' mumbled Ram with a sweet in his mouth.

'I think she did,' said Denni. 'She just wanted to give us the run-around.'

'Once upon a time,' said Ram, 'old girls who did knitting respected the police.'

Denni smiled. 'Once upon a time or so the fairy tale goes, criminals said, "It's a fair cop, Guv."'

A young constable entering the interview room gave Denni a lecherous look as he handed her a folder containing details of Maria Seaton's young life. She smiled at him, not knowing if she meant thanks for the folder or for the lust in his eyes.

'That lad has fancied you for ages,' said Ram.

'Has he? I hadn't noticed.'

'You little liar.' Ram laughed. 'Half the blokes here fancy you.'

'What's wrong with the other half?'

'Must be newly wed or gay,' Ram said, throwing her a sherbet lemon.

As she began reading the file her mood shifted to sombre. Maria had had more foster parents than most kids have holidays. In early childhood she had been abused sexually by a stepfather. The result of which was that the rest of her short childhood was spent in care. From then on, her life had been spent skiving from school, running away and various bouts of petty theft. Reports from social services said she was: 'Likeable and bright, but insecure, unreliable and easily led.'

The 'easily led' seemed almost prophetic now, and yet Denni didn't believe that as an adult woman on the game Maria couldn't spot a dangerous man. Or had that been his attraction?

Fifteen

Alexis Openshaw shivered. She could feel a slight draught from the patio windows. She'd been out and although she hadn't walked far she felt chilled. Carefully she altered the dial of her central-heating system, turning it slightly to the right. Satisfied when she heard the sound of the boiler firing up she called, 'Barney – food!' Barney padded softly into the kitchen. It was fried liver and biscuits tonight, his favourite. She'd cooked it earlier and the flat still smelt slightly. She placed the bowl in his corner near his basket that he rarely used and switched on the radio.

With Barney gulping down his food and some Chopin playing on Classic FM, Alexis began to relax. She'd just finished a shift at the Samaritans. Four hours of calls that varied from the outright suicidal to the chillingly obscene. Sometimes the calls replayed in her head just as she was trying to sleep, especially if she hadn't been able to help. She'd once been a caller herself, when her husband had left her years before.

There was another reason she was a little on edge. She'd had a feeling someone had been following her home from the Samaritans' office. If anyone walked too close behind her Barney would always become agitated, turning, even growling. But tonight he'd seemed his normal calm canine self. She pushed her little niggle of fear to the back of her mind. Here in her flat she was quite safe. There was an intercom system and the residents of the other five flats were friendly enough. She'd lived at Oak Tree Court on the ground floor for a year, her first year with Barney and her first year as a Samaritan. Her life had been transformed: she had one or two good friends and no money worries. Her husband sent her a generous maintenance cheque every month, a salve to his conscience – she would have preferred his friendship to his money but money *did* make life easier for her. She smiled to herself. Maybe the person following her was Rob, her ex, keeping an eye on her, and perhaps Barney sensed he meant no ill intent.

Her internal phone rang. She wasn't expecting anyone and it was nearly midnight.

'It's Denni. Are you going to let me in?'

She opened the door when she heard the outer door click close. Denni hugged her close, her cheeks cold.

'I'm so pleased to see you, Denni. Nothing wrong, is there? You don't usually come this late.'

'I saw your light on. Sorry I haven't been round lately. I'm working all hours since the murder.' Barney wearying of wagging his tail for her attention now gave a short bark. 'Hi, Barney. How're you doing?' She stroked his shiny black head and rubbed his chin. His tail continued to wag and his eyes shone.

'Go through to the lounge and put your feet up,' said Alexis. 'I'll put the kettle on.'

'I've bought some wine.'

Alexis paused for a moment. 'Great. I'll find the opener. You know where the glasses are.'

Denni walked the short distance to the lounge. Barney as always stayed with Alexis. The room seemed familiar, not because of the number of times she'd visited but because she'd chosen or helped to choose the furnishings. 'I want it bright,' Alexis had said and it was, with orange-coloured walls on two sides and blue on the other two. In front of the window stood a pine table covered by a white lace cloth, in the middle of which a thin black vase held several white roses.

'The roses look spectacular,' said Denni as Alexis came in with the wine.

'I thought they would,' she said. 'They smell good too. Have you got the best glasses out?'

'Not yet. I was too busy admiring your roses.'

Denni took the best crystal glasses from the cabinet. 'Shall I pour?'

'No.' Alexis laughed. 'I need the practice. You hold the glass and I'll manage the wine. Just tell me when.'

Denni had known Alexis for three years. They'd stood together in a long checkout queue one Christmas time. They'd got talking and found they had more in common than a third-full trolley and a preference for ice cream rather than Christmas pudding. They'd gone for a cup of coffee together afterwards and their friendship was cemented over three cups and a lot of laughter.

Eighteen months later Alexis had been badly injured in a car crash and had been in hospital for several weeks. When she eventually returned home her scars had healed and were beginning to fade. Except that she was blind. Before the accident she'd owned and managed a florist's shop, which she'd then had to sell. She'd not had a paid job since. Her husband Mark, unable to cope, had left her and at thirty-five she had taken lessons in Braille and stretched out her days accompanied by Barney.

Occasionally she talked about her blindness and Denni always marvelled at her lack of self-pity. Once she'd had lovely greenish eyes, now she wore dark glasses to cover them. She was tall, slim and still very attractive with long dark hair that always shone, full sensual lips and great legs. Somewhere, Denni felt certain was the right man for her and Alexis needed a partner for so many reasons. She looked down at Barney sprawled asleep at his mistress's feet. Barney was loyal and faithful, good natured and affectionate. But he couldn't read or drive a car or . . .

'Come on, Denni, stop daydreaming, tell me what you've

been up to,' Alexis said. 'Tell me who you're shagging now. And how your mother is.'

Denni laughed. 'I can see being a Samaritan hasn't made you any more refined.'

'It's broadened my mind,' said Alexis. 'I hear about so many problems rather like you do, I suppose. People in . . . deep shit.'

'I haven't got a sex life at the moment,' admitted Denni. 'I'd like to say all these sexy exciting men were trying to get my knickers off permanently but not one of my so-called boyfriends has lasted longer than a bag of sugar.'

'In your case that's about a week.'

'Pathetic isn't it? And, as for my mum she just keeps drinking and smoking and refusing to see the doctor.'

'You do your best for her, Denni – she takes up most of your spare time. And you're doing better than I am on the male front. Do you know there are men who are attracted to women with disabilities, not in spite of them?'

Denni laughed. 'You're talking to an ex-psychiatric nurse. I had a patient once who was aroused only by hairy legs and thick ankles.'

Alexis downed her wine quickly. 'Pour me another, will you? That one's already gone to my head so it must be good. When you leave, do me a favour, Denni – make sure I'm in bed. Now tell me all about this murder – should I sleep at night?'

'We think he's local.'

'Nuts?'

Denni smiled. 'Probably,' she said, as she poured more wine.

'Have you any suspects?'

Denni shook her head and said wryly, 'This is real life. We're waiting on forensic reports but so far nothing.'

Alexis heard the slight edge to her friend's voice. Now she could no longer see facial expressions she listened far more intently to the rhythm and tone of words.

'You sound worried, Denni. What's wrong?'

'There's been a rape, a young girl . . . a child.'

'Are you involved?'

'I've interviewed her. We're doing a check on all known sex offenders in the area.'

Alexis again thought she sounded dispirited. 'No wonder you sound tired.'

'There's no fooling you, is there?' Denni sighed. 'I feel shattered most of the time. There's a missing woman too. Walked out in the middle of the night leaving her baby behind.'

'I heard about that. Do you think she's dead?'

'I'm probably prejudiced but her baby is gorgeous and she wasn't depressed. So yes, I think it's more than possible that she is dead.'

'Same person?'

Denni paused.

'What's wrong?' asked Alexis.

'You've just made me think.' She sipped her wine thoughtfully. 'We've been investigating two cases separately, when perhaps we're dealing with one killer. We just haven't found her body yet.'

'Don't start worrying about it now, Denni. I'm sure you'll catch him soon. You've told me before Tom Rydell is a good bloke.'

'He's on the odd side.'

'Brings out the maternal in you, does he?'

'No!'

Alexis laughed. 'Let's change the subject. Would you be an angel and read my post?'

'Of course. Where is it?'

'Usual place. Kitchen drawer.'

Denni thought Alexis's kitchen drawer was one of the least cluttered in the Western world. But it had to be tidy and half empty so that she could find things. On the left of the drawer was placed a pair of scissors and a ball of string.

Above those a small torch in case anyone should need it. In the middle she kept her unopened mail. And on the right she kept her spare door keys. Denni picked up the small bundle of mail and then noticed the house keys weren't in their usual place.

'Alexis,' she called out, 'where are your spare keys?'

'On the right hand side of the drawer,' Alexis called back. 'The ones I use are on the hook.'

A few moments later Alexis stood beside Denni, her practised hands exploring the drawer.

'Are you sure they were there?' asked Denni.

'Of course I'm sure,' Alexis replied. 'I have to be. I keep everything in the same place.'

'We'd best not panic,' said Denni, 'before we're absolutely sure.' She lifted out the drawer, checked the cupboard below, the cutlery drawer, and even the fridge.

'They're not there, are they?' murmured Alexis anxiously.

'No, but don't worry,' said Denni calmly. 'I'll stay the night and in the morning I'll get the locks changed.'

'I feel sick,' Alexis said. 'Some bastard has been in my flat.'

Denni took her by the arm and led her back to the sofa. 'Let's forget it now. I'll read your post. Just leave it to me. We'll get it sorted.'

Alexis wasn't convinced. It wasn't just that someone had been in her flat – it was that they had planned to come back. She tried to think. Could someone have slipped past her as she opened the flat door? But Barney was always with her and he would have alerted her. Someone in the flats? she wondered. She had left another set of keys with the elderly lady who lived in the flat opposite. But she was totally reliable.

She still felt slightly queasy but she drank the rest of her wine and waited as Denni began opening the mail. For Alexis, having to rely on someone to read her personal mail was one of the worst trials of being blind, it invaded her privacy in a way that was hard to bear. She could have no secrets and no debts.

Denni, still feeling uneasy because Alexis was so vulnerable, began reading aloud: a summary of bills, a letter from an elderly aunt, a letter from the building society, a flyer from a mobile artist, a flyer about driving tuition.

'That's a joke,' said Alexis, failing this time to keep a trace of bitterness from her voice.

Eventually she finished. Alexis seemed crushed. Smaller. Barney sensing something was wrong nuzzled close to her legs. Alexis stroked his head.

'You, my darling,' she murmured, 'are my comfort and consolation – and you too of course, Denni. You don't skimp on reading my mail. Some people who read for me think they have to act as censor as well.'

Denni felt helpless. There was nothing she could do at the moment. In the morning she could get a locksmith in, a personal alarm and a can of mace.

'Would you consider a personal alarm?' she asked.

Alexis managed a smile. 'I'd *consider* Arnold Swarzenegger as a personal bodyguard if it would help. But who takes any notice of alarms? Car alarms are just a bloody nuisance.'

Denni tried hard to lighten Alexis's low spirits but Alexis remained polite but preoccupied. Eventually Alexis asked, 'What if he comes tonight before the locks are changed?'

'I'll be here and Barney will bark. He won't stand a chance.'

Alexis didn't seem convinced. The wine had made her a little unsteady and Denni helped her into bed. She checked on her half an hour later and found her curled up, head half under the duvet, sleeping soundly.

In the spare room, Denni couldn't sleep. She had nothing to read and although she tried to conjure up her latest romantic hero she couldn't actually *see* him in her mind's eye. She tossed and turned and fretted instead. How the hell had those keys been taken? She'd checked all doors and windows and there was no sign of a break-in. She'd also slipped the safety chain on the flat's front door.

Eventually she closed her eyes, aware of the foreign night sounds of someone else's home: noises from other people's flats, doors closing, footsteps. She kept the bedside lamp on, comforted by the light. How must it be for Alexis alone and always surrounded by darkness?

Sixteen

Vernon Greenly hardly heard the knock at the door above the sound of rain and his mother wheezing. He'd propped her up on pillows, noticing how the grey colour of her face now matched her hair. He rushed downstairs expecting their GP but instead Liam King stood there soaked and scruffy.

'What the hell are you doing here?'

'I 'aven't seen you around,' he said. 'So I thought I'd pay you a visit.'

Vernon glanced out at the pouring rain and empty lane. 'You can't come in. The doctor's due any minute.' He thought for a moment. 'Go round the back and wait in the shed.'

'Don't be long, mate,' said Liam. 'I'm perished.'

'I'll be as quick as I can.'

Just as Liam walked through to the back garden and before Greenly had even shut the front door the doctor drove up in a silver BMW. He didn't lock his car door and he was obviously in a hurry.

Upstairs Mrs Greenly coughed and wheezed and with the most perfunctory of examinations Dr Arnecoat pronounced that she should be in hospital.

'Just for a couple of days,' he said, putting his stethoscope back into his black bag and closing it shut with one hand.

Greenly glanced at his mother waiting for her to protest. She said nothing. The doctor was already leaving. 'Could

117

be pneumonia,' he said as he walked down the stairs. 'I'll send for an ambulance.'

'Vernon,' his mother called weakly from upstairs.

'I'm coming, mother, I'm coming.' Greenly, however, wasn't moving. He stood still at the bottom of the stairs, panic tight as a metal vice clenched his chest. What was he supposed to do now? He couldn't leave Rusty for long periods of time. He couldn't stand hospitals, the thought of them made him feel faint. Would she be coming back home . . . ever?

When he did go back to stand by his mother's bed he felt like a young boy waiting for instructions. Between gasps, she said, 'There's a case packed in my wardrobe . . . you don't have to come with me.'

Relief flooded through him. She glanced at him briefly then half closed her eyes and from between bluish grey lips she muttered, 'Don't . . . do anything . . .' And then she stopped. He could still hear her breathing so he knew she wasn't dead but the realisation that she *could be* left him unable to move. Already he felt lost, abandoned. He stood for some time just watching her. It was only Rusty's whining that finally caused him to move.

'Hang on, Mum,' he said. 'They'll fix you up in hospital.' At that moment he believed they would.

As he opened the back door for Rusty, he remembered Liam was in the shed. Barking excitedly, Rusty ran to the shed door. When Greenly opened the door he noticed the warm damp smell of sweat and male odour. 'You'll have to go,' he said. 'My mother's very ill.'

Liam who'd been sitting in a garden chair stood up and, judging by his expression, was about to argue. Then, as if realising he was on a loser, he said grudgingly, 'Sorry about that. When can I come back?'

Greenly paused, debating with himself whether or not it was a risk worth taking. 'OK,' he said. 'Come late, about ten. Try not to be seen.'

The ambulance came a few minutes after Liam had left. The crew placed his mother in a carrying chair and he watched helplessly as they carried her away from him. It was one of the bleakest moments of his life.

Donna Grant paced the living-room floor carrying a screaming Ben. He'd been crying ever since his father had left at eight o'clock. It was now nine thirty. She didn't know what to do. She'd tried him with a bottle, but he'd refused to suck. She changed his nappy but still he cried. His face was bright red and she wondered if he could be teething. She'd rung her mother at work who'd suggested some Calpol, but it hadn't worked.

At ten forty-five she took Ben up to the nursery, still screaming, and put him in his cot. Then she closed the door, went downstairs and switched on Radio One loudly enough to drown out his miserable wailing. This wasn't what she'd expected. Since leaving school nothing had turned out as she planned. Her A level grades had been lower than she'd hoped, her year out travelling had been cancelled due to two friends letting her down. Then the jobs she'd applied for she hadn't got. Eventually she'd found a job waitressing at a chips-with-everything place. She spent most of her time clearing tables and listening to complaints. Even her social life hadn't improved. Boys her age who she liked seemed frightened of her. Truckers and baldies tried to flirt with her at work but she had perfected some really nasty put-downs: she'd already had two verbal warnings.

Donna had thought looking after Ben would be a great job. She could ring friends, watch TV, listen to music. Instead, old Bolten had given her a list of jobs to do, as well as looking after his screaming brat. She was to tidy up and vacuum and dust and do the washing and prepare vegetables for an evening meal. She finished at five thirty. She smiled to herself. She'd start his list of jobs at five and if she didn't finish them – tough shit.

*   *   *

Rhoda couldn't concentrate on work. She stared out onto the car park at the back of her office. It had started to rain and for some time she observed the rain bouncing on the car roofs and watched the puddles growing on the tarmac. If someone had asked her how she felt her only answer would have been that she didn't feel in the here and now. Physically her body sat at her desk, but she didn't feel present in the flesh. Her mind couldn't fixate on contracts to type or memos or filing or client phone calls. She could think only of Ben and Sara. She'd rung the day before to speak to the new 'nanny' and she had hardly been able to hear her replies for Ben's screams. Rhoda had been back home for two days. Initially, she'd felt relief, now she felt guilty and worried. Was an eighteen-year-old with no experience the right person to look after Ben? What if Sara never returned? Was she being selfish in not looking after her grandson?

The internal phone rang and she picked it up automatically. It was Clive the senior partner. 'Rhoda, could I have a word?'

In his office he sat at a desk of files and stared at her above his half-glasses. He was past retirement age, forgetful and vague at times but well-intentioned and consulted by staff so often that Rhoda was surprised at how much work he actually managed to complete.

'Sit down, Rhoda,' he said. His voice was low, his eyes concerned. 'You look pale. Should you really be here?'

She wanted to say that she wasn't really *here* at all but she said, 'I can't stay at home on my own. I just keep worrying.'

'Of course you do,' he said. 'Only natural in the circumstances. Have the police made any headway?'

She shook her head. 'They seem to be concentrating more on the woman found in the barn.'

'It's all very distressing for you,' he said. 'Have you thought about employing a private detective to find your daughter?'

She hadn't. Inspector Rydell seemed competent enough. Now Clive had made her wonder if she could do more. 'I'll think about it,' she said.

'Good . . . good,' murmured Clive, slipping his glasses back into position. 'I can recommend someone.'

Rhoda went back to her office feeling slightly more anxious. Was she doing enough to find Sara? Was a private detective the answer? Much worse was the thought that she was letting Sara down by not looking after Ben. She'd read that people with a strong bond – twins, mother and child – could sometimes sense that their loved one was either dead or alive. She'd tried to commune with Sara at night just before she slept but nothing came. There was only a void, a black hole where eventually she found sleep.

Seventeen

Denni had arranged for a locksmith to change Alexis's locks and planned to call in that evening. She'd just finished talking on the phone when Rydell came in looking pleased.

'Forensic have come up with something.'

'Great,' she said. 'Are you going to tell me what?'

'It doesn't sound much, but it could help.' He paused. 'A couple of dog hairs were found on her body. Only one drawback, the pathologist is sure they come from two different dogs.'

'Rusty,' said Denni. 'Shall I get a sample?'

'I'll come with you later. The super's called a press conference.'

'Why?' asked Denni. 'Has he got anything to say?'

Rydell shrugged. 'Someone – probably Liam King – has been talking. I think he's told them how he found the body. I'm supposed to quell the news hounds by saying we have a new lead.'

'Are you going to tell them about the dog hairs?'

Rydell smiled. 'I'm saying as little as possible.'

'What about Fenton?'

'The super's asked that I read out a prepared statement and Fenton didn't even make the audition.'

Denni laughed. 'Who's the blue-eyed boy being groomed for stardom at the next interview board then?'

'I shall remain modest,' said Rydell.

'Good,' said Denni. 'One Fenton is enough for any force.'

*   *   *

The news conference took place at two p.m. The room was noisy, the voices excitable and some of the faces recognisable. Rydell saw a few London-based newsmen among the small group of local reporters and knew their experience bred a fierce cynicism. He took a deep breath, paused waiting for silence, welcomed them briefly and then read his equally brief statement. There was a short silence when he'd finished.

The first to ask a question was a youngish reporter on a national Sunday tabloid – Rydell had committed her name to memory and a quote came into his mind about terrorism – 'kill the women terrorists first'. She had a soft rounded face, was a bottle-blonde and had a nickname: Miss Tongue-lash, or so he'd heard.

'Inspector,' she said. 'How do you account for the fact that a London prostitute was found dead in West Mercia?'

Rydell fixed her firmly in his gaze. She was in a good mood, he could tell.

'I can't account for it, Mandy,' he said, 'but I have to presume that the perpetrator has connections in both locations.'

There was a low mumble rather than the usual loud free-for-all, whether in surprise that he knew the reporter's name or simply because her colleagues were wary of her verbal sadism, he didn't know.

She spoke again. 'West Mercia police are well known –' she paused for effect, 'for their poor murder clean-up rate.'

Was she guessing or did she know? 'It is true,' he said, 'that over the past ten years we have had three unsolved murders. On current figures that's one above average.'

'Is that due to shortage of money or manpower?' someone from the back row shouted.

'Neither,' said Rydell. 'One explanation could be that in

West Mercia we have more cunning murderers.' There was a low rumble of dissent.

'It couldn't possibly be,' said an unseen speaker, 'that the CID are a bunch of . . .' The last word was lost by sounds of laughter.

Rydell, unfazed, said, 'If anyone has a question rather than a comment I'd be pleased to hear it.'

It was Mandy who spoke again, and this time more loudly. 'What about the missing woman? Is there a connection?'

'They are two separate inquiries –' he paused, 'and we're grateful for the coverage you have already given Sara Bolten and we'd appreciate your help in the future.'

Rydell felt a tiny moment of triumph as the room fell silent. Then Mandy spoke again.

'What about the baby?' she asked.

'What baby?' he queried, wondering how the hell she knew.

'Maria Seaton's baby.'

That information hadn't been disclosed publicly and Rydell assumed that Sabine must have told her. Knowing that didn't help him. Before he could string together an answer the voices began to clamour: 'Do you expect to find the baby dead?' 'Rumour has it the baby was fathered by a Tory MP. Is that true?' 'Do the police think the baby has been murdered?'

He was about to give a noncommittal answer when Mandy called out, 'Could the baby have been the motive for murder?'

Rydell swallowed hard. With one question he had been landed with all sorts of possibilities. The elaborate 'burial' had led him to think 'psycho' when perhaps he should have been merely thinking, evil cunning bastard. 'We are looking for a devious killer.' He looked directly at Mandy. 'We *are* making progress and we have definite leads, which, of course, we cannot disclose at the moment. An arrest will be made in the near future. That is all I have to say.'

Rydell immediately regretted his words. He could picture the headlines the following day: BARN KILLER. ARREST IMMINENT.

Later, after a de-briefing and de-bollocking by Fenton and the super, Rydell met Ram and Denni in the canteen to discuss strategy. Ram seemed depressed and quiet but no one asked him why. 'I'm not getting far on the arson front, Guv,' he said.

'What about you, Denni?' asked Rydell.

'I've got to find this rapist and I'm working my way through the lists of known sex criminals.'

'I'm going to lean on Bolten,' Rydell said grimly. 'Threaten to dig up his patio. And I think we'll have to see Sabine again and get some client info. Even if we have to put someone on surveillance. Nab the punters at source and see if one of them admits to knowing Maria on a more personal level.'

'If Sabine was telling us the truth,' said Denni thoughtfully. 'She doesn't seem to have known much about her friend's sperm donor. You'd think being a couple they'd have discussed a good set of genes.'

'I hadn't given it much thought,' said Rydell, 'but I am thinking now about the baby angle.'

'Baby farming?' queried Denni.

'Worse. Paedophiles.'

The thought made Denni feel sick. She knew that some paedophiles deliberately targeted single mothers for the sole purpose of sexually abusing their children. Would an experienced prostitute like Maria be taken in by one? She didn't think so. Sabine and Maria had their life together well arranged. Maria had to have been taken against her will. And suddenly it became glaringly clear.

'Guv . . . I think Sara Bolten is still alive.'

'Could be,' he said blandly.

'No. You don't understand. *He's* got her. It all fits. Sara wouldn't have left her baby. She went with him willingly to save her baby.'

Rydell turned to Ram. 'What do you think?'

Ram looked nonplussed. 'Sorry, Guv. My girlfriend's place has been done over. She's in a bit of a state.'

'Just keep your mind on the job, Ram,' said Rydell irritably. 'Denni thinks Sara is being held captive. What do you think?'

Ram thought for a moment and proffered a crumpled bag of humbugs in their direction. They both shook their heads. 'Problem is,' said Ram, 'where's he keeping her? Is he even in Harrowford? We assume he's local because he knew about the barn but Maria lived in London so he might—'

'Go to London occasionally,' interrupted Rydell. 'And he must have decent premises. Large house, outbuildings. Could even have an accomplice.'

'Do you think we need a profiler?' asked Denni.

'At this moment,' said Rydell, 'we need a bloody miracle.'

At six p.m., they drove out of Harrowford towards Marston, the street lights soon giving way to the dark gloom of empty country roads, stark trees and a general wintry forlornness.

Greenly looked agitated when he answered the door. Rusty stood beside him wagging his tail. 'I'm on my way to the hospital,' he said hurriedly. 'My mother's very ill.'

'Sorry to hear that. Is she in the General?' asked Rydell. 'We'll give you a lift – later – after we've had a chat. You don't have a car, do you?'

Greenly looked across to Denni. A nervous flick of a glance. 'My wife kept the car,' he said. 'I haven't bothered to get another.'

'Have you had any more thoughts about finding the body of Maria Seaton?' asked Rydell, sitting down uninvited.

Greenly furrowed his brows, deliberately, thought Rydell, to look surprised. 'What thoughts was I supposed to have?'

'Don't mess with me, Mr Greenly. If you had nothing to do with the murder then you have nothing to fear.'

Greenly squared his narrow shoulders. 'I rang the police. If I'd killed her I'd hardly have drawn attention to myself.'

'Many murderers want recognition. Perhaps you *wanted* to be caught.'

'Don't be ridiculous,' he snapped. 'I'm not a violent man.'

'We've only your word for that. Perhaps we could have the address of your ex-wife and get a character reference from her.'

A flicker of anxiety crossed his face. 'Do you really think, Inspector, that I'm the type who would associate with a prostitute?'

'Just the type,' said Rydell. 'Until you prove otherwise.'

Greenly looked towards Denni hopefully as if somehow she would be an ally.

'Did you meet up with Liam King for sexual purposes?' she asked.

'I'm not gay and I don't use prostitutes—'

'And you don't have a girlfriend?' she interrupted. 'Where exactly *do* your interests lie, Mr Greenly?'

'It's not a crime to be celibate.'

'No,' she agreed. 'But are you sexually interested in children?'

'Good God, *no.*'

He seemed genuinely shocked by the idea and Denni knew he was at a low enough ebb for her to press home her advantage. 'So, Mr Greenly,' she said softly. 'You're not gay nor a paedophile nor a user of prostitutes. So that only leaves bestiality, arson and voyeurism.'

'I didn't start that fire. We—' he broke off, aware that the 'we' had trapped him.

'There's no point in telling lies,' said Denni. 'We do have

witnesses who would testify to seeing you and Liam King together on several occasions.'

His mouth opened and closed. He seemed about to speak when the loud trill of the telephone stopped him.

Rydell followed him through to the hall phone. The call was brief and as Greenly put the phone down his hand trembled and the colour had drained from his face. 'My mother – I have to go at once.'

In the car Denni was concerned that Greenly would expire before his mother. He was ashen, sweating and breathing rapidly. At first she thought it was a panic reaction to his fears of his mother dying, but it was Greenly himself who explained.

'I get into this state just at the thought of hospitals.' Those were the only words he spoke until they arrived at the hospital gates. Then he gasped, 'I'll manage . . . thanks for the lift.'

They watched him walk the short distance from the car to the front entrance. His gait was nervous and unsteady and they waited until he disappeared into reception before driving off.

'I feel quite sorry for the poor bugger,' said Rydell as they waited at traffic lights. 'I did manage to snaffle a few of the dog's hairs before the phone rang. We'll see Liam King tomorrow. I think he'll tell us everything we want to know.'

'I didn't even see you touch the dog,' said Denni in surprise. One dog suddenly reminded her of another. 'Could you drop me off, Guv, at my friend's place in the town. She's worried about her keys. They could have been stolen.'

'Hasn't she got a spare set?'

Denni noticed the slight trace of irritation in his voice. 'She has, but she thought she was being followed then she found her keys were missing.'

'She sounds neurotic.'

Denni wanted to say – *you should know*, but she didn't. 'No, she isn't neurotic. She's blind.'

'Oh,' said Rydell.

At first she thought Alexis's lights were off but then she saw a chink of light between the curtains' edges. 'I'll only be a few minutes,' she said as Rydell turned into the forecourt.

'I'll come with you,' he said as he switched off the ignition.

Denni rang the intercom and waited. Alexis was as always slow at answering, hurrying was something sighted people did. 'Hi, it's me,' she called out.

When they got to Alexis's door Denni heard the safety chain being drawn back and as the door opened Alexis stood there smiling, saying, 'It's lovely to see you. Guess what?'

'Alexis – hang on a minute. I've got my boss with me, Inspector Tom Rydell.'

Alexis laughed. 'Thank God I'm dressed. I'm pleased to meet you – may I call you Tom?' She put her hand out to find his. A large hand found hers and much to Denni's surprise Rydell bent to kiss Alexis's hand.

'Of course you can call me Tom,' he said. And since no one else did, Denni was even more surprised. Alexis smiled, then placed her hand on Rydell's arm. 'Come on in and meet Barney.'

Barney, as if on cue, sprang forward rubbing himself against Rydell's legs and dribbling slightly. 'He loves men,' said Alexis by way of explanation.

'Does he meet many?' asked Rydell.

Alexis grinned. 'No, that's the point. Men have novelty value.'

Rydell, encouraged by Alexis to go and sit in the lounge and relax, left both women in the kitchen. 'You seem brighter,' observed Denni.

'I am. That's what I was going to tell you. I found my keys.'

Denni, remembering the thorough search she'd made, said, 'Show me where.'

Alexis walked over to the cutlery drawer. 'I must have put them in the wrong drawer.'

'When did you find them?' asked Denni.

'Lunchtime. I found them in with the spoons. It's weird, isn't it? Perhaps it's my age – ultra-early senile dementia.'

'Very weird,' agreed Denni. 'You've still had the locks changed?'

'No. The locksmith came after I'd found them. He said it happened all the time although I was probably more careful than most.'

Denni wasn't sure what to say, somehow she felt uneasy. Alexis put the kettle on for tea.

'It must be catching,' said Alexis. 'A neighbour, Lyn – she hasn't lived here long – mislaid hers too. She said she always hung hers on a hook. Then she found them on top of the washing machine.'

'When was that?'

Alexis thought for a while. 'I only found out today. It was nearly a week ago.'

Denni didn't want to frighten Alexis but she still had uneasy niggling doubts. 'Don't forget to put the chain on when we go, will you?'

Alexis smiled and her hand touched Denni's. 'No, Mum, I won't forget.'

'I'm serious. I'm in police mode.'

'OK. I'll put the chain on – but on one condition.'

'What's that?'

'You let me cook you both a meal.'

Embarrassed, Denni murmured that she wasn't hungry. 'Don't lie to me, Denni, you're always hungry. I want to cook. I like showing off.'

'OK. You win. I'm starving.'

'Leave me alone then and I'll fix you something.'

Denni joined Rydell in the living room. He looked

comfortable and relaxed on the sofa. 'She's so tidy,' he said admiringly.

'She has to be,' said Denni. 'Which is why I'm suspicious about the keys. She's always so careful.'

In less than fifteen minutes Alexis had produced a pasta dish with a sauce made from mushrooms, bacon and tomatoes, plus salad and bananas baked with rum. After the meal Denni observed Rydell closely. Not that he noticed. His eyes were firmly fixed on Alexis.

Before going home, Denni called in to see her mother. She lived in a two-bedroom bungalow about five minutes' drive from Denni's home. 'Hi, Jean,' she called out as she entered – she'd long ago stopped calling her Mum.

'What you doing here?'

'Just checking you're OK.' There was no reply. The television was on but if Denni had asked her mother what she was watching she wouldn't know. The room was stiflingly warm, tobacco smoke and whisky making it smell pub-like. Her mother sat hunched up over a large ashtray on a stand. On the table in front of her was a half-empty bottle of whisky and a full glass. The evening was still young for Jean. Most nights she didn't bother to go to bed. She'd simply raise the foot of her recliner chair and watch TV through the night.

'Have you eaten?' Denni asked. Without taking her eyes from the screen, Jean shook her head. Denni went out to the kitchen to make her cheese on toast – her staple diet. As she was waiting for the cheese to melt, she thought of her mother's wedding photos. She'd been thirty-two when she'd married, slim, with a great smile and sparkling eyes. Now she was thin and frail, her eyes as dull as a muddy puddle. She rarely smiled and the tremor in her hands meant she continually dropped her cigarettes.

'Try to get to bed, won't you,' said Denni, as she handed Jean the cheese on toast.

'Are you going home now?'

Denni nodded. 'Unless you want me to stay.'

'Please yourself,' said Jean, as she took another slug of whisky.

'I'm off then. See you tomorrow.'

'Bye,' said her mother grudgingly.

Thoroughly depressed, Denni drove home. She felt better after a hot bath and once in bed she began reading to chase away thoughts of her mother. She managed to read two chapters before she fell asleep. But she didn't dream of Wilbur Smith's Africa, she dreamt of rapists and fire and being chased by masked men.

At first when she heard the noise she thought it was still part of her dream. Eventually, realising, she picked up her bedside phone.

'Denni – rouse yourself. I'm driving towards the old industrial estate – Leaward Park, South Harrowford. There's a factory on fire and there's been a report of a body being taken in there.'

Her throat was dry and she didn't answer immediately. Rydell's voice broke in again as she was about to speak. 'Denni – have you taken that in? Get a move on.'

'Yes, Guv. I'm on my way.'

Eighteen

R am left the Incident Room at Harrowford Station early because he found he couldn't concentrate. He'd been sifting through arson reports, checking Personal Descriptive Forms but he knew he wasn't giving it his best shot. Now he lay on the bed in his room and waited for the phone to ring. The call earlier in the day had been brief – a message from a colleague of Paula's saying her flat had been ransacked and she was staying with friends and that she would ring him after nine p.m. And so he waited, staring at the mouldings on the high white ceiling and listening to the rain and the slight movement of tree branches brushing against his window.

He'd met Paula, a physiotherapist, in the Manchester Royal Infirmary. She'd treated his whiplash injury, and he'd fallen for her the moment she laid hands on his neck. They'd been dating for a year and he saw her as much as possible. Working undercover had always made him feel theirs was a clandestine affair and it was three months before he'd told her. He'd got the impression she didn't believe him, so he never discussed his work and she never asked. His job was 'the other woman' but at times it had felt more like a wife and six kids.

It was at moments like this when he wished he smoked or drank spirits. He drank beer or lager to be sociable, but he never drank on his own. He had never felt so alone or so powerless, his inability to be with Paula and protect her made him realise just how much he loved her.

Ram's experience of women had been limited. As a child

he'd been in awe of his mother, perhaps because he saw little of her because she was always either working or studying. He associated her with his dreams because of her habit, when he was a child, of coming into his bedroom when he was asleep. She, unlike most other mothers, wouldn't be encouraging him to sleep but to wake. 'I dreamt about you, Mummy,' he would say and she would laugh and say she was his dream princess. Her bright saris and exotic make-up *did* make her a young princess in his eyes. Occasionally he wondered if putting her on a pedestal had hampered him in his love life.

Ram had long since realised he was a disappointment to her. His father having died before he was five, he'd had very little male influence in his life. A few uncles or cousins he met at family events but that was all. His mother concentrated her efforts on her medical career and over the years had tried to interest Ram in medicine. He wasn't academic enough to be a doctor, no medically related careers appealed and he showed no sign of marrying and producing any grandchildren. He'd been an aimless accountant until joining the police force at twenty-four and he hadn't regretted it until now. It was no wonder his mother despaired.

Now he was based in Harrowford, a large town sur-rounded by countryside, and in a strange way he missed the buzz of Moss Side. It may have been a forgotten remnant of the last century with its poverty, squalid houses, street gangs, petty criminals, drug users, minor pushers, vicious thugs and pimps all thriving together like rampant weeds on vacant land. But it had been exciting. Meanwhile, the law abiding lived as best they could. In Moss Side to have a gun in the wardrobe or a stash of dope under the floorboards or a year's supply of knocked-off lager wasn't that unusual.

Paula lived outside Manchester itself in Ashton-under-Lyne surrounded by hills and fields. He'd wrongly assumed she was safe there in her dark stone terraced house overlooking the small town. He consoled himself that it was probably nothing to do with him – maybe it was kids.

She rang at ten p.m., her voice distant, cool. 'I'm staying with my sister in Bolton,' she said.

'What happened? What did the police say?' There was no response. 'Talk to me, Paula. You know I'd be there with you if I could.'

'Do I?' she said.

'Don't piss me off. Just tell me.'

'I came home early with a migraine,' she said. 'As I came in the front door they left by the back.'

'You weren't hurt?'

'No, Ram, I wasn't hurt but it feels like I was. They –' she began to cry. Ram hearing her sobbing felt as if he'd been kicked.

'Look, I can't stand this, Paula, I want to be with you. I'll come up.'

'No,' she said sharply. 'Don't do that. It's you they want.'

'Tell me about it. What did they do?'

She sniffed and was obviously trying to pull herself together. 'Everything is wrecked,' she said dully. 'My clothes, my furniture, my television. They threw paint everywhere. There were used syringes –' she broke off – 'even in my bed.'

'The bastards,' he muttered, his vocal cords sounding as raspy as sandpaper on wood.

'On the walls,' she continued, 'they wrote in red paint – Black Bastard Pig – We'll Get You.'

'I'm so sorry, Paula. I'm gutted.'

'You're gutted,' she said caustically. 'I've lost everything.'

'Come to Harrowford,' he suggested. 'I'll look after you.'

There was a long pause. 'I'm sorry, Ram. I'm very fond of you. You're a really nice guy but . . .'

135

'But what?'

'You're a policeman.'

'You knew that from the beginning.'

'I didn't know what it would mean then. And I do now. I've never been scared in my life before . . . I'm thinking of working abroad for a while – probably Australia. They need physios there. Sorry.'

As the line went dead Ram still held the receiver in his hand. He sat without moving for some time replaying the conversation in his head as if somehow it could have had a different outcome. Australia. Bloody Australia. The other side of the world.

When he did move, it was to walk slowly in zombie fashion to the nearest pub. There, sitting on a barstool, he drank morosely and alone. He downed five double whiskies and learnt why people drank spirits: the effect was quicker than beer, it was less strain on the bladder and it was a cheaper way to reach oblivion.

When he returned to the guesthouse all was quiet. There was no sign of Bridie and he navigated the stairs carefully, holding on to the banisters like an old man. Once he was safely lying on the bed he thought about Australia. He had money. He could go out there. It was a large country but there wasn't a huge population, he could easily find Paula there – no problem. He wasn't going to give up on her. Given a chance she would grow to love him. It was just a question of time.

The word time came back to him when he heard a ringing tone. He thought at first it was his alarm clock, but it was the telephone. It could be Paula, he thought.

'Hello?'

'Move yourself,' said Rydell. 'There's a fire. Suggestions of a body being taken into a disused factory.'

'I've had a few drinks, Guv.'

'I don't care if you've had a bucketful – you can still speak. I'll send a car for you. Ten minutes.'

At least Ram thought he was ready – even his shoes were still on.

Alexis had insisted on leaving the washing up, preferring to do it once Tom Rydell and Denni had left. When she was sighted, washing up had been a doddle but then most things had been a doddle. Now she had to be totally organised and methodical. First she placed the plates and dishes in a stack on the right of the sink, saucepans she left on the cooker till last. Cutlery she placed in a plastic basket. She filled the washing-up bowl with really hot water and then squirted washing-up liquid in and swirled it round with her hands. Before her accident she'd always worn rubber gloves, now she couldn't bear the loss of sensitivity. She placed the openwork slatted basket into the bowl and began washing each knife, fork and spoon carefully. She had a horror of stale food being on her utensils. Guests rarely left food and most were thoughtful enough to scrape their plates but even so she used a scraper to clear any residue. Pans she washed and scoured thoroughly and then traced her fingers around both inside and out before a final rinse.

It was while she was putting away the plates she thought about her keys. When she'd finished and everything was put in its usual place, she checked the kitchen drawer again. Her keys lay where she'd left them. She would never have left them in the cutlery drawer. Someone had definitely been in her flat. But who? Both the gas and electricity men had been to read the meters. She knew their voices; they did their job and left.

She racked her brains for a recent stranger. There was a man, called Nigel, who lived upstairs and was fairly new to the flats, but he was hardly ever in. She'd spoken to him once or twice. About three months before, he'd fixed her doorbell. She'd last spoken to him about a month ago on a Saturday. There had been snow and he'd asked her if she wanted any shopping. He'd bought her some bread and some dog food. He seemed perfectly normal; he worked long hours as a manager in a plastics factory, had a girlfriend and seemed very respectable.

There was the milkman too, of course. She had a pint of milk delivered every day and on Friday lunchtime she paid him. He'd never been inside the flat, he stood at the door and she always paid him in pound coins. Barney liked him, which in her opinion was as good a reference as any.

Alexis couldn't think of anyone else. And at least she hadn't thought she was being followed again. It must have been all in her mind. Blindness bred mind games. Interpretation was everything and she seemed to have made the wrong one.

Vernon Greenly, anxious and on edge, tried to relax into a moulded hospital chair. The six-bedded bay was stuffy and oppressive. He sat watching his mother breathe. He didn't want to be there. One of the nurses had told him that she was *aware*, but she didn't look it to him. Awkwardly, he had tried to hold her hand but she hadn't responded. The other patients were also old and asleep, bar one, who called out an unintelligible name over and over again. A musty smell hung in the air with overtones of boiled cabbage, and outside in the darkness he could hear the wind whistling, or thought he could until he realized it was his mother's lungs wheezing.

Eventually the night sister came to his bedside. 'Your mother has had some morphine, to keep her comfortable. She should sleep all night.'

'Will she wake in the morning?' he asked.

Did he imagine the slight shake of her head? She looked very young, slim with her fair hair tied back in a ponytail. 'Would you like to see a doctor to explain your mother's condition?' she asked

He shook his head. 'What is there to explain? She's come to the end of the road.'

She smiled. 'You can stay overnight. Either here, or in the day room.'

'No,' he said. 'I couldn't do that. I'll come back in the morning.'

It was the excuse he needed. He managed, with a struggle, to kiss his mother's forehead. It felt cool but not as cool as her hand.

He rang for a taxi from reception and waited on the forecourt shivering with cold but relieved to be outside in the well world again.

Once he was home he had some digging to do, to get rid of the evidence. He looked at his watch. It was nine thirty. Liam would be round at ten. He could help him: hold the torch, and do some of the digging. He felt cheered by the thought – so cheered that he managed a brief smile and a, 'Thanks, mate,' as he clambered into the warmth of the mini-cab.

Nineteen

R ydell and Denni heard the scream of the fire engines and saw the huge columns of smoke long before they arrived at the industrial estate. Three appliances were already in action. The main building, which looked like a low-level office, was fully ablaze with great leaping flames breaking glass and spilling forth noxious-smelling smoke. Audience participation was high as a road of semi-detached houses fronted the factory. The residents stood at their front doors in dressing gowns watching the proceedings in silent fascination.

Rydell parked his car well away from the fire area. As they walked into the factory gates a uniformed police sergeant approached him. 'It's a shoe factory. The smell is the glue according to the owner. He says there's nothing likely to explode. I shouldn't get too close though.'

'What about the body?'

The burly sergeant shrugged. 'The fire crews are having to use breathing apparatus. Another couple of appliances are on their way. They don't want to take risks with their crew for the sake of a corpse.'

'Who saw the body being taken in?' asked Rydell.

'No idea, boss. We had a call from a bloke calling himself Reg Fields. The address he gave is being checked out, so we're none the wiser at the moment. Could be a hoax of course.'

Rydell nodded. 'We'll just have to wait and see.'

The hoses were being played mainly on the main building,

which was burning the most fiercely. For several minutes Rydell and Denni watched – there wasn't much else they could do. As more appliances arrived the new fire crews were pointed in the direction of the smaller buildings. They quickly fixed their masks and cylinders into position and with hoses at the ready went into action. They reminded Denni of films she'd seen about cavalry charges, only the fire crews went into battle with hoses instead of swords.

Ram turned up just as the crews went out of sight towards the buildings at the back.

'God, you look awful,' said Rydell.

'I haven't shaved, that's all,' mumbled Ram. 'Where's the body, Guv?'

'No idea but if it's in the main building it'll be burnt –'

'To a crisp,' suggested Ram.

'That's one way of putting it,' said Rydell.

Denni, watching the action intently, noticed a man wearing a dressing gown creeping towards the main building with a video camera. She was about to go after him when a crashing sound reverberated across the whole of Harrowford, or so it seemed. Someone shouted, 'The roof's caved in.' After the first thunderous noise came loud crackles and sounds as if wood was being split. At first Denni didn't sense any additional air of urgency, but then she saw three fire-fighters going into the building via a side entrance which could only mean that a colleague was trapped inside. The men seemed to be inside the collapsing building for a long time. All three police officers waited and watched. No one spoke. Denni couldn't keep still, she stamped up at down, not with cold but nervous agitation. If she'd had any nails left to bite she would have bitten them. But her nails after years of abuse had ceased to grow to a biteable length.

An ambulance with siren sounding and blue light flashing drew up and the paramedics quickly organised themselves, but they also could do nothing but wait.

Just as Denni had almost given up hope, three men, staggering with the effort of dragging their injured colleague, appeared at the side entrance. One gave the thumbs up and then went down on his knees. Other fire-fighters who were spraying their hoses over that section now stopped to help and Denni lost sight of the injured man. She did get one glimpse as they took off his helmet – it wasn't a *he*, it was a she.

Once the ambulance had driven away the crews carried on normally and it was only a few moments later the senior officer came over to Rydell and said, 'Round the back, brick-built hut. They've found something, but they haven't touched it yet.'

All three walked round. Denni was already putting on surgical gloves and steeling herself. The hut was bigger than she expected. The door was open, the inside black with smoke and the ground was wet from the water from the hoses and it smelt acrid and sour. By the light of her torch she saw, propped up against the far wall, a charred and wet bulky carpet. A noosed rope was loosely cast round the top. They looked at each other.

'I'll do it,' said Denni.

Rydell was already on his two-way radio summoning the scene-of-crime officers and the police surgeon. Denni removed the rope necklace carefully and placed it in a clear plastic bag that Ram held out for her. She took a deep breath and began to peel back the sodden carpet slowly and carefully. A charred carpet was one thing, a charred face quite another. *But there was no face.*

What stood there was easy enough to recognise. Sacks of potatoes. Two, one on top of the other secured by wide brown masking tape and topped with a bow of purple rope. There was silence for a moment then Rydell muttered, 'The bastard! He's laughing at us.'

Sheer relief and a strong sense of anti-climax made Denni want to laugh too but she controlled the urge. 'I don't think so,' she said. 'I think he's practising.'

'Practising what?' asked Ram. 'Arson?'

Denni shook her head. 'Disposal of a body. He wants to get it just right next time.'

Rydell immediately phoned the police surgeon and cancelled his visit. The scene-of-crime teams he would need anyway, and between them and the fire investigation team he reasoned forensic should come up with something. Somehow he didn't find that very reassuring. He'd worked on cases before where forensic supplied all the clues – DNA fingerprints, hairs, fibres et cetera – and still the killer hadn't been found.

'What do we do now, boss?' asked Denni.

'Wait for the SOCOs and then try to find the witness who saw the so-called body.'

When the team finally arrived, they seemed to find the situation amusing. 'I've heard of a chip-pan fire,' said one of the officers donning his protective whites, 'but I've never heard of a baked-potato fire.'

Rydell didn't find it amusing. They were hunting a pyromaniac and a murderer: a killer with a sick mind. Worse, they didn't have a single suspect.

He stood well back half hidden behind the curtains. The binoculars gave him a clear view of the action. The fire crews were like worker ants, going backwards and forwards, backwards and forwards. The pointed flames reminded him of mountain tops, high and sharp. The colours were spectacular, orange black and grey – surging upwards to heaven.

It was easy to guess that the group of two men and one woman were CID. They stood around trying to look important. He knew they were no nearer to finding him. He had no criminal record and there was no reason for them to be suspicious of him.

His planning hadn't been perfect. Maria had been a mistake from the start. He'd only invested time in her because of his baby. Treading on eggshells, spending a small fortune on her, telling lies. No one should tell lies. He'd thought she'd grow to love him, but she was like the others – treacherous. He knew there was no one he could trust. He could only trust himself.

He'd made more plans. He'd recognised the right woman this time: one who would be grateful; one who wouldn't try to escape; one who would love him and his baby.

Sara was serving his purpose at the moment but she was trying to be too clever. She'd tried to seduce him – the silly bitch. Did she think he had no self-control? He'd wanted to kill her then. All women were whores. Some were more honest about it. Maria knew she was a whore, but now she was redeemed. He smiled to himself. He was an important person – a redeemer. He could take bitches and make them angels. One on his right hand, one on his left – and on his shoulders?

The fire was nearly out now, drizzles of smoke instead of bright flames. Soon the fire crews would leave and then Mr Plod would come knocking but there would be no answer.

Alexis had heard the sirens in the night and had guessed it was a serious fire. Fire was her constant dread. She pulled all plugs out at night and checked the position of each dial on her cooker, then with her hand she checked that her cooker top wasn't warm and that the oven was off. Barney of course alerted her to any sounds that disturbed him. Just lately she had allowed him to sleep on the bed with her at night. She felt safer that way.

Yesterday it had rained and she hadn't left the flat. She found bad weather difficult: she was afraid of falling and Barney seemed nervous in rain and pedestrians were far less likely to be helpful. Sometimes she wondered if without Barney she would have become agoraphobic. She *had* sensed someone was following her but she dismissed the idea. Being blind was bad enough, she told herself firmly, but getting neurotic as well would be a real pain.

Today, the small back garden wouldn't be enough for Barney. Whatever the weather, she'd take him to the park. There she could let him run free and she would sit on a bench for a while and let him have some fun.

She switched on the local radio and listened to news of the fire. Probably an insurance fraud, she thought, as she loaded her washing machine. She dare only wear her clothes once: being blind could be a messy business and everything she bought had to be machine washable. She felt grateful to washing-powder manufacturers for their new compressed discs of washing powder. In the past, however careful she was some of the powder always seemed to land up on the kitchen floor.

At just after ten, she and Barney began walking towards the park. A chill wind encouraged her to walk briskly. She counted her footsteps: two hundred and seventeen to the first of the shops, which was a baker's, a shop easy to recognise by its irresistible smell. On the way back she would buy fresh bread.

She knew the park quite well from her sighted days. It was circular with four entrances, a huge variety of trees and flowerbeds and a policy of all dogs being kept on leads. Except for Barney. She had an arrangement with the park keeper who had a soft spot for her and Barney.

Today it was eerily quiet, apart from the wind rustling noisily through the trees, there were no voices or footsteps. Even the ducks on the pond were quiet today. Near the second entrance was a small playground with swings, a slide and a roundabout. Even in winter some mothers braved the weather to bring their pre-school children to play but today she could hear no children. She wondered if there were dark clouds: rain had been forecast for the afternoon.

They walked round the park via the footpath and Barney knew to take her to the bench nearest their entry and exit gate. Once Barney had delivered her to the park bench she took off his harness and he knew that was his signal to run free. He barked excitedly and bounded away.

She'd been sitting for only a few minutes when she began to feel cold. She stamped her feet and crossed her arms. She could hear Barney snuffling and the occasional sound of his feet padding against grass. The trees creaked, she realised, rather than rustled. In her mind's eye trees were never leafless and stark but always green and abundant. Today, perhaps because of the cold and the quiet, she thought of gaunt dead trees with cracked black trunks. She imagined her cheeks and nose were turning blue.

After a while of straining to hear Barney she stood up. Usually that sent him lumbering in her direction, excited and wanting to be fussed. His response to the fussing was to be rather wet-mouthed and dribbly which she tried to discourage. She'd noticed when she wasn't wearing her glasses that he would lick her eyelids as though telling her he knew quite well the problem was her eyes.

She called out, 'Barney, time to go.'

She waited. A long way off she heard a dog bark. She called again, louder this time. 'Barney . . . Barney.' She listened for his answering low bark that indicated he'd heard but had been delayed by an interesting smell. She blocked out the sounds that didn't relate to her dog. She tried to use her ears like aural binoculars focusing on the one noise she wanted to hear but no sound she heard related to Barney.

She called his name again and again, louder, more insistent, more desperate, 'Barney, please!'

From her coat pocket she took out her white stick and shook it out to its full length. Then, making for the path, she began to retrace their initial walk – tap-tapping and calling. She passed no one and heard no one. She wanted to double up and sob, but she had to keep walking. Panic and fear welled in her stomach making her feel sick. Her normally dry eyes were welling with tears. She shouted, 'Barney,' until she was hoarse and by the time she'd circled the park, hopes of finding him began to fade. Not having Barney with her was like becoming blind all over again. In some ways worse. He was her eyes, her companion, her friend and in all the world she loved no one more.

She stood by the bench, oblivious now to the cold, and screamed, 'Help!' but no one came. She tried to think calmly but couldn't. In her panic, she stumbled back against the bench. She righted herself and remembered his harness. With the flat of her hands she felt along the wooden seat, there was nothing. On her hands and knees she raked the ground with her stick, then she used the flat of her hands, trying to be systematic. First the front, then the back, then the sides. It was after that she knew Barney hadn't just failed to return or run off – he'd been stolen. 'Please, someone help me,' she cried out aloud, but she knew there was no one there and she was wasting valuable time. The blackness that she was so used to crowded in on her. Obstacles existed where logically there were none. The fear was as great as if she were moving towards a cliff edge knowing it was near but not exactly where. As she left the park she gave one last croaky call even though she realised it was useless. Barney had been taken.

She walked fast towards the baker's, swinging and tapping her stick frantically, aware tears were streaming down her face. The bakery assistant was very kind.

'Would you like me to call the police?' she asked. Alexis nodded and managed to say, 'Ask for DS Caldecote – she's a friend.'

Someone found her a chair, but minutes passed and she couldn't sit still. 'I'm going back to my flat.'

A woman's voice asked if she would like someone to go with her.

'Yes,' she answered miserably.

Once back home, Alexis sat by the front window still wearing her coat. She felt numb. She could no longer cry; she could hardly think. Anger against the criminal predominated. Anger felt safer than worry, less painful. But it didn't last and gnawing anxiety took its place.

The phone rang to say DS Caldecote was out of the office, but Police Constable Dave French would call in ten minutes or so.

When he rang the bell Alexis rushed to answer the door. His voice sounded young and unsure. 'I believe you've had your dog stolen, madam,' he said.

'Guide dog,' she corrected him.

'I'll take a few details.'

As she walked into the front room she stumbled which she rarely did in familiar surroundings. She felt embarrassed when he took her elbow and guided her to a chair. It was like being an old woman.

'What exactly happened?' he asked.

She explained.

'Why do you think he's been stolen and not just run off?'

She couldn't explain that she *knew* Barney wouldn't run off and leave her. He probably wouldn't have understood that amount of trust in an animal. She merely said, 'The harness was taken.'

'You didn't see anyone?'

'No. I'm blind.'

She sensed his embarrassment. 'I know some partially sighted people can see shapes,' she said, 'but I'm totally blind which is why –' her voice wavered.

'Don't upset yourself,' he said. 'Did you hear anything?'

She shook her head.

'Is the dog wearing a collar?'

'Yes, and a microchip.'

She could hear his pen scratching on his notepad. 'Barney's a black Labrador, he's four years old. He's got flecks of white under his chin.'

'Have you got a photograph?'

'I've got a small painting. People tell me it really looks like him.'

'OK if I take it with me? I might be able to get some posters fixed up for you.'

She nodded. 'It's in the bedroom above my bed.'

He left shortly afterwards. His last words and his tone sounded less than hopeful. 'We'll keep an eye out for him. Inform the local dog warden. We'll be in touch.'

Alexis sat down and sobbed. Some of the initial shock had dissolved, to be replaced by the thought that she might never see Barney again. It was only after crying for some time that she asked herself the question. Why would anyone want to steal Barney? And did it have anything to do with sensing that she was being followed?

Twenty

'You're on "Pervert Patrol",' DCI Fenton informed Denni and Ram the next morning. 'Check the slime hasn't moved.' According to the gaffer who chose his words more carefully, 'In this inquiry your visits are to eliminate those with alibis and maximise our suspect potential.'

'All he really means is – let's nail the bastard,' said Ram as they began the drive to the first address, a run-down care-in-the-community home on the outskirts of town. Denni scanned her list. There were three convicted paedophiles, two flashers and two known rapists living in or near Harrowford.

'In my opinion,' said Ram, 'all those convicted of sex offences should be castrated.'

'Surgically deactivated?'

He shrugged. 'Does it matter how it's done, as long as it stops them?'

Denni kept quiet. She liked a debate, but not when she was driving.

Rosedale was an ex-guesthouse now providing a home for alcoholics, the mentally ill, recidivists and two sex offenders. Sex offenders were kept to a minimum because of fears of public outrage. The manager, Alan Halls, in his forties, was good-natured enough, but looked as run down as his establishment. He always had at least two days of stubble, wore faded jeans and had only a meagre selection of sweatshirts.

This time he surprised her. He was dressed in a paint-spattered boiler suit. 'I'm decorating,' he explained.

'Supervising really. Community service orders – drunk drivers. They paint as if they're still half pissed.'

'We've come to see Joe and Martin. Routine rape inquiry. Not that they're suspects.'

'Thought you might pay them a visit,' he said. 'They're in their rooms. They haven't been any trouble.'

'This is DS Ram Patel by the way.'

Alan gave him a smile and a brief appraising glance. Denni had known for some time that Alan was gay. He had just ended a long-term relationship and was obviously on the pull.

On their way upstairs they passed two decorators in the hallway using rollers to paint the walls. Denni and Ram carefully avoided ladders and trays and pots of paint. Underfoot the hall floor was covered with newspapers. Denni glanced down noticing they were the 'biggies' – *The Times*, *Telegraph*, *Independent* and *Guardian*. She knew Alan read the *Guardian*. She wondered where he got the others. On the way out she decided she would ask him.

Joe and Martin had adjoining rooms on the second floor. They rarely worked. Martin was an ex-bus driver; Joe had once had his own shop selling bikes. Both had served long prison terms. Martin was approaching forty, surly and resentful; Joe was nearer sixty and Denni thought he'd probably lost the abnormal desires that had ruined his victims' lives and his own.

Martin scowled at the sight of Denni. 'What do you want? You know damn well I haven't moved. Who's your brown friend?'

'This is DS Patel, so try and make a good impression, Martin.'

'Sarky bitch,' he muttered. 'I suppose you want to come in.'

The curtains were pulled and a portable television provided the only light. The room was spacious but cluttered with magazines, full ashtrays and plates with half-eaten food. The threadbare carpet had a sticky feel and the air smelt as foetid as a bag full of unwashed socks.

Martin stood with his back to the television. He wore a grey jogging outfit with a hood. If he ever did jog, it hadn't improved his paunch. 'I was just going out for a run,' he said.

Denni raised an eyebrow at the overflowing ashtrays.

'I'm planning to get fit – run every day. Give up smoking.'

'Did you hear about the rape, Martin?'

He nodded. 'Yeah, I read about it in my local paper.'

Denni stared at his round face and small watery blue eyes. 'Not your style, I know. But now you've taken up running . . .'

'I couldn't run as far as that,' he said hurriedly. 'I'm puffed out after two hundred yards.'

'As far as what, Martin?'

'The Kestrel Estate. And I don't rape fifteen-year-olds.'

'Too old for you, are they?'

As Ram stood in the seedy room he glanced down at the magazines strewn on the bed and a wave of revulsion made him feel physically sick. Among war and martial arts magazines were ones about babies and toddlers.

'I'll wait in the hall,' he said.

'What's wrong with him?' asked Martin.

Denni shrugged. She didn't hate all paedophiles, some she could feel sorry for. Martin wasn't one of them. He'd never shown any sign of remorse, but then she reasoned if you had no conscience how could you feel remorse?

Martin gave a brief laugh. 'Does he think I'm the devil?'

'No,' said Denni. 'He thinks you're the biggest scumbag he's ever met and if he sees you jogging within a mile of a child he'll probably run you over.'

'I don't know why you come calling,' Martin snapped. 'You've got my DNA and fingerprints on file and I'm not going to risk being banged up again.'

'Next time,' she said, 'you won't be coming out. A third offence – you'll stay in prison – for life.'

'I'm on the straight and narrow now.' He paused and ran his fingers over his flattened nose. 'And I've got a steady girlfriend.' He obviously noticed the expression on her face and he smiled. 'Don't worry, she hasn't got any children – yet.'

Outside the room, the air seemed relatively fresh. Ram was sucking a humbug.

'I've had enough already,' he said.

'Joe isn't quite as bad,' she said, jabbing her thumb towards Joe's door. 'He has a few interests, so he's not quite so fixated.'

The room next door smelt fresh, the bed was made, there were two potted plants and Joe had been writing letters. He was a short, dapper man wearing a white shirt and a beige cardigan with trousers that had razor-sharp creases. Thick silver white hair added to his respectable appearance. 'Hello, Denni. You're looking well.'

'And you're a creep. Are you still behaving yourself?'

He smiled. 'I'm old now. You know I'm past it.'

'Just carry on proving it.' She introduced Ram and then asked, 'You've read about the rape?'

He nodded.

'And?'

'There's a rumour,' he said, patting a stray hair in place. 'A new man.' Denni knew his 'new man' wasn't the nineties model. 'As you know,' Joe said with a knowing smirk, 'I always try to help the police.'

'For a price,' she said. 'So tell me what you've heard.'

'A score will do it,' he said. 'I am a business man.'

She took a ten-pound note from her pocket. Joe for some reason began to look uncomfortable. Perhaps she'd complied too easily or did he really expect a score?

'It may not be kosher,' he muttered.

'Get on with it, Joe, or I'll rip this tenner into shreds.'

153

'Someone gave me a name,' he said hurriedly. 'Greenly. Not for the rape. He's been doing some digging in his garden. It could be that missing woman.'

'So this is your "new man"? God, you're a disappointment.'

'Word on the rapist is that he's just starting or he's just moved here. He likes them young or young-looking. Greenly was named because he's a loner and why dig in the middle of winter? You do your digging *before* the frosts come.'

'Well, that's hardly worth a tenner,' she said, 'but keep your sly old ears and eyes open and I might be able to get you considerably more.'

'I'll do my best.'

'You do that. Take care.'

As they walked downstairs Ram muttered, 'I don't know how you could be so pleasant to him.'

'Joe was a victim himself,' explained Denni. 'From the age of five, in a Roman Catholic children's home. Abused, not just by one priest, but two. He joined the army at sixteen to avoid temptation but the damage was done.'

Alan came out of his cubbyhole office to offer them tea. The decorators had vanished. 'No tea thanks,' said Denni. 'But I do have a question.'

'Fire away,' said Alan.

'Where did you get the old newspapers from to cover the floors?'

Alan's expression was a cross between amazement and amusement. 'Nothing escapes a detective, does it? I'm impressed. Well, as they used to say – it's a fair cop. I admit it. I nicked them.'

'Where from?'

'Next door. They put out their newspapers in a box for recycling once a month so I nicked them.' He laughed. 'Have I committed as criminal offence?'

'Not that I know of, but one day I might be thanking you for helping to solve a nasty crime.'

He didn't look convinced.

*   *   *

Their last call of the day was to a middle-aged rapist who had
spent most of his adult life in prison. He had been suffering
from depression since his release two years earlier. Denni
found him more sinister than most. He seemed nervous and
ill at ease when she spoke to him, but was he more relaxed
with men and birds? His home was a miniature aviary. He
lived in a cottage, left to him by his mother, in a hamlet
north of Harrowford.

'You do the talking this time, Ram.'

The small front room of the cottage had been given over
to caged birds: budgerigars, canaries, love birds, cockatiels,
all ruled over by a mad parrot called Hector who spent most
of his time on Norman's shoulder. Windows were never
opened and consequently the still air smelt of feathers and
bird shit. Norman himself had a bird-like quality – that of
a predatory crow. His hair was slick and black, his eyes
small and dark, his nose was sharp and beaklike. Denni
ruled him out as Stephanie's rapist. He was too short –
a mere five foot two, he also had a penchant for big
women.

Ram didn't waste any time. The usual preamble about
reasons for their visit then the initial questions. 'Where were
you on that night?'

Norman, parrot Hector stamping on his shoulder, smiled
a sly smile. 'I had a couple of bird fanciers here. I don't go
out much. A bit more since I went on the Prozac.'

'Criminal bird fanciers?' asked Ram.

Norman shook his head unfazed as the parrot stared
menacingly at Ram. 'Very respectable people, bloke who
works at the bank, a school teacher and another chap,
an artist.'

'I'm impressed,' said Ram sarcastically. 'What time did
they leave?'

'Just before midnight.'

'How did you meet these "respectable" people?'

'I advertised in a bird magazine.'

'Was this their first visit?'

'No, second.'

'I'll want their names and addresses.'

'I know their names and I've got their phone numbers. I don't need their addresses.'

'That'll do.'

Norman placed the parrot on the floor and began rummaging through papers on a table. Hector stalked up and down like a guard dog. Ram felt mesmerised, not by the patrolling but by the parrot's beady intelligent eyes.

'Here they are,' said Norman flourishing a slip of paper.

Ram wrote them down quickly in his notebook. 'We'll be ringing them of course.'

'You do that.'

Just as they were leaving the parrot spoke, 'Fuck off, pigs. Fuck off, pigs.'

Outside Ram took a deep breath. 'Too many visits like that could shorten my life.'

Denni laughed. 'I feel the same. Shall we go to the pub for a pint?'

'I've never seen you drink a pint yet.'

'There's always a first time,' she said.

It was late afternoon, dark and raining when they got back to Harrowford Police Station. As far as they were concerned the day's work was over. Denni felt ready for a hot bath, a meal and bed. The duty sergeant shattered any such simple dreams. 'Denni – don't go creeping past me. Message from young Stephanie's mum – could you visit this evening? And before I forget, someone called Alexis phoned to say her dog's been lost. I sent round a PC.'

'Lost,' repeated Denni. 'How could she lose him? And it's not any old dog, Sarge – it's a guide dog for the blind.'

'No good getting arsey with me,' said the sergeant. 'It's not my fault.'

Rydell sat glumly at the office computer. 'Any headway?' he asked.

'No suspects for the rape, Guv. But at the Rosedale there was a pile of newspapers in the hall. The manager had nicked them from his next-door neighbours.'

'Why?' asked Rydell pointedly.

'To protect the floor from paint.'

'Oh.'

'It could be significant.'

'Tell me how.'

Rydell still hadn't taken his eyes from the computer screen. 'The faggots of newspaper,' she explained, 'around Maria's body.'

At last he responded. 'What are you suggesting?'

'He may have done the same thing.'

Rydell shrugged. 'You're making an assumption that our man is a *Sun* reader and has to nick the *Telegraph*.'

Denni nodded. 'You're right. Big assumption.'

Rydell managed a smile. 'I've had all the newsagents in Harrowford contacted for a list of subscribers who have the *Telegraph* delivered so that might yield something – although I don't know what.' He paused. 'You can do some paperwork now you're here. We've had three more reported sightings of Sara. Her husband has had to take time off from school and he's thinking of having the baby fostered. And we've been allocated more help from other divisions –'

Denni held up her hand. 'Enough, Guv. My brain's still addled from the pervert patrol. I've been asked to visit Stephanie, the rape victim, this evening and Alexis is in trouble.'

'What sort of trouble?'

'I've only just heard. Her dog's missing but I haven't got any details yet. He may have been stolen.'

'Thieving bastards . . . you go to Stephanie's. I'll go round to see Alexis.'

Denni felt a little put out, after all Alexis was supposed

to be *her* friend. 'I'll see Stephanie first and then I'll get to Alexis as quickly as I can.'

'Fine.'

Rydell began straightening his desk. Placing new piles of reports and computer printouts in neat piles, he logged off his computer and covered it, then he removed the electric plugs. Denni noticed his ritual was speedier than usual.

'Where's Ram?' he asked at the door.

Denni shook her head. 'No idea. He came in with me but I was delayed by the desk sergeant.'

'Probably feeding his face in the canteen,' said Rydell. 'Don't forget to switch the lights off when you go.'

Stephanie sat hunched up on her bed, her hair lank, her eyes hollow. Her mother looked equally haunted. 'She won't talk to me,' she said. 'She's not sleeping and she won't leave the house even with me.'

'Stephanie, do you remember me?' Denni asked. There was a barely perceptible nod, but it was a reaction. At least she wasn't catatonic.

'I'm going to ask your mum to leave us alone and then you'll talk to me, won't you?'

This time there was no reaction, but once her mother had left the room Denni noticed her shoulders relaxed slightly.

Denni sat on the bed and held Stephanie's hand. It remained limp and cool.

'I know you don't want to talk,' said Denni. 'So I'll talk and you can listen. Is that OK?' There was no answer, but Stephanie's eyes met hers. 'I'm going to be honest with you. We haven't caught him yet, and I know you're worried he'll come looking for you.'

There was no need for any answering words. Denni sensed her fear. 'But rapists don't usually seek out their previous victims. They look for new ones.'

A tiny voice asked, 'Is that really true?'

Denni nodded. 'Another thing to think about, Stephanie.

He came at you from behind. It was dark. Why should he even remember what you looked like?'

It was obvious from her expression that she hadn't thought of that. 'Just imagine being in a line-up of young girls all more or less dressed the same – would he be able to pick you out? I don't think so.'

Stephanie thought about that for a while. Eventually she said, 'Should I go back to school?'

'I think you'd feel better if you did.'

'I'll never be able to go out at night again, will I?'

'You will. In time. With a crowd of mates. Everyone has to be careful.'

'Has it happened to you?'

'I was attacked once in the grounds of a hospital but I was lucky because someone came along.'

'Was he caught?'

Denni nodded. 'About a month later he attacked someone else. He was caught within two weeks.'

'Were you scared?'

'I was a gibbering wreck for a week or so, but gradually I started going out with friends. Fairly soon I was back to normal. I did have some bad dreams for a while.'

'I have bad dreams and I'm frightened to go to sleep.'

'You could try some mild sleeping tablets for a while.'

'Yeah. Mum says I should go to the doctor.'

'You could give it a try.'

When Denni left shortly afterwards, Stephanie walked downstairs with her and her mother's relief was obvious. 'Thanks for coming. I know you're busy.'

'If I get any news,' said Denni, 'you'll be the first to know.'

Rydell opened the door to her at Alexis's flat. 'She's very upset,' he said. 'I don't think she should be alone.'

'I can hear you talking about me,' called Alexis from the front room. 'Make yourself some tea, Denni.'

Alexis had taken off her dark glasses and her eyes were red and swollen. Denni sat beside her friend and gave her a hug. 'How did it happen?' she asked.

Alexis related the result of her trip to the park. 'Why would anyone do such a thing? He's a pedigree dog, but he's been spayed so they can't use him to breed – I don't understand.'

'It couldn't be personal, could it?' asked Denni.

'Do you mean have I any enemies?'

'Knowing you, it's very unlikely but did you ever—'

'Sleep with a friend's lover,' she interrupted, 'cut down someone's favourite tree, park the car in the wrong place – no. I haven't upset anyone enough to do this.'

'What about your ex-husband?' asked Rydell.

A flicker of a smile played on Alexis's lips. 'He's out of the country at the moment. He's a nice guy anyway. He just couldn't cope with a blind wife.'

Silence fell. No one knew quite what to say. Eventually Denni said, 'Posters. We'll need lots of posters.'

'The constable who came round said he'd do that.'

More silence, broken by rain against the windows. 'I've got a feeling,' said Alexis, 'that I'll never see Barney again.'

A trite reassurance wanted to emerge from Denni's lips, but she said nothing. They hadn't found Sara Bolten yet. If they couldn't find a young mother, what hope was there of finding a black Labrador?

Twenty-One

R hoda had been carefully applying her make-up at seven thirty a.m. when her son-in-law rang. She'd just reached the mascara stage and had counted some extra lines around her eyes.

'I'm not going into school today,' he said.

'Is Ben all right?'

'Yes, he's fine. I've lost my child-minder. She couldn't cope.' Rhoda's guilt surfaced yet again but before she could say anything he went on, 'I've rung social services.'

'Whatever for?'

There was a long pause before he said, 'I want to have Ben fostered.'

Shock made her mouth dry. 'You're not serious?'

'In truth, Rhoda, I'm the one finding it hard to cope. Only my job will keep me sane. I'm not very good with babies. I can't sleep. I'm not eating. For God's sake, I've lost my wife and as time goes on I'm more and more convinced she's dead.'

Rhoda watched in the magnifying mirror as her tears filled her eyes, threatening to add mascara to the other lines on her face. 'People like us don't get involved with social services,' she muttered.

'They do if they're desperate.'

She knew then that she couldn't think rationally, all she could see was her daughter's face. For Sara, if not for Ben, she had to do the right thing, the only thing.

'Give me today,' she said, 'to make arrangements. Tomorrow you can bring him here.'

'It's a big commitment,' he said dully. 'Are you sure?'

'I'm sure.'

Rhoda sat for some time staring at her face in the mirror. Her life from now on would be that of a single mother – disturbed nights, continual worry, the toddler stage when she wouldn't be able to leave him for an instant. David would initially feign interest but he'd gradually grow apart from Ben – until another woman turned up and then he'd decide he couldn't live without his son. The future seemed fraught. Her relationship with Philip would be in jeopardy and she would miss her job. But she'd made her decision and she knew Sara would be proud of her.

At the office she saw the senior partner first thing.

'I'll be very sorry to lose you,' he said. 'What does Philip think about it?'

'He doesn't know yet.'

'I'm sure he'll be supportive. You're really having a hellish time, aren't you?'

She nodded, thanked him and went in search of Philip.

Philip looked up from his desk. 'What's wrong?'

She told him.

'Couldn't he go into a nursery?' he asked.

'He's too young.'

Philip was silent for a while. She knew he was about to make a suggestion. Problem-solving was a way of life to him. 'We could always hire a private detective to find Sara.'

'The police are doing their best.'

'It doesn't seem to have achieved much.'

Rhoda felt at a loss. Since Sara had disappeared her brain seemed to have shut down.

'Let's compromise,' he said gently. 'We'll give the police two more weeks and then we'll decide.' He walked her to the door eager to get on with his day's work. He gave her a brief hug. 'Whatever happens,' he said, 'we'll cope.'

The 'we' gave her reassurance. At least he didn't expect her to cope alone.

Rydell would have liked to have done *something* towards finding Alexis's dog, but what could he do? As Denni said, they couldn't manage to find a missing person – what hope did they have of finding a missing dog?

Forensic reports and fire reports were now filtering through covering everything from a DNA profile to rope analysis. He glanced at them quickly and requested a database check on the DNA.

Denni's report of her interviews with the sex offenders puzzled him. A grass, sex offender or otherwise, knew ten quid's worth of information was going to be fairly useless. Rydell didn't think for a moment that Greenly had been burying a body in his garden so to be fingered he had to have upset someone in some way. Complete waste of time or not, he had to investigate Greenly's digging activities. He reasoned that no one had seen him actually doing the digging, that it was only hearsay, but nonetheless . . .

He asked a burly PC called Ian Plackett to accompany him. His muscles were more developed than his brain, but he had a certain threatening presence that might save time.

Greenly looked scruffy and unshaved. 'My mother died yesterday,' he said, beckoning them both inside. Rydell murmured his condolences.

'This won't take long,' he said. 'As long as you co-operate.'

Greenly looked puzzled. 'What's it about? I've told you I know nothing about that fire.'

'We've had a . . . report,' said Rydell, 'that you've been burying something in your garden late at night.' He paused. 'My large colleague is very good with a spade. He gets to work before we send in the bulldozers.'

Just for a moment Greenly's expression seem to doubt Rydell's veracity but then he shrugged as if in defeat. 'Yes,' he said. 'I was burying something – plants . . . several of them of the genus – marijuana. My mother tended them, quite unaware of what they were.'

'Why destroy them now?'

Greenly didn't answer immediately. 'It just seemed an appropriate time – before the funeral.'

'I don't believe you,' said Rydell. 'I think you wanted to keep your customers to a minimum. No doubt Liam King got greedy and wanted to supply his mates.'

Greenly eyed him anxiously. 'Are you going to charge me?'

'What do you think? King I can understand – he's strapped for cash – but you were just greedy. Now your mother's dead she's probably left you something in her will and you don't want to risk it anymore.'

'No . . . I –'

'You want to say something in your defence?'

Greenly shook his head.

'We'll need to take a statement from both you and King.'

'I won't be kept long, will I? I do have my dog to think about.'

'It shouldn't take too long,' said Rydell. 'Once you're at the station would you have any objections to being DNA tested?'

'Is it painful?'

'Not at all.'

'Fine then. I haven't done anything wrong.'

'Nothing at all, it seems,' agreed Rydell, 'except for growing and supplying an illegal substance.'

As they drove back to Harrowford, Rydell knew that DNA testing would be unnecessary, Greenly was so unperturbed by the idea it verged on relief. It seems he did have a secret but it had nothing to do with the drugs or the murder. In Rydell's mind there were only two other areas – sex and money. If he hadn't been so involved with finding a murderer he might have felt compelled to follow it up. A drug conviction would have to do for the moment.

Later in the day Denni caught up with him. She looked slightly flushed and excited.

'Do you want the good news or the bad news, Guv?'

'Whatever,' he said. 'But I would like a cup of coffee with it.'

In the canteen they sat amongst the debris of the day's fry-ups and numerous empty cups. 'Fire away, Denni.'

'The bad news is that there's no identification of the DNA from Maria's body.'

'And the good news?'

'There is a match on it.'

Rydell's interest quickened. 'Who with?'

'Stephanie's rapist. And I've been thinking—'

'Hang on, Denni,' he interrupted. 'Don't rush me. I've got to think this through.'

Rydell drank his coffee slowly. 'There is something else,' said Denni, unable to wait for his thought processes to be caffeine assisted. 'Our man is firing blanks so Maria's baby wasn't his.'

Rydell looked up from his cup. 'Let's suppose he doesn't know the baby couldn't be his and that the baby is still alive. What would he need in its life?'

'A woman.'

Rydell smiled. 'You're sharp, Denni, but what's the psychology given that he's recently raped a young girl and murdered the baby's mother?'

The sudden sound of plates being cleared made her pause. 'I suppose the old chestnut – Madonna and whore – could apply. He –' she paused again and murmured, 'do you realise what we're saying?'

'I think you're ahead of me.'

'He's murdered the child's mother,' she said. 'Maybe because he found out he'd been duped. He's left with no one to care for the baby who he's grown attached to so he has to find a replacement.'

'Go on,' urged Rydell.

'So he targets someone suitable, someone already with a child, and substitutes her.'

'That someone being Sara Bolten.'

'And it must mean she is still alive.'

Rydell nodded thoughtfully. 'But why the elaborate fire raising? Why the rape? Why now?'

'It may not be his first rape,' suggested Denni. 'Maybe they weren't reported.'

Rydell didn't seem convinced. 'It really doesn't matter why, does it? We have to find Sara. He's local, he's mobile and he's got premises. And for God's sake he's got a past.'

'What about house-to-house searches?' asked Denni. 'Or mass DNA testing?'

'Nothing wrong with the idea,' he agreed. 'But the Gaffer won't spend that sort of money this early in an investigation. We could try an appeal via television. Michael Sams was caught that way.'

'Pity we don't have a recording of his voice. It was Sams's ex-wife who recognised his voice, wasn't it?'

Rydell nodded, remembering the case in 1992 and the awful suffering of the girl he kidnapped. 'A coincidence our victim is a Stephanie too,' he murmured. 'How's she doing?'

'She's feisty, she'll do well in court. She's bright too, good memory and she heard his voice.'

'I wonder,' muttered Rydell almost to himself, 'if we could do a voice fix like we do a photofit.'

'Have we got a specialist?'

'No. But finding one would be a damn sight cheaper than the alternatives.'

As they left the canteen Rydell said, 'I want you and Ram to keep plugging away at anyone, friends, neighbours, acquaintances, the milkman, tradesman, carpet layer – any-one who knew Sara Bolten.'

'We've already tried most of those, Guv.'

'Try again. In all of Harrowford he could have taken his pick of young mums. He chose Sara for a reason. Somewhere there has to be a connection or something in common between Maria and Sara.'

'I thought it was just their looks.'

Rydell shook his head. 'There's something we've missed. This man has to have an occupation, a source of income. He runs a car, goes to London, and uses prostitutes . . .'

'We don't know that. Maybe he befriended her.'

Rydell stared at Denni for a moment and then walked off deep in thought.

Twenty-Two

*N*ow *he'd stopped taking his medication he felt much better: more alert, more aware. And he'd got far more work done. Not everyone who suffered from his condition could cope as well as he did. He was an honest man and he'd never cheated anyone in his life. Sometimes late at night before sleep came he would go back over his early years. He'd made two major mistakes. The second of those mistakes – truanting – he'd compensated for by being bright and talented. At sixteen he'd left home taking his mother's stash of money. She'd always said she was saving it for him, anyway, and some good had to come out of her life. As a child he'd had more rich uncles than most kids had toys. Some stayed a few nights, some weeks, one stayed a year. But his mother got bored. She was beautiful and fun-loving and fickle. No one man could hold her prisoner – until he came along: rich, good-looking and possessive. That time, when he was sixteen, he'd asked her to choose. And she had. She'd chosen him! Bitch, bitch, bitch!*

He'd never seen her again to talk to but he watched her from a distance. Then they'd moved abroad and she'd left him the house. He'd gutted it, renovated it and sold it at a large profit. Then he'd bought three other houses which he rented out. And he was a damn good landlord: his tenants thought he was wonderful; if a tap dripped he fixed it immediately.

The police would never guess it was him. He imagined they'd be looking for a working-class yob, instead of someone special. He was outwitting them and the time was approaching and he knew they hadn't made the right connections. He was far too clever for their small minds. He would have made a good detective.

After the factory fire a young PC had come to the door asking questions. He'd explained to the lad that he was the landlord and was getting the house ready for renting. The plod had shown a real interest and asked him about the rent. 'Give me a ring in a couple of weeks if you're still interested,' he'd said. 'I've been looking for somewhere for ages,' said young plod. 'I don't want to take on a mortgage just yet but I do want to live with my girlfriend.' He'd offered him first refusal.

The idea of a cop living in one of his houses gave him a buzz. Lots of things gave him a buzz now. Since stopping his medication he was really coming alive. Feeling powerful. As the psychiatrist had told him, 'You have a good insight into your condition. With medication you'll be able to live a perfectly normal life.'

Why would he want to live a perfectly normal life? He wanted to live an extraordinary life. He wasn't ordinary. He was special.

Twenty-Three

Heavy snow had fallen all day. Alexis felt the chill in the air, heard the slushing sounds of the cars passing by. Sometimes she imagined she could actually hear the sound of snow falling, like soft whisperings in her own darkness.

She felt restless and uneasy with only Barney to occupy her thoughts. He'd hated snow as much as she did: she was afraid of slipping and she guessed he didn't like his paws being cold and wet. The thought of him being lost or hurt or starving made her feel real physical discomfort: a tight chest, a pounding headache and a sick churning in her stomach.

At about seven, one of her co-workers from the Samaritans would collect her for her weekly evening shift. She resented the loss of independence: Barney had given her freedom; now she felt once more imprisoned by her lack of sight.

When she answered the door to 'Ray', she managed to smile. In the Samaritans you were given a name and callers and staff kept to that name. Hers was 'Julie'.

'Any news about Barney?' he asked in his gravelly but soft voice. She had never felt the contours of his face. If he was good-looking she didn't need to know and if he was ugly it didn't matter. Voices and personality were the only criteria that mattered when you couldn't see.

'No news yet, Ray. I'm glad to be doing a shift. Other people's problems will put mine into perspective.'

He laughed. 'What an optimist you are. I've done an extra shift this week and it hasn't made me feel any better.'

Outside it was wet and cold. Alexis asked Ray to describe the scene as they walked.

'I'm not very good at this,' he said holding her arm far too tightly. He was a tall man with big hands and heavy footsteps. 'The snow's drifting down,' he said hesitatingly. 'The sky's black. There's a good two inches of fresh snow on the pavements but the road is just wet, with snow only in the gutters.'

'What about the house lights and the trees?' she asked.

He stopped. 'Pretty. Snow looking like white confetti on the trees and . . . I wish I was curled up in front of a coal fire.'

'Can you see someone doing that?'

'Yes,' he said.

But she knew he wasn't telling the truth because the houses were back too far from the road. The Samaritans had taken over the ground floor of an Edwardian house. The office area had been carpeted and painted a soothing pale green or, at least, described as soothing to Alexis. The rest of the house crumbled away empty and gathered dust. It smelt of age and damp and relied on an array of convector heaters to keep the place warm.

'Mind the steps,' warned Ray. Her toe hit the first one. There were only four steps but they were deep and felt slippery although going up felt far safer than going down.

Once they were in the office they took over the respective desks of the two outgoing volunteers. It was about eight when the phones got really busy. Bad weather on its own didn't cause desperation, but bad weather combined with illness or poverty or loss did. She'd taken three calls by nine o'clock. One had rung off after five minutes of silence. Sometimes the silent callers rang again when they felt calmer or they could no longer hold back. On the fourth call the voice said, 'Hello, Julie.'

Just for a moment she didn't recognise the voice. It had been at least a year since she'd heard it. 'Is that you, H?'

She'd only ever known him as H. She'd met him twice for a cup of coffee. Samaritans could befriend if they had established rapport and met first in a public place. Any such meetings were always logged.

He laughed. 'Don't tell me you've forgotten me already?'

'Of course not. Your voice sounds different.'

'I'm on a mobile.'

'You sound better,' she said.

'I'm really fine. This time I'm ringing to help you.'

'How?'

'Barney.'

'You know where he is?' In her excitement her voice rose an octave.

'Not exactly but I've got my suspicions. I can't explain now. Could I ring you at home later?'

She hesitated. 'I don't finish till midnight.'

'That's fine. I'll speak to you then.'

She hesitated again but not for long. H had been depressed after the break-up of a relationship, but she'd known him slightly even before he'd called the Samaritans. If anyone would recognise Barney, H would. He already had her number.

'Great. Thanks,' she said.

As soon as she'd put the phone down another call came through. This time she knew the voice immediately. It was a woman who rang often. She was sobbing and incoherent. It was going to be a long call. Sometimes the calls just *seemed* long. Tonight was one of those nights.

Ray's wife, Liz, always came for him in the car after his shift. Ray helped Alexis into the back of the car and although her excitement about Barney was hard to suppress she kept quiet while Ray's wife talked and talked. Thankfully it was a short distance to her flat. Ray led her to the front door and murmured, 'Is it any wonder I make a good listener?' before he dashed off.

Alexis checked her telephone messages. There were none.

Then she took off her coat and sat by the kitchen phone waiting. She waited and waited. Maybe H's suspicions had been wrong and now he hadn't got the nerve to tell her. At one o'clock she left the phone and wandered into the lounge wondering what to do. She couldn't go to bed, she couldn't relax enough to listen to the radio or a talking book; she'd just decided to have a bath when she heard the main door downstairs open. She listened to the footsteps that stopped outside her door. She moved nearer to the door to check she had put the chain on. It seemed a long time before her doorbell rang.

'It's H,' he said in reply to her, 'Who is it?'

Quickly she undid the safety chain and flung the door open. 'Sorry I'm so late,' he said. 'I had to be sure that it was Barney. Now I am.'

'Where is he?' She tried to keep her voice calm but when he didn't answer immediately she asked again. 'Where is he? Is he OK?'

'He's fine,' he said, gently squeezing her hand. 'Calm down. I'll take you to him now.'

'Thank you. Shall I call the police?'

'Not yet. Once you've identified him we'll call the police. Get your coat.'

He helped her slip on her coat, then took her arm. 'Have you got your keys?' he asked. She walked with him into the kitchen, took the keys from the hook and placed them in her coat pocket.

'Do you want your handbag?' he asked.

What for? was almost on her lips but then she remembered her white stick was in her handbag. Never leave home without your stick was an essential rule of being blind.

Outside the air seemed colder than ever. Alexis felt the snow on her face but only for a few seconds because he had parked just outside the front door. As he helped her into the passenger seat of the car she felt totally aware that it was late at night. She could hear no traffic or footsteps.

But she could hear H breathing. She felt excited and yet anxious. It might *not* be Barney. There were still so many questions she wanted to ask but she took a deep breath and thanked H as he shut the passenger door.

When she'd been sighted she'd enjoyed driving, now being in a car was quite a rare event and she couldn't fail to notice the plush comfort of the seat, the generous leg room; and the solid but smooth sound as he closed the door meant that the car was expensive. The engine had a soft purr and she guessed by how easily it manoeuvred that it had power steering.

'What make of car is it?' she asked.

'It's a BMW.'

'You must be very successful. You used to have a van.'

He laughed. 'I am. I work very hard. And I've still got the van.'

'Where did you see Barney?' she asked.

'In a shed. He was taken out and then brought back very late.'

Alexis felt totally mystified. 'Where is this shed?'

'Lady Luck is with us there,' he said. 'It's my next-door neighbour. Bit of a recluse, an oddball.'

He drove on. Alexis could feel her excitement mounting. 'How far is it?' Normally she would have chatted but now only Barney occupied her thoughts.

'My house is another ten miles or so.'

'Does he look well? He hasn't been badly treated, has he?'

'He looks fine. Don't worry.'

Alexis was aware that she was being driven along a straight main road but soon that changed to winding country lanes and the smell of manure crept into the car. Impatient to see Barney, the now slower speed of their journey irritated her. Eventually the tarmac sound changed to rough gravel, and he was driving even more slowly. 'Where are we?' she asked. He didn't answer but stopped quite suddenly, then turned to the right for a short distance, then stopped again.

'We're here,' he announced. 'Journey's end.'

Ram studied arson with the same sense of commitment he had studied the misuse of drugs. Knowledge is power, he told himself as he scanned computer printouts and newspaper reports. One recent report from the *Daily Express* had a byline: TWO PEOPLE KILLED EVERY WEEK AS ARSON SOARS. The home-affairs correspondent went on to report:

> Two people die every week in fires started by arsonists who cost the public £1.3 billion a year.
>
> A disturbing government report out today shows that the 3,500 blazes started deliberately in an average week injure 50 people and cost society at least £25 million. But while fire-raising offences have doubled in a decade, the culprits are only caught in 16 per cent of cases and only one in a hundred results in a conviction.

Ram sighed and stared out of the window watching the snow drifting down. It was so easy to think of Paula and what she might be doing at this moment. He looked away from the window and stared at his notes, willing himself to be focused.

Most arsonists it seemed were young and didn't have murder on their minds. The report quoted the Home Office minister as telling fire-fighters, in what seemed to Ram a totally self-evident statement: 'Arson is a complex crime. Its effects are devastating. It can lead to financial losses, but more important is the cost in terms of human life and misery.'

Ram thought about the individual cases he'd researched. Arson as a means of disposing of a body was relatively common. But this perpetrator wasn't using fire to hide a crime but to highlight it. The nooses were purely for show.

175

Hangman's nooses – an eye for an eye – a fire for a fire. The attacks were for revenge but revenge for what? A fire in which people had died seemed the most likely explanation. When in doubt, he thought, go to the experts. The local fire brigade would have detailed fire reports going back years and with any luck something that would trigger another 'pathway'.

He didn't hear Denni enter the room, he was so deep in thought.

'Are you OK?' she asked.

'Doing what?'

'Thinking at this time of night.'

Ram wearily rubbed his eyes and felt the stubble on his chin. 'I was remembering what an old boss of mine used to tell us.'

Denni sat down, resting her elbows on the desk. 'Which was?'

'His name was Waghorn so his ideas got known as WWs: Waghorn's Ways. He said the way to think of a murderer was to imagine him in the middle of a dark forest.' Ram took a scrap of paper and drew a stick man in the middle surrounded by lollipop trees. On the outskirts he drew a dropped cigarette end, a knife dripping blood and a set of footprints. '"And where does that get you?" he'd demand and before anyone could answer he'd say, "Clues are evidence – they *prove* your case. But take the wrong path through the forest and you'll lose the bastard. Pick up the clues along the way but fan out your men along different paths and one of them will find him in that forest."'

'Very profound, I'm sure,' said Denni. 'What he really meant was you couldn't see the wood for the trees. I feel so knackered I'm past caring.'

'Do you fancy a drink?' asked Ram.

Denni shook her head. 'Sorry, my chubby friend. All I want is my bed.'

Ram laughed. 'Sounds good to me. And less of the "chubby".'

'I'll see you tomorrow,' she said. As she got to the door she remembered why she'd come looking for him. 'Early start tomorrow, Ram. The Gaffer, according to rumour, is ordering a major search for Sara: barns, sheds, farm buildings, empty houses. He wants the police to be highly visible because he thinks chummy might get rattled and make a move.'

'If she's alive,' muttered Ram, 'it might panic whoever's got her.'

Once Denni had gone he realised just how much he dreaded going back to the guesthouse where a cold impersonal bed smelling only of him waited. He knew he wouldn't be able to sleep. On a cold winter's night, he thought, a man of his age, of any age, should be tucked up with a warm woman.

He left the station about ten minutes later to find his car covered in snow. Brushing off the soft surface snow on the windscreen only revealed the ice underneath. He retrieved a scraper from the glove compartment and switched on the ignition or at least tried to switch on the ignition. A dull click resulted. He tried again. He rocked the car back and forth in case the starter motor was jammed. Then he gave up. He knew nothing about the internal parts of cars and he didn't nurse any ambitions to ever find out. He began walking towards a pub popular with the force. It was a good excuse and a far better proposition than one side of a double bed.

He was walking fast. The pub was in a side street a few hundred yards away. There seemed to be no one about and he looked forward to the warmth of the Frog and Fiddler. Then from a side street on his right three lads appeared, young but big. He didn't hesitate, he walked on. He heard only one voice as they laid into him. 'Paki bastard,' one of them screamed into his face before his fist followed. He felt a blow to his back and chest, one to his jaw, several to his kidneys and then someone shouting 'Oy! You!' He heard the sound of running footsteps, fluid welled in his mouth and he knew it was blood. He spat it out and started to crawl. He was making for the pub, but how far he got he didn't know. A woman's voice was urging him to stay awake. He didn't want to, he wanted to drift away into the blackness. He felt no pain. He felt warm and far away.

When he woke up he was propped up in bed. The white sheet covering him and the plain room shouted hospital. Every bone, every joint ached. His mouth had been replaced by a sewer and he couldn't summon the energy to speak. He closed his eyes, he didn't want to speak, he just wanted to sleep.

'Ram. Wake up.'

He wanted to say 'sod off' but he recognised Rydell's voice. So he said nothing.

'Come on, Ram – talk to me. I know you're still alive.'

'Am I?' croaked Ram. 'It's hard to tell.'

'Your mother is on her way.'

This time his eyes shot open. 'Am I that bad?'

'Apart from stab wounds to your chest and back, two broken ribs, bruised kidneys, a loosened tooth, a black eye and a hairline fracture of the skull – not bad at all.'

'I'll need a day off, then,' murmured Ram. 'Did you catch the bastards?'

'We caught two of them and we know the name of the third.'

For some reason Ram felt disinterested. He struggled to remember what he wanted to tell his boss. 'The fires . . . not a professional arsonist,' he mumbled between lips that felt big as sausages. 'A victim maybe or revenge for a fire . . .' he trailed off, unable to hold his train of thought.

'I get your drift,' said Rydell. 'Get some sleep. I'll see you tomorrow.'

*   *   *

Denni had already been to the hospital in the early hours. She and Rydell had been rung immediately. Ram had been in theatre having his stab wounds investigated and patched up. Luckily his heart and lungs hadn't been punctured which the surgeon cheerfully described as being due to a 'short knife and good padding'. And if his kidneys didn't 'conk out' Ram would be out in a few days.

Back in the incident room Denni had begun to feel overwhelmed with the workload. She'd meant to give Alexis a call but it had slipped her mind. Ram being attacked had upset her, she had few friends and two of them were in real trouble. She picked up her desk phone and, while her guilt was still foremost in her mind, she dialled Alexis's number. There was no news about Barney but at least she could visit her later in the evening. There was no reply. She left a brief message saying she'd call round after work.

Rydell had already decided that she should concentrate solely on Stephanie for a day or two. Newly drafted staff were being sent to London to mount surveillance activities on Maria's old flat plus checking the Haddon Farm again and revisiting Sara's friends and neighbours. Rydell was irritated that forensic were taking so long comparing dog hairs and coming up with a rope report, but they both knew that in a murder inquiry information dripped in steadily. Usually that steady drip was enough, but if Sara was still alive it might not be.

The voice man Rydell had found might help if Stephanie's memory was good enough, but he was an amateur, although he'd helped West Mercia police before. He was a hypno-therapist professionally, but he'd taken a special interest in speech and dialects as a hobby. He needed to interview Stephanie and he said this would take at least an hour.

Denni spoke to Stephanie on the phone. She was willing but worried. Her detailed memory of the event was beginning to fade. She tried to explain to Denni. 'It's all blurred in my mind. Like it was a bad dream. Honest, I don't think I can remember what he sounded like now.'

'He'll help you remember – his name's Richard Howard. He might want to help you remember by hypnotising you. How would you feel about that?'

'Would I be unconscious?'

'Not at all. You'll be perfectly aware of what he's saying to you. Afterwards you'll feel great – really relaxed.'

'Have you tried it?'

'Yes. I've tried it. To give up smoking.'

'Did it work?'

'So far. It's been two years.'

'All right then,' she agreed. 'You'll be there, won't you?'

'I'll be there. I'll collect you for two o'clock. Will that be OK?'

There was a pause and a childlike voice said, 'I'd like to be home before dark.'

Richard Howard's office exuded a muted peacefulness that had a marked tranquillising effect on Denni. The slatted blinds of silver grey were closed; pink shaded lamps glowed softly next to two grey reclining chairs. There was neither desk nor telephone. There were large fronded plants on the floor and from somewhere a tape played the sound of the sea gently lapping some imagined shore. Richard himself sat on an office chair. He wore a beige cardigan and brown slacks. His bald head had a shine and his face was somewhat pudgy but he had a voice as soothing as warm honey and whisky.

'I'm Richard,' he said to Stephanie. He spoke to her very gently for a few minutes explaining that under hypnosis she might remember her attacker's voice more clearly and that when it was over she would feel relaxed and happy. She shrugged slightly as if to say it was unlikely, but she seemed calm and Denni gave her an encouraging wink and she managed one in return.

'You take the other recliner, Denni, and relax,' said Richard. It was an offer that she couldn't resist.

Stephanie lay back in the chair and Richard drew his chair nearer and murmured, 'Close your eyes, Stephanie.' As Denni too reclined back she didn't need to be told, her eyes were already lead lined.

'Breathe very gently – in and out. And listen carefully to my voice,' he intoned slowly. 'You are on a warm beach, the sun is shining. You close your eyes. The sea is lapping gently backwards and forwards. You have no cares. You just feel very very sleepy. Now you are falling asleep, fast asleep.' There was a pause. Denni was nearly asleep but she still listened.

'Raise your right hand, Stephanie,' he said. 'Good girl. Now lower it.'

Denni could hear the girl's gentle breathing. 'Now, Stephanie, you are quite safe here. I'll be with you and if you want to stop we'll stop. Do you understand?'

'Yes,' came back a drowsy voice.

'It's evening. You're at home with your mum and you're going out to meet a friend. How do you feel?'

'Great. I'm hoping to see this boy I like.'

'Did you see him?'

'No, he didn't turn up.'

'So what did you do?'

There was a slight pause. 'After a while I started walking home.'

'What was the weather like?'

'Cold. Windy.'

'Were you frightened being on your own?'

'Yeah, a bit. The alleyway was dark but I didn't see anyone.'

'Now, Stephanie. I know you were grabbed from behind, but what I'm interested in are his actual words and his accent. Was his voice loud or soft?'

'It was soft.'

'Was he whispering?'

'At first he was.'

'What did he say?'

There was a long pause. 'He had his arm around my neck . . . he said, "Keep still, bitch. I'll kill you if you don't." He's so close I can smell him.'

'I'll say those same words now and I want you to tell me if I sound anything like him.'

He whispered the words with a furious intensity that made Denni shudder. The words themselves were common enough warnings from rapists but actually hearing them from a male voice tinged with such menace was still a shock.

Stephanie, still calm, murmured, 'I don't know. A bit like him, I suppose. I can hear him breathing in my ear. He's dragging me. That smell . . . it's on his clothes.'

'The smell bothers you?'

'Yeah. I've smelt it before . . . when . . .'

'When was it, Stephanie? When you were younger?'

Denni could hear Stephanie's quiet breathing and she thought for a moment that she'd actually fallen into a really deep sleep but eventually she said drowsily, 'My mum's boyfriend was still around so I was about eight or nine. He was decorating. He had paint tins and brushes and rolls of wallpaper everywhere. I wanted to help him and there was a jar of . . . I thought it was water on the floor. He said, "Be careful, Steph, that's not water in that jar – it's turps." And that's what *he* smelt of . . . it was the *same* smell.'

Twenty-Four

H had led her along a path. 'Soon be there,' he said, giving her arm an encouraging squeeze. She'd heard the wind blowing through trees and felt snow falling on her face but she heard no traffic sounds. Underfoot felt a little slippy and she was glad he held her arm. He stopped and she heard him open a door. 'Wipe your feet,' he said with an edge of laughter in his voice. He'd gently pushed her ahead of him and she immediately listened for sounds of Barney. She held out her arms and called out, 'Come on, Barney – its me.'

When there was no response she turned her head. 'H – H – where is he?' Her voice trailed away. Her hands flailed around to find him. It was then that she heard the dull clang of an up-and-over garage door followed by a click as he turned a key in the lock. His soft footsteps fading away made her shudder with the full realisation of how easily she had been tricked.

Alexis stood with trembling arms outstretched in the black void. She wanted to scream for help but she reasoned the only person to come to her might be him. She stood for a long time trying to stay calm, trying to control her breathing and her thoughts, listening intently for any sounds which might help her. There was only silence and the smell of damp and a sour airlessness. If she'd thought she'd felt lonely and afraid in the past, now she experienced a feeling of such bleakness as though the world had retreated and she was the only one left. 'God if you're there – help me please,' she whispered.

Still feeling the air with her hands she found the metal door. She pounded the surface with her fists. The loudness was reassuring but futile, but at least the door gave her a point of reference. She could edge round the walls, try to get a picture in her mind of where the hell she was. The *why* would have to wait.

With her back against the wall and her hands stretched out on either side of her, she began edging along. The floor felt like concrete, and whatever she was in was very cold or else she was now in shock. She guessed it was a garage because of that door but fear made her doubt even the stability of the floor. After a few steps her left foot knocked against something light. She bent down to feel it – an empty plastic bucket. Picking it up she moved back to the door and placed the bucket by the door edge. If he came back, opening the door would knock it over.

There was nothing else in her way along that one wall. Somehow she had hoped along the next wall to find a window or another door but there was nothing – just bricks. She faced the walls using her hands in wide sweeps to find another way out: a window, a hole – anything. It was then her foot caught something. Her hands found the corner of the wall. She bent down to touch what she'd felt with her feet. It felt like old rags and next to them were tins. She felt the rims and recognised them as paint tins. Lifting up one tin she felt its weight in her hands and decided it was nearly full and could be used as a weapon. She retraced her steps to the door and placed two of the cans next to the plastic bucket.

Turning sideways she paced her footsteps to the first corner. At a guess it was fifteen feet. She continued walking round feeling the walls trying to find a light switch but the walls were blank and, apart from a pile of old newspapers, there seemed to be nothing else around the room's perimeter.

If this place had no lights, she thought, it *might* be to her advantage unless of course he came back with a torch. At least if he kicked the obstacles she would be instantly alerted. In the circumstances that was only a grim consolation but she felt comforted that he couldn't creep up on her unawares.

Gingerly she explored the middle of the space, her toe hitting first some sort of mat then touching something springy. She guessed it was a mattress. She sat on it, aware of its thinness, it was hardly even a barrier to the chill of the concrete floor. She smelt or imagined that she could smell damp. Running her hands over the bare flock either side of her it felt reasonably dry except for one patch. Was it urine or blood or simply wet?

Now she was sitting down and she had some idea of her surroundings her mind flittered like fast-juggling balls. Why? How long? Who else? Had he killed the woman found in the barn? Was this the barn? Had he killed the missing woman? For God's sake, had he killed her on this mattress? She jumped up suddenly, stood for a moment and then made her way to the door. She paused there feeling its metal ridges, as if somehow they held the answer. H wasn't that tall and she was younger than he was. Perhaps if it was very dark she could outwit him, even outfight him. Physically she was strong. It was better to die fighting, she told herself. A woman fighting for her life could be as strong as any man.

She began hammering again on the door and shouting for help. She continued hammering until her arm ached.

'Come on, you bastard,' she screamed. 'Come and get me.'

She gradually grew hoarse and her anger began to give way to despair. Was he anywhere near? Why could no one else hear her?

How long she sat on the floor she couldn't know because she'd removed her Braille watch at home just before she planned to have a bath. It seemed a long time, but she couldn't judge how long. She'd grown stiff and her cold feet had developed pins and needles. She stood up and stamped her feet and marched on the spot to an imaginary drummer.

The mattress had become her island, so she sat down again, upright and alert. The cold soon made her begin to shiver violently so she wrapped her arms around herself and rocked gently backwards and forwards. Keeping still was impossible. Strange, she thought, she could actually feel desperate for the man who might well be planning to kill her. Her real dread was that he had simply abandoned her.

After a while she eased herself back on the mattress and turned sideways to draw up her knees and try to keep warm. It didn't work. Her feet even in boots felt painfully cold. She stood up again and stamped her feet and walked a few steps forward. The sound of her feet on the concrete was a welcome noise in the overwhelming silence. With a certain amount of confidence now she walked up and down beside the edge of the mattress. When she felt a little warmer she sat down. As she tried to settle herself yet again she felt the edge of a blanket and gave it a pull. It was caught on something. Her hands reached out to investigate.

It took a fleeting second before the horror registered, for her hands to recognise the hairy softness of Barney's body. Only a low moan emerged from her throat as shock made her struggle for breath. She sank down on the floor, feeling for his head, uncaring that the sticky gelatinous mess on her hands was blood. His body was stiff and unyielding, but she cradled him in her arms like a child and rocked backwards and forwards. She couldn't cry, she just kept rocking him. Her brain, her whole body became numb. She couldn't think, all she could do was murmur his name.

Eventually her arms went into spasm and she could no longer hold him. Gently she placed Barney back on the mattress. She felt sick now, bile rising in her throat making her heave. She began deep breathing, tried to think clearly, and told herself that survival depended on her getting out. She had to focus on escaping. There was nothing she could do for Barney now. She couldn't even cry.

Rigid with fear now she no longer felt cold. But nagging

doubts crept back into her mind. What if he didn't plan to come back? What if for some reason he couldn't? What *was* his mad plan? Her worst fear surfaced, she would be left here to die a slow and lingering death. Buried alive to die beside Barney's corpse.

Twenty-Five

*H*e'd done it. Got her. He hadn't been able to sleep but then he didn't need much now. It had all gone to plan. He stood at the window staring out over snow-covered moonlit fields and then in wonderment at the stars.

Once the police knew she was missing they'd pull out all the stops. He guessed that would take a day or two and then they'd start searching and doing spot checks. Now was the time to get rid of the whining bitch in the cellar. First though, she could write that letter – that would throw them off the scent. Then she could have a bath as a reward. He laughed. He might even fuck her first. She wasn't fit to be an angel. She'd had a couple of paddies and sworn like a street slag. Maria may have been a tart but she did have self-control.

Once Alexis realised that it was their destiny to be together he could allow her more freedom. She could even be allowed to sleep in his bed. She'd been alone and now being with him would make all the difference to her life. She was special and she needed someone special like him to make her happy.

His eyes would see for her. He would be her interpreter.

But first the cellar had to be cleared. He'd noticed in the last day or two that his baby angel had looked at him in a strange way and when he took her from the bitch she would begin to screw up her face and snivel. Perhaps her mind was being poisoned against him.

Now that he didn't need so much sleep because his mind was clear he could plan ahead. Prioritise.

Alexis would have to stay where she was at the moment. It would give her time to get over the dog. In his line of work he'd seen far too many people get attached to their pets. They were all going to die at some point, so what difference did sooner make? The Angel of Death was the powerful one. Not God. If only people could understand that. He'd never thought that he was God but he could be the Angel of Death. Strange, he thought, how people blamed God for disasters and plagues when they should be blaming AD. What did they think 1999 AD stood for? Not Anno Domini, that was for sure.

He was so clever he could actually hear his own laughter bubbling away inside.

Twenty-Six

So much had been going on, Denni very nearly forgot to call in on Alexis. After seeing Stephanie home, she'd gone back to the station to key in her report. Rydell had thrust some forensic reports in her hands and had expected her to read them and probably inwardly digest them. She was so hungry, she could have eaten the paper they were written on. 'Could you give me a résumé?' she asked. He'd shrugged in irritation. 'My team always want spoonfeeding.'

'A fork would do,' said Denni. 'I haven't eaten all day.'

'Come on then,' said Rydell, as he straightened the sheaf of papers by tapping them on the desk and then placing them parallel to another pile. 'I'll treat you to a pub meal.' Denni murmured her thanks, but she couldn't stand by and watch his little rituals. 'I'll wait for you downstairs, Guv.' He looked up in surprise. 'You haven't asked about Ram,' he said. His tone was neutral but she sensed he was disapproving.

'I was planning to see him tonight,' she said, 'but I also want to see Alexis. There just aren't enough hours in the day.'

Rydell smiled. 'Tell me about it . . . give me five minutes.'

It was more like ten. In the front office Ram's attack, it seemed, was the talk of the station. 'Poor old Sabu,' said the duty sergeant who was Scots but known as Scotch, not because of his nationality but because he drank so much of it. The general consensus was that it was a racist attack.

190

For Denni, a thug was a thug. Racism was just an excuse for a mindless yob to beat hell out of someone different. 'Anyway,' said Scotch, 'at least one of the bastards is banged up. His story is Sabu reminded him of a bloke who attacked his sister, but at least he's not denying it. Said he was drunk and out of his mind.'

'There's no chance he'll get away with it?' asked Denni.

'Not with his form.'

'Is he local?'

'No. A Mancunian.'

Denni was about to comment on that as Rydell arrived and now that *he* was ready there was no time to waste. They walked quickly in the chill night air to the nearest pub, the Quill and Pen, a quiet pub with as much life as a public library but with a good line in substantial pies. And a real coal fire.

They sat at a corner table near the fire, took off their coats and peered at the menu as if they had never seen it before. It wasn't a menu that reflected any health warnings. Rydell went off to order drinks and food and Denni sat forward wearily with a hand supporting her head.

'Don't go to sleep on me,' he said as he placed a white wine spritzer in front of her.

'I'm not sleeping well,' she murmured raking a hand through her hair and sitting more upright. 'I feel exhausted, but when I get into bed I have to read and then I wake up in the early hours and start thinking.'

'Too much adrenaline,' said Rydell. 'Try sleeping on the sofa with the TV on.'

She sipped her drink. 'I've tried that. I still wake up about three a.m. feeling eighty-five, crawl to my bed and then lie awake. And it makes me feel like my own mother.'

Rydell stared at his beer. 'The job was part of the reason my marriage cracked up,' he murmured. 'My ex-wife worked in an office and it was fine for a year or so. She

191

was busy and she didn't resent my long hours, my running irritated her, but basically we were happy.'

'What happened?'

'She got pregnant. After a few months she had to give up her job. She swelled up like a balloon and my long hours did become a problem then. She found it hard to adjust . . . and then—' he broke off.

'What happened?' asked Denni softly.

He cleared his throat and stared at her for a moment. 'She had a difficult long labour. Our son Paul suffered lack of oxygen to the brain.' He paused again and added bitterly, 'Technically he was born dead but they brought him back from the edge.'

'Is he very handicapped?'

Rydell shook his head slowly. 'Not any more. He died when he was four.'

'I'm sorry.'

'Don't be. God forgive me but I think it was for the best. It's just that I—'

'What?' she prompted.

'I can never put things right now.' He swallowed hard and then drank his beer. 'I don't want to talk about it anymore. I spend my life trying to forget.'

'Some experiences you can never forget – too important I suppose.'

'You sound as if you know from experience.'

She nodded. 'I do but like you sometimes I can't talk about it. It's too painful.'

He drained his glass, smiled bleakly and said, 'Right then, let's change the subject.'

Denni smiled back. 'I could tell you about my love life but its non-existent.'

'Why's that?'

'The moment men find out I'm in the police they divide into two camps and show their true colours – wimps or control freaks.'

'It's best to stay within the force,' said Rydell thoughtfully as if it had just occurred to him.

Denni laughed. 'Restricts our choice though, doesn't it? And we could face a lifetime of talking shop.'

The arrival of puffed-up pies halted their conversation and once they'd eaten, Rydell asked her about progress with Stephanie. 'It was no go on the voice front,' said Denni. 'But she did remember one thing and it could be important.'

'Which was?'

'He smelt of turps.'

Rydell finished his beer but still held the empty glass. 'Let's add two and turps and make him a self-employed painter and decorator. He would have transport, might do jobs in London, could target women. It's a possibility.'

'He could also have just been doing a little DIY.'

He'd obviously thought of that so he ignored her suggestion. 'I'm having another beer. You'll drive, won't you?'

She nodded. After all, what choice did she have? When this case is over she vowed, I'm getting legless and if I get laid as well that will be a bonus. She'd had neither social nor sex life for ages and although she hadn't the energy for either at the moment she held at least a few treasured memories of a time when she did.

Rydell returned with more beer and a coffee for her. 'To keep you awake, Denni,' he said, 'while I tell you about the forensic reports.' He pushed a hand through his hair and took a taster gulp of beer, probably to check it was as good as the last, and said, 'We've got a match on one of the dog hairs.'

'Rusty?'

'Correct. Fenton wants Greenly and King in for questioning tomorrow and I'm in the doghouse myself for not having had his garden dug up properly.'

'It's a bit worrying, Guv, isn't it?' she said. 'About the dog hair on her body.'

'Too bloody true. But I'm convinced Greenly isn't our man.'

'What makes you so sure?'

Rydell looked at her sharply as if in some way she was being disloyal. 'Greenly is a man devoid of imagination, of that I'm certain. The bastard we want is cunning and imaginative.' Then he added angrily, 'For fuck's sake, he's mad.'

Denni sipped her coffee. 'Greenly's obviously a practised liar. He convinced us he hadn't even been near the body.'

'Yeah, yeah, I get your drift. Don't labour it. Maybe I've cocked-up but I'm not going to bang him up for thirty-six hours and lose that time when we should spend it looking for Sara Bolten.'

'What about the rope analysis?' she asked, wanting to get off the touchy subject of Greenly.

'The expert view is that the basic three-ply nylon rope was never used for climbing, no traces of grit or grass. The opinion seems to be that it was used for bondage. The ends had been heat sealed to stop them from unravelling and traces of moisturising cream were found. It seems bondage enthusiasts often get their rope from yachting suppliers.'

'Could we get a print out on customers?' she asked, seeing clearly at that moment breakthrough heaven. 'It could have been mail order or the Internet.'

'I'd thought of that. But there is another possibility.'

'What's that?'

'He nicked it from Maria's place.'

She sighed. 'In that case it just seems to highlight him as one of Maria's punters.'

'Could be,' he agreed. 'Maybe she didn't know he'd taken the rope, depends on the quantity she'd bought. She may not have noticed a few missing metres.'

'If our man is a painter and decorator,' suggested Denni, 'it might explain Sara opening the door to him.'

'Knots,' said Rydell.

'What?'

'The knots – a standard hangman's noose on Maria,' he

explained, 'but on the bags of potatoes he used the scaffold or gallows knot. According to the report that's also used as a knot to tie angling rods to fishline. For Maria's wrists he used a timber hitch to secure her.'

'So he could be a painter and decorator or a fisherman?'

'Or just a bondage enthusiast. At least we can check out fishing licences.'

Denni finished her coffee and yawned. The sudden in-take of food and the warmth of the fire had obviously stultified her brain. It was eight thirty and sleep was still a long way off. First they planned to visit Ram, and then she was calling in on Alexis. With any luck she'd be offered a bed for the night and Alexis might just welcome the company.

At the hospital the night nurse had bags under her eyes and appeared in irritable control. 'You can only stay for a few minutes,' she said. 'His mother's been here all the afternoon.'

'How's he doing?' Rydell asked.

Her narrow shoulders shrugged. 'Not that well. There's a possibility of some kidney damage. We're monitoring him very carefully.'

As she walked away Rydell turned to Denni. 'Is that serious?'

She shook her head thoughtfully. 'The kicking he got might have bruised his kidneys and that would make them more prone to infection. Antibiotics and rest should do the trick.'

They found Ram, eyes closed, one sheet barely covering him and with an electric fan on a stand whirring noisily by the bed. There was only one chair. Denni leant over and kissed his cheek. He was burning up. He opened his swollen eyes to reveal a dull feverish stare.

'If I had hair it would be standing on end,' he said.

'Drink plenty,' urged Denni. 'It might make it grow.'

He half smiled. 'I would, but they only provide water.'

Denni took a professional interest in the chart at the bottom of his bed and when she looked up again Ram looked asleep. He murmured something and she sat beside him and held his hand. 'Say it again, Ram,' she urged.

'Cloth ears,' he mumbled without opening his eyes. 'I asked if you'd caught him yet.'

'Only one of them. The other two were marathon runners.'

'Not them,' Ram said, shaking his head. '*Him.*'

Denni squeezed his hand. 'Not yet. You've been here hours not days. To catch *him* we need you back as soon as possible.'

Ram lay motionless and in repose his long eyelashes and round face gave him a childlike look. His answer wasn't childlike though. 'I'm knackered. And I can't think straight.'

'Don't worry about it. You'll feel better tomorrow.'

Ram smiled wearily. 'Yes, nurse. Tell Rydell there has got to be a link.'

'He's here with me. What do you mean?'

'I'm ill,' muttered Ram. 'I'm not sure what the fuck I'm talking about. But there has to be a link between someone we've spoken to in Harrowford and the murderer . . .' He trailed off and, although they waited for a few minutes, Ram began to snore and there didn't seem much point in staying.

As they walked out of the ward Denni turned to Rydell but she noticed all the colour had drained from his face. She took his arm and once outside the cold air seemed to revive him. 'I can't stand hospitals,' he said. 'I've never fainted yet but I feel as near as dammit.'

Once back in the car his face soon resumed a normal colour. 'He is going to make it, isn't he?' he asked.

Denni smiled. 'He's tough. But he might be in hospital for a while.'

She drove out of the hospital car park realising that once

Rydell knew she was going to see Alexis he'd want to come too. He did.

The flat was in darkness with the curtains closed. A residue of snow lay thinly over the communal gardens. Light from the other flats accentuated the bleak frontage of Alexis's flat. 'That's strange,' said Denni. 'Alexis might be blind but she keeps her lights on to deter burglars. And she goes to bed late because she doesn't sleep that well.'

As Denni pressed the intercom bell, Rydell asked, 'Why doesn't she sleep well?'

'Blindness, it seems,' she explained, 'alters the melatonin levels in the brain so it alters the body clock.' She pressed hard on the bell again. As they waited, Denni stamped her feet anxiously. Something was wrong, very wrong. She pressed the bell of the adjacent flat belonging to Mrs Dora West. Dora held the spare keys. She took a long time to answer but Denni knew she moved slowly with bowed arthritic legs. 'Hello. Who is it?' she asked nervously.

'Denni. A friend of Alexis.'

'Do I know you?'

'We have met. I'm the policewoman friend.'

'I remember,' she said. 'You're the buxom one.'

'Could you let me in and open Alexis's door. She's not answering.'

'Oh dear. Yes, of course.'

Dora pressed her entry button and they entered. Denni's eyes flicked anxiously towards her friend's door, but then Dora's flat door clicked open a fraction still with the safety chain on. Dora wore a pink dressing gown that nearly touched the floor and her face was obviously in the process of being moisturised. Little patches of cream hadn't quite been rubbed in.

'I hope she's all right dear,' she said, handing Alexis's spare keys to Denni and looking with a degree of suspicion at Rydell. Once Rydell had been formally introduced Dora smiled and slipped off the safety chain. 'I thought it was unusual not to have seen her today. She went out last night. I think it was her Samaritans night.'

'What time did she get back?' Denni asked.

Dora shook her head. 'I've no idea. I go to bed early with a sleeping tablet and I'm fast asleep then till four or five in the morning. Sometimes the young people above me play music and that keeps me awake but not last night.'

'Thank you. We'll ask the other residents.'

Dora lingered at the door while Denni fumbled with the keys. She felt sick. Rydell seemed to notice and he turned the key in the lock. 'I'm right behind you,' he murmured. She took a deep breath as she swung the door open and called, 'Alexis! Alexis!'

Twenty-Seven

D avid Bolten's post arrived just as he was leaving. A quick glance showed it was only bills, except, that is, for one letter. The bluey grey envelope felt thick, like vellum. He turned it over and stared at his own name and address. It was Sara's writing, a pseudo italic style but totally recognisable. Hurriedly he opened it and then stood in the hallway reading the words of his missing wife. The wife he had become convinced was dead. The actual words danced in front of his eyes and he read them twice.

Dear David

I know how worried you must have been but somehow I couldn't bring myself to ring you. I'm settled in a very pleasant cottage in the south of Ireland. I think about Ben all the time and wonder how you're coping. I'm sure you're managing really well, you're such a good cook and you were always better at changing nappies than I was.

I'm sure you're asking yourself why I left in such a hurry in the middle of the night. I just couldn't go on. I was very depressed although I tried to hide it. I did tell Harriet I felt as if I were going mad and she wanted to tell you but I persuaded her not to.

I'm living with a friend and hoping to get acting jobs.

Please don't try to find me. Ben is better off without me and you'll meet someone else soon.

Tell Mummy I'm sorry to have given her such an horrendous time. Please give her a Hug from me. Give Ben a kiss and lots of Hugs for me.
Sorry
Love Mole

There was a postscript: 'A friend posted this in London.'

Having read the letter twice he abandoned his plans to visit Rhoda and Ben and instead dialled Harrowford Police Station and then, tapping his foot and drumming his fingers on the telephone receiver, waited for someone to pick up the phone. Eventually a human voice answered to tell him DI Rydell wasn't available but would be in by ten a.m. He felt irritated about that until he remembered it was Saturday.

He placed the letter in a plastic food bag and debated with himself about ringing Rhoda. He decided against it. He was convinced Sara had written the letter but it wasn't her style and she was obviously trying to get across a message. He could sense her desperation and any anger he once felt about her leaving was now replaced by guilt and a stomach-churning anxiety.

He drove to the police station in thin spiky sunlight that made him squint. Luckily traffic was light because his concentration was poor. Not since the actual night Sara had gone missing had he felt so shocked. He knew Sara well enough to know the letter had been written under duress and that she was trying to tell him something, but what? And who the hell was Harriet?

The young constable on duty in the reception area nodded at him in an off-hand way. 'Take a seat, sir. As soon as Inspector Rydell comes in I'll let you know.'

Bolten sat on a bolted-to-the-floor plastic chair and ignored the comings and goings of staff, the steady stream of people complaining of lost or stolen purses or damaged cars or damage to their person. He didn't care about anyone else's problems, he wanted action, dynamic action. Not the wishy-washy efforts made so far.

At ten thirty his patience grew thin. He joined the queue of three people waiting to speak to the constable. When it came to his turn he began blustering with pent-up frustration.

'I was told Inspector Rydell would be in at ten. Has he decided to take a day off? If so I would be grateful to be told . . .' he paused. 'My time is just as valuable—' he broke off, suddenly aware of how pompous he sounded. The young policeman's face remained impassive. He was young but obviously used to all sorts of criticism and abuse. Bolten was wasting his time.

'I'll check his office,' he said, picking up the phone.

Now that Bolten had calmed down a little he read the officer's name badge: PC Andy Harris.

'You're in luck, sir. He's in the interview room. Take a seat, he shouldn't be too long.'

Disgruntled, Bolten sat down convinced PC Harris took sadistic delight in keeping people waiting.

The news of the blind woman's disappearance had permeated Harrowford Police Station as fast as high-speed ducted air. DCI Alec Fenton called an eight a.m. emergency meeting and off-duty officers, mostly volunteers, had arrived by seven thirty and were milling around, cups of coffee in hand, waiting for instructions. Fenton, easing his bulk through the small crowd, glanced at Denni and said with his usual lack of charm or tact, 'Sergeant, your eyes look like piss holes in the snow.'

She stared back at him with a blankness she felt from within. The night had been long and sleepless, most of it spent either in Alexis's flat or in the Samaritans' office. Denni had balked at rifling through Alexis's belongings because it seemed like a serious invasion of privacy but Rydell had insisted, saying: 'Be objective, Denni, forget she's your friend. Treat this – incident just like any other.'

'This isn't an incident,' she'd said. 'This is an abduction.'

'Yes. And it's the second one, so let's get on with it.'

The flat had seemed so dark and desolate that turning on all the lights only seemed to illuminate its emptiness. There was no sign of a forced entry or a struggle. Denni, by a process of elimination, worked out that Alexis was wearing a camel hair coat and her new black boots. She'd always refused to wear a fluorescent armband as Denni had suggested but always wore light-coloured jackets. Her handbag was missing and with it her small Dictaphone on which she had taped addresses and telephone numbers. There was only one indication she might have left in a hurry or had been trying to tell them she was leaving under duress and that was her Braille wristwatch, which lay on the table by the telephone.

'She always wears her watch, even at night,' said Denni.

'She'd take it off for a bath.' Rydell was right of course. If she'd been planning a bath then she wasn't expecting anyone to call and yet she'd let him in. Denni found no sign of her having taken a bath – no damp towels or condensation.

In the kitchen Barney's empty dog bowl on the floor was unremarkable but oddly a tin of dog food and the tin opener had been taken from the cupboard and placed side by side on the work surface. 'You don't think we might have jumped to the wrong conclusion?'

'In what way?' asked Rydell as he dialled 1471 to check her last phone call.

'Perhaps she's had a tip-off about Barney and has gone to investigate?'

Rydell smiled at her. She supposed it was meant to be reassuring, but it felt more like a 'stop clutching at straws' smile. He gazed at her steadily. 'She wasn't here this morning when you rang, was she? She's not the type just to go off, is she? Even disregarding her blindness.'

Denni shrugged, knowing Rydell was right. 'She's not the

sort either to open her door to a stranger. She would have to know and trust him.'

'Or he had news of Barney and she took a chance.'

Denni fell silent, desperately trying to think of any man Alexis might know, trustworthy or not.

'Last number to ring here was 3 p.m. today,' said Rydell and then reeled off the number. Denni recognised it. 'That's her mother. She lives down south. They speak to each other nearly every day.'

'It doesn't help us much. We'll need to get a printout of all her calls. She could have been waiting for someone to ring,' muttered Rydell. 'Equally she could have had a call from the Samaritans' office telephone.'

'In which case,' said Denni, 'she may have been waiting for him.'

'Or waiting for him to phone.'

'There are several male Samaritans volunteers,' said Denni thoughtfully. 'She'd trust them implicitly.'

Rydell nodded. 'We'll check them out, however respectable they may seem.'

They had left the flat and driven straight to the Samaritans' office. The night sky was clear and it felt cold enough to freeze tears. Inside the house 'Freda' and 'George' manned the phones in the office and neither knew that Alexis was missing. There was a shocked silence as they absorbed the news. They had little time to get over their shock as both phones rang simultaneously and Denni and Rydell were left waiting for intervals between calls. The time between them was depressingly short.

All the calls were logged and in a brief lull they glanced at the individual call books. Only a single letter, the duration of the call and occasionally a comment such as 'abusive' or 'silent' identified callers. Freda, who wore large dangly earrings and had her grey hair in a bun, handed them Alexis's call book. 'It's a bit of a mess, but she does have a system. She cuts out a small square at the side of the page, lines up her ruler to it and then writes above the ruler.' Denni was impressed. Occasionally Alexis had overwritten but it was still legible. Not that it helped except that one call did have FTC written by the side.

'What's this mean?' asked Denni.

Freda smiled. 'First time caller.'

'We'll need to talk to the chap working with her on Thursday,' said Rydell. A worried frown crossed Freda's round face. She glanced across at George who although listening to a caller still seemed to know what was going on. He gave her the nod and she wrote down 'Ray's' real name and address.

It was by now one thirty in the morning. William Fortune or 'Ray' lived about ten miles away in Lower Waddeston, a small village of twenty or so houses, one pub and no shop. They passed only two cars on the way and the clouds gathered and sleet began to fall. The orange glow of the streetlights failed to compensate for lack of moon or stars.

Denni banged on the front door and waited, shivering with cold, tiredness and hunger. She *was* trying to be objective but her only thoughts had revolved around the cold and the dark: if she felt like this how the hell must Alexis be feeling? It was hard for her to talk to Rydell because she was feeling emotional and it was better to keep quiet.

Eventually William Fortune answered the door in a red plaid dressing gown. He was tall, with a full head of spiky grey hair and a slight stoop. When his wife came downstairs in a neck-to-floor matching red plaid to stand beside him Denni understood why he stooped. Jenny was about four feet eleven and although she spoke quietly it was rapid fire.

'Police? At this time of night? What's happened?'

Rydell explained. Denni noticed the shocked expression on William Fortune's face, but he said nothing. He didn't get a chance.

'Poor Alexis. She's got enough to cope with. She's such a brave person you know. She's –'

Ray put a hand on his wife's shoulder and she paused. 'Do come in,' he said. The 'pause' didn't last long. Even as they walked into the house she carried on talking. 'What is the country coming to? First she has her guide dog stolen then someone steals her. I mean, you'd think having a dog would be some sort of protection.'

Rydell visibly gritted his teeth. 'She's missing, we believe abducted. The person or persons involved may have lured her away from her flat with news of Barney.' He was aware he sounded just like a cop but his cold official tone didn't stop her.

'I'm not really surprised,' she carried on. 'Fancy a blind woman being a Samaritan. All the callers are disturbed. Someone has probably been stalking her for ages. My husband's had some strange experiences, I can assure you—'

Rydell held up his hand. 'That's enough, Mrs Fortune.'

'Call me Jenny,' she said, looking puzzled by his tone.

'Sergeant, take Mrs Fortune into the kitchen. I'm sure she'll make us all a cup of tea.'

Denni smiled and said briskly, 'You lead the way.'

Rydell felt more relaxed in the silence that enveloped the room. William also seemed relieved. 'I savour a peaceful moment or two,' he said with a slight shrug. 'They don't come very often. She's been "nervous" since she lost two babies.'

'That's understandable,' said Rydell.

The sitting room had the atmosphere of dust-free tidiness that made Rydell feel at ease, but he was aware of its lack of personality. Jenny Fortune was, he thought, a woman who made a career of cleanliness, of preparing a nest that would never be.

'It's a real shock,' said William, shaking his head. 'I'm very fond of Alexis.' Then very quietly he added, 'Very fond.'

Rydell mentally noted the massive understatement for it was obvious, just by his wistful tone of voice, that he was in love with her. 'I can't do anything about it of course. My wife needs me. She's been hospitalised a few times. And anyway, Alexis thinks of me as a good mate – nothing more.'

'Tell me what happened on Thursday evening.'

'Nothing untoward. I picked her up from home and walked with her to the office. A chap in the village works in a pub – he gives me a lift in and my wife gives me a lift home.'

'Did she come straight down or did you go to her flat?'

An expression of annoyance or anxiety crossed Fortune's face. Rydell wasn't sure which but he did recognise a man who was trying to keep his emotions under control. 'Why do you want to know, Inspector?'

'Answer the question.'

There was a pause. 'I don't want my wife to know, but sometimes if I arrived early we would have a coffee together. And a bit of a chat. Both poor lonely sods I suppose—' he broke off and smiled wryly. 'Hard to imagine being lonely with a wife like mine but believe me, it is.'

'Did you have coffee that night?'

'No. She was still upset about the dog and she didn't suggest it.'

'What happened at the office?'

'It was a run-of-the-mill Thursday night. We always seem to get more calls towards the end of the week.'

'Are they all suicidal?'

Fortune shook his head. 'No, thank God. Depressed, worried, poor, drunk, mentally ill, homeless, betrayed, battered, frightened. You name the human condition and we get the call.'

'And was that night different in any way?'

'I don't think so . . . Alexis and I didn't really have any sort of break from calls. Some last for a long time and some callers ring back . . .' he paused. 'Now I remember that she did have a very short call just before we left. I don't know what was said, but I got the impression it was either a friend or a thank-you call – we get those sometimes.'

'Was that why she didn't log it?'

'Possibly. Our relief shift had arrived and my wife was waiting outside – she's always early.'

'Tell me what made you think Alexis's last call was – friendly?'

'She smiled; she looked sort of relieved.'

'As if someone had found her dog?'

'Yes . . . yes exactly. Why didn't I think of that?'

'Can you think of a reason she didn't tell you?'

He gave a brief nod. 'My wife. Alexis could have had a broken leg and she wouldn't have had a chance to say.'

'If it was a "caller" have you any idea who?'

'Alexis was a very good listener and I know she did befriend a few who she thought she could help. Sometimes she met people during the day at the office.'

'Are there records?'

'Should be logged in her call book. Only first initial though. Our service is confidential.'

Rydell nodded and when Fortune's wife reappeared, he wanted to be away, daylight couldn't come quick enough for him. He wanted every nook and cranny searched, every barn, outhouse, empty house and especially the homes of all known sex criminals. He wanted every plod in West Mercia to drop traffic control and piddling cases and find both women before it was too late. Deep down, though, his fear was that it was already too late.

In the car Rydell said, 'You were a hell of a long time making tea, Denni. I bet you managed a cup or two.'

'You wanted me to keep her out of the way, didn't you?'

'Yeah, I certainly did. Did she rabbit about anything in particular?'

'Actually, she's a nice woman. She was telling me about her time as an in-patient at Four Fields Psychiatric Hospital.'

'Scintillating.'

'Don't sneer. I bet you don't even know where it is.'

'Does it make a difference?'

'It's on the outskirts of London. Half private, half charity run.'

'So?'

'There's more. Vernon Greenly was a patient there at the same time.'

'Was he indeed?' murmured Rydell thoughtfully as he U-turned the car. 'We'll pay him a visit. Perhaps he's been a touch too clever for us. And we need to find out about his knotting skills.'

It was nearly three a.m. when they arrived at Greenly's house, the lights downstairs were on, the curtains were gone and the windows were covered with newspaper. Greenly answered the door in paint-spattered jeans and a grey jogging top. His annoyance was obvious.

'I haven't broken my bail conditions,' he said. 'This is police harassment. Growing marijuana isn't exactly crime of the century.'

'We're not here about your drug empire,' said Rydell. 'We just want to talk.'

'It's three in the morning.'

'You're up. We're up. What better time could there be?'

Greenly scowled and wiped the palms of his hands slowly up and down the sides of his jeans. 'Come through to the kitchen. You can see I'm decorating.'

There were two chairs and a stool in the kitchen. Denni sat on the stool. Rydell and Greenly sat either side of a blue Formica table.

'Are you planning to sell the house?' asked Denni.

'I'm not sure. Depends if I get a custodial sentence.'

'Where's your dog?' asked Rydell.

'Asleep on my bed. Why?'

'Not much of a guard dog, is he?'

'Rusty's slightly deaf.'

'Doesn't stop him exploring, does it?'

Greenly stared at him. 'What's that supposed to mean?'

'I'm talking dog hairs.'

There was a flustered silence and a few nervous blinks before Greenly spoke again. 'If you've got something to say, Inspector, why not just say it?'

'Dead body in barn. Dog hairs found on leg of victim. Hair from your dog. Conclusion: you are not only a would-be drug baron but also a liar.'

'Smoking a bit of hash doesn't make me a drug baron,' Greenly snapped. 'And I don't think dog hairs make me a murderer.'

'I notice you haven't denied being a liar.'

Greenly wiped a hand wearily across his face. 'I didn't kill her but Rusty did find the body.'

'If that's the case why not admit that the dog found the body?'

'It was less complicated.'

'You're annoying me, Greenly,' said Rydell. 'Do you realise that you and King are our only suspects? Let me put forward the scenario: the pair of you kidnapped Maria Seaton. King stole a car for the purpose. Maria was kept prisoner in the farmhouse and then when she grew difficult you killed her and set up the scene to look like a mad arsonist was to blame.'

There was only a short pause before Greenly smiled, cocky and sure of himself.

'If you *really* thought that, Inspector, you'd present me with more evidence than just dog hairs. I didn't know the dead woman – how could I – she wasn't local, was she?'

'I believe you were once in Four Fields Hospital?'

'So what?'

Rydell glanced across at Denni, a look which said, you take over.

'Were you sectioned?' she asked.

'I was not.'

'So after the initial observation time you would have been allowed out?'

He nodded uncertainly. 'Yes.'

'Where did you go?'

'The nearest pub, local library, the park.'

'London?'

'Sometimes.'

'Did you visit prostitutes on those occasions?'

'Not possible,' he said with a self-satisfied grin.

'Why not?'

'I was accompanied by a hairy male nurse and two other patients.'

'Right – that's it, Greenly,' announced Rydell. 'We've both been very patient, but my patience has run thin. Go and fetch Rusty perhaps, we'll get more sense out of him.'

Greenly didn't move.

'You heard,' said Rydell. 'Bring him down.'

Disbelieving, Greenly sat rigid as though tensing his body would help him resist the urge to obey.

'I'm waiting,' said Rydell, staring coldly. 'Rusty is a material witness. The police dog pound will keep him for a short period – seven days usually and then as he's old he'd probably be put down.'

'I think you're talking cobblers,' Greenly snapped. 'But then you're probably just enough of a bastard to do that.'

'Believe it,' said Rydell calmly. There was a slight pause during which Rydell continued to stare unblinking.

'OK. OK,' Greenly said eventually. 'You win. I'll tell you exactly what happened. I met Liam at the bottom of the bridle path. I let Rusty off the lead and when I heard his frantic barking we rushed to the barn. For some reason I thought it was the police.'

'Why would you think that?'

'We had some marijuana hidden there. It was a meeting place for us. Anyway, there was the body. We were in shock. Neither of us had ever seen a dead body before. She was like a statue, a beautiful one. Whoever had put her there had tried to start the fire but it had gone out.'

'And then what?'

'We stood there – it seemed a long time. There was no rush, we could see she was dead. Rusty was still excited trying to get nearer to her.'

'Are you sure it was just Rusty getting excited?'

Greenly looked down. 'My mother's dead now – it hardly matters. Liam is gay and in love with me. I've been married, but I can't say I was ever totally sure that I wasn't gay but I'd never had a chance to find out. Liam opened my eyes.'

'And your flies by the sound of it.'

'Crude but correct.'

'So you delayed phoning us?'

'We heard a noise – a van, I think, but I couldn't be sure because of the storm. By the time we left the barn the van or whatever had gone and the farmhouse was burning.'

'So *then* you deigned to ring us on your trusty mobile?'

'It still took ages for the fire brigade to arrive. It took the police even longer.'

'Oh dear, what a shame. I wonder how you passed the time?'

Greenly stayed silent staring at the floor.

'Come on, Sergeant,' said Rydell abruptly. 'Let's go before I say something I might regret.'

Denni stood up. 'I'd like to ask a question of Mr Greenly just before we go.' His eyes shifted to hers expectantly. 'Do you have a cellar?'

There was a slightly too lengthy pause for the answer to be 'no'.

'We can always search the house now,' she said. 'You're on bail so we don't need a court order.'

'I haven't got much choice, have I?'

'None at all,' said Denni. 'Lead on, Vernon. We'll be right behind you.'

Twenty-Eight

*H*e liked to keep abreast of the police investigation.
Abreast – a breast. He found himself laughing. It
was so good to feel this alive. So far they hadn't offered
a reward. That could well be their next step, and a major
search. Not that they would ever suspect him. He had no
criminal record. And if they did catch up with him it would
be too late.

Sara Bolten had served her purpose. The silly cow had
tried to send a coded message and thought he hadn't
guessed.

Now that she was no longer breast-feeding she was
getting his daily dose of the God Lithium. It was having
an effect. Making her into the zombie he once was. Now
she had stopped asking him to let her and the baby have
some fresh air. Silly bitch didn't realise there was no such
thing as fresh air. Everything was polluted. The earth, the
sea, the air – all polluted.

He couldn't leave his new angel where she was for much
longer. She'd be getting hungry and thirsty by now and he
had to get rid of the dog. Everything had to be synchronised.
Synchronised – that was an interesting word. He liked words.
Words that rolled round his tongue. He especially liked words
from the bible. 'I go to prepare a place for you. In my father's
house there are many mansions.' He laughed. He was sure of
one thing, the Elysium fields wouldn't be polluted.

The Lord is my shepherd. I shall not want. He maketh me
to lie down in green pastures. He restoreth my soul.

213

There you are then, Sara, you'll soon be there in those green pastures. Your soul restored. Along with Maria and his best beloved who'd gone before. Best beloved. First love. It had been real. It had changed him and now he was resurfacing like a phoenix. In his blind angel he had found her *again.* She *had been perfect. The one bright jewel of his life.* She *who still waited for him. Maria, Sara and Alexis would all be with him. But* she *would hold his child. Like a Madonna. Serene. Happy that he had found his way home.*

Twenty-Nine

D CI Fenton's voice carried to the back of the room and beyond. 'I expect every man . . . and woman to stop bickering about overtime payments and lack of staff and find the nutter.' He paused to see if his words quelled the rumble of discontent. There was a momentary lull before loud mutterings started again. The only time, thought Denni, he'd ever been PC was when he was one. Fenton didn't mince his words and the promotion ladder had been pulled away from him mainly because of his vocabulary. He was nobody's police showpiece but he had value in Denni's eyes – no aspiring cop wanted to be anything like him.

'We're pulling out the stops,' he continued, 'a full-scale search will begin today. DI Rydell and DS Caldecote will concentrate solely on Maria Seaton's murder in London. We all know our second missing girl – Alexis – is a friend of the sergeants and we don't want any hysteria to develop – do we?'

Denni, fists clenched, smiled at him and between her teeth muttered, 'You bastard.'

Fenton continued talking but actually said little and eventually pulled out sheets of paper with names of the search teams and their operational patches.

'And finally,' he said, 'there is now a reward offered by an anonymous donor. So if police work fails, as it has so far, maybe someone will get greedy.'

He thought he was being funny and there was a slight titter but his attitude made Denni despair. Fenton and his type made her sometimes feel as if she was in the wrong job. Deep down though she'd long ago realised that once past thirty a job was a bit like the old concept of marriage – you made your bed et cetera.

'Is he serious about us not investigating Alexis's disappearance?' she asked Rydell when Fenton left the room. Before he'd had time to answer a PC nudged his way through the crowd milling around the lists now pinned up. As a space developed she could see that the notice board now displayed a photograph of Alexis with Barney, alongside those of Maria Seaton in death and Sara Bolten with her baby. Denni had taken that particular photo and now to see it pinned up made her shiver, as if the photo on the station board made Alexis's disappearance a reality. She feared Sara was already dead and she tried not to dwell on Alexis's fate. It was just a question of time though, she was sure, before they found a body. The voice of the constable broke into her morbid thoughts.

'There's someone to see you, sir – downstairs – David Bolten. He's been waiting some time.'

When they found him in reception he was staring resignedly at his feet. 'Sorry to keep you waiting,' said Rydell.

'I've had a letter from Sara,' he said abruptly.

'Genuine?'

'Oh yes,' he said as he produced the plastic food bag containing the letter from his jacket pocket. 'It's her handwriting. But I'm sure it was written under duress. It's not her style.'

Rydell put out his hand, but Bolten seemed unwilling to let it go. 'Could we go somewhere else? I seem to have spent ages sitting here – thinking.'

'There's a cafe around the corner,' suggested Denni.

In the Healthy Choice Coffee Lounge, a place not frequented by male members of the force because the coffee was expensive and the bread and cakes used only wholewheat flour, Bolten showed them the letter. Denni, who always carried disposable gloves, handed a pair to Rydell and with the utmost care they opened and read the letter.

Bolten sipped at his coffee and watched their faces to judge their reaction. 'My wife's a bright woman: I've never called her "Mole". Harriet doesn't exist, she never calls her mother "Mummy" and my so-called cooking and nappy changing were not a feature of our married life.'

'We'll need other comparative samples of her hand-writing,' said Rydell.

'I've got some with me,' he said, producing a small bundle and handing them to Rydell.

Rydell slipped off his rubber gloves and looked steadily at Bolten. 'I'm sure she is bright but he's very cunning. He probably noticed what she was doing but he didn't care. It could well be a ploy to distract us from whatever else he's doing.'

'He's abducted that blind woman, hasn't he?'

'We're convinced she has been abducted,' agreed Rydell, 'and we assume it's the same man, so it may be bad news for your wife.'

'I see,' murmured Bolten. 'Do you have *any* suspects?'

It was Denni who answered then. 'No,' she said gently. 'But the evidence is mounting steadily. Every day means we get a little bit closer to him.'

'Will you be in time to save Sara?' he asked plaintively. Denni could only guess how he was feeling, but she recog-nised that feeling of powerlessness. Not being able to help her friend felt bad enough; losing a wife and the mother of your son must, she thought, be much worse. It was the not knowing, the only being able to imagine that gnawed away as sharp as teeth in the pit of her stomach.

Bolten stood up suddenly, his remaining coffee spilling into the saucer. 'You will let me know as soon—' he broke off, his voice cracking. Rydell stood up and shook his hand.

They sat for a few moments watching him walk away, shoulders hunched, the slight wind lifting the fine hair that remained at the sides of his head. He seemed shorter as if the letter, which should have raised his spirits, had defeated him.

Rydell stared uneasily at the coffee in the saucer and resisted the urge to mop it up. 'Poor sod,' he murmured. She wasn't sure if he meant Bolten or himself. Then standing up, he said, 'Come on, Denni, let's get to London.'

'Could we see Ram before we go?'

'You see him, I'll wait in the car.'

Denni bought humbugs and toffees at the hospital shop and was delighted to find Ram sitting by his bed reading the paper.

'You're looking chipper,' she said delightedly.

'The antibiotics have kicked in,' he said. 'So I'm saved from dialysis.' He pointed to the paper's headline: MAJOR SEARCH FOR MISSING WIFE.

'What's all this about?' he asked. 'Why pull out all the stops now?'

'Another woman has gone missing – believed abducted. Same MO, no signs of a struggle, no reason and no contact.'

'Who is she?'

'My blind friend – Alexis.'

Ram looked angry. 'The bastard needs to be stopped before –'

'I know,' she said. 'Rydell and I are off to London again – Fenton says we're to concentrate on Maria and not to get involved with trying to find Alexis. He thinks I'm too emotionally involved.'

Ram folded his paper and laid it on the bed. 'Do me a favour, Denni, wait outside the ward. I need to –' she didn't wait for him to finish. 'I'm on my way.'

She'd been standing outside the ward for about ten minutes when Ram appeared fully dressed.

'You can't leave just like that, Ram.'

'I bloody can. I've signed myself out. I'm going back to work.'

'You're not fit,' she protested.

'I never was. I'm not as young as I once was but I'll never be as young as I am now. Same goes for fitness.'

He took her arm and they left the ward and walked slowly out of the hospital. Denni felt she should have tried harder to persuade him to stay especially as he seemed unsteady on his feet. As the automatic doors opened an icy blast caused Ram to stagger slightly like a drunken man.

'They haven't discharged you already?' asked Rydell in surprise.

'It's a miracle,' said Ram straight-faced. 'The doc said I was fit for anything.' He glanced warningly at Denni.

Rydell looked with slight suspicion on them both, then sighed and said, 'We'll give you a lift home.'

In the front seat Ram sank back looking tired and jaded. 'Home?' he said. 'I haven't got one. My only home at the moment is Harrowford nick and I'm going back to work now.'

'I've been thinking about that,' said Denni. 'I know you hate the guesthouse and since the Manchester mob found you I think you'd be safer staying at my place. I've got a spare room.'

'Are you serious?' asked Ram. 'Do you realise I burn joss sticks every day and eat curry for breakfast?'

'Can you make a *good* curry?'

'Good? My curries are superb.'

'Did your mother teach you?'

He laughed. 'She has trouble with toast. I was taught to cook by a Mrs Blenkinsop. She didn't take holidays, she went to restaurants and when she had a superb meal she chatted up the chef and got the recipe. So now I can cook.'

'We're here,' announced Rydell outside Harrowford Police Station. 'Take it easy,' he advised Ram. Denni handed over her house keys. 'I don't expect we'll be back till the early hours so make yourself at home.'

Ram grinned. 'Thanks. See you.'

Rydell had driven several miles before he spoke. 'Do you think it's wise to put Ram up?'

'How do you mean?'

'You know damn well. Gossip.'

'It doesn't worry me and I don't think it would worry Ram.'

'It might harm your promotion prospects.'

'I don't see how. I'm not planning to seduce him. I'm more likely to be nursing him. And even if I was to ravish him twice nightly we're both the same rank so it's not exactly unknown.'

'You'll get some racist comments. It's jealousy, of course, but knowing that won't help.'

'I'm doing a pal a favour, that's all. Can we drop the subject now, Guv?'

In Palmer's Green it was raining, but it seemed to Denni a warmer rain than fell in Harrowford. Sabine opened the door in full dominatrix gear, all shiny tight leather accessorised with silver spikes on her neckband and on the leather around her wrists. Her boots were thigh high with platforms and spurs. Rydell was, for a moment, mesmerised.

'Do you come bearing news?' she asked.

He shook his head. 'We've come seeking more information.'

Her heavily mascaraed lashes flicked towards Denni. 'Hello, sweetie,' she said with well-practised huskiness. 'We'd better get comfortable. Follow me.' They followed her as she led the way tossing her head back slightly and making her dark hair bounce as impressively as in a hairspray ad.

Rydell refused to sit, remembering his discomfort the last time, and Sabine chose to perch on a table ensuring her boots looked particularly impressive. 'I've told you everything that might help,' she said. 'Don't you think that if I had a name I would have given you it – especially if I thought he was a client?'

Denni sat on the floor cushions. 'The killer was someone she trusted,' she said. 'Someone she met, perhaps outside the house. Someone you didn't know.'

'She would have told me if there was anyone,' Sabine snapped. 'We didn't have secrets. Men to her were only a combination of cash and sperm dispensers.'

Denni ignored that. 'He may have stolen some rope from here. The type he used to tie up Maria was typical of the type used in bondage.'

'Typical maybe, but not exclusively for bondage use.'

'Let's just say it matched the rope we found here. Which means she must have let him in.'

Sabine crossed her long legs in a defiant gesture that matched the look on her face. As she did so, the leather squeaked slightly. 'It's the name of the game – letting strange men in.'

'But you did say she was careful and I'm sure she was astute and experienced enough to spot a real weirdo.'

'Sergeant,' she said smiling. 'For a cop you're a nice chick. But you're not making your point clear. She obviously didn't realise he was weirdo or she wouldn't have let him in.'

'Perhaps that is the point I'm trying to make,' conceded Denni. 'He could have been a casual acquaintance. Maria couldn't have been "working" all the time. Where did she go when she went out – pubs, clubs?'

Sabine shook her head. 'We went out together occasionally. Nice restaurants. She went shopping about three times a week. She was always buying.'

'Clothes?'

'We buy our work gear mail order and she rarely bought fashion items although she loved kaftans and ethnic clothes.

It suited her artistic temperament I suppose.'

'I didn't know she was artistic.'

'Didn't I say? A bit of a sore point really with me. She couldn't paint an egg box, but she thought she had real talent. Her stuff was a bit – modern for me. Erotic she called it, but I'm afraid I couldn't see it. It gave her pleasure though. She loved the art shop in the High Street. She was always buying stuff from there.'

'So the owner would remember her?'

'Oh, yes. I think she always had a chat with him. Adrian Woods. The shop's called World of Art.'

Rydell's trance-like state ended swiftly. 'Thanks for your help, Sabine, we'll be in touch.'

Outside it was dark and drizzling. 'That was a bit abrupt,' said Denni.

'It's four thirty. World of Art might close at five.'

The shop was easy enough to find and it was the only one that wasn't festooned with Christmas glitter. There were two customers inside browsing amongst the easels and boxes of paints. The quiet atmosphere reminded Denni of a library although Adrian didn't look much like a librarian. He wore a lilac shirt and lilac jeans teamed with a maroon embroidered waistcoat. The ensemble was completed by dark-rooted blond hair worn in a ponytail and one large earring. He was well into his second adolescence – fiftyish – lost somewhere in the sixties or seventies with enough lines on his face to prove it.

When the two dithering customers had been reduced by one Rydell introduced himself.

'Police?' repeated Adrian with as much surprise as if they had suggested they were from the Star Ship Enterprise.

'We're enquiring about a customer of yours – Miss Seaton.'

He couldn't resist glancing past Rydell's shoulder as his

only customer walked out without buying. 'Doesn't ring any bells.'

'Maria?'

He smiled. 'Maria. I haven't seen her for ages.' His face clouded. 'What's wrong?'

'She's dead,' said Rydell bluntly. 'Murdered.'

'Good God! I am sorry—' he broke off as if suddenly wondering why he should be visited.

'I'm surprised you didn't know. Local prostitute goes missing and is then found murdered – very newsworthy.'

He seemed relieved. 'Wrong Maria. The Maria I knew was an art student.'

'Don't you read the papers, Mr Woods?'

'No. Is there a law that says I should?'

'Or watch TV?'

'I don't have a television set.'

'Radio?'

'I paint in my spare time. I enjoy photography too. The media dulls our artistic side. An artist sees the world differently.'

'Well, Maria isn't seeing the world at all,' said Rydell tersely. 'So perhaps you'd answer a few questions for us.'

'Of course, of course. I just can't believe that she was – on the game.' Woods seemed genuinely surprised and Rydell had always found shock was the hardest reaction to fake, whereas grief was one of the easiest. 'If I can be of any help,' continued Woods, 'although I don't see how.'

'How often did she shop here?'

'She used to come in about once a week. She didn't always buy anything but we'd have a chat.'

'What about?'

'Art of course. Art materials. Nothing really personal.'

'Do you work here alone?'

'Yes. It never gets that busy.'

'Did she ever come in with anyone or talk to any of your other customers?'

He thought for a moment. 'There was one chap she talked to. To be honest I think he had the hots for her. He told me he was longing to paint her. She was a very striking woman.'

'Did she seem to like him?'

'Oh, yes. She told me she was thinking about the portrait as a surprise present for a friend of hers, but he was quite expensive.'

'A professional then?'

Woods shrugged his narrow shoulders. 'I assumed so. He knew his paints and brushes. He only ever had the best.'

'Name?' asked Denni, trying to keep the excitement from her voice.

Silence.

'There's the rub. I can't remember. Names are not my forte.'

'Can you remember what he looks like?'

'Of course I can. I could draw him if you want.'

Denni looked at Rydell in a mixture of suppressed excitement and triumph. This was the breakthrough they'd been waiting for.

'Wonderful. We'd be very grateful.'

'He had very striking eyes,' he said thoughtfully. 'Rather pretty in fact. A deep cobalt blue with the blackest of lashes.'

'Was he local?'

Woods shook his head. 'He said he lived in the country. He came in about once a fortnight on a Wednesday.'

'When did he last come in?'

Realisation suddenly dawned. 'I've been slow. He hasn't been in since Maria stopped coming. He's the one, isn't he?'

'He could be,' agreed Denni. 'Your drawing of him could save lives. He's abducted two other women.'

'Give me an hour. I'll give it my best shot.'

224

In the middle of Palmer's Green High Street Denni punched the air excitedly.

'Calm down,' said Rydell. 'He may have a face but we still don't have a name.'

Thirty

The cold was even more intense now. Her feet had been numb but now each toe burned and throbbed. Sleep was impossible. She sat for a while then stood and marched on the spot, she walked up and down, she rocked backwards and forwards, and she lifted pretend weights. Exercise is good for you, she told herself, and it wasn't only her muscles that benefited: it *did* help to relieve anxiety. Continuous brisk exercise dulled her brain as effectively as alcohol. It was impossible to think constructively while she moved, or to worry. In moments of stillness the fear returned.

If he planned to rape and kill her, why wait? Denni would know she was missing by now. The police would be looking for her. Why the hell hadn't she logged his call? The initial might have helped. Was H for Hell or Harry or Henry? Should she try to make him see she was a person not just a victim or should she remain aloof? Was fear his turn-on? If so, would she give him the satisfaction? If he couldn't succeed in making her afraid, would he feel less powerful or would he strive harder to instil fear? This is your own stupid fault, Alexis, she told herself. Her blindness had led her to believe she could 'read' people better than a sighted person. A form of arrogance that she was paying dearly for.

She thought back to H's first call more than a year ago. He hadn't known she was blind at first. It was only when he came to the office – the office – someone must have seen him. He'd come two or three times. Each time she'd been with Mark. Mark who was now backpacking somewhere in the Antipodes.

She began walking on the spot slowly trying to remember conversations she'd had with H. That first call more than a year before he'd been silent for a long time, eventually when he'd begun to speak it was in a dull monotone. Someone he loved had died, he didn't say who but his sadness and depression had seemed a perfectly normal reaction to being bereaved. During one of his office visits he had talked about his first love: how beautiful she was, how her long dark hair tumbled to her shoulders, how she was kind and gentle, how much they loved each other. Strange, now that she looked back, the words he'd used like, 'my angel', 'my baby', 'my first love', belonged not to middle-aged man in the present but a grown man remembering in soft focus an adolescent love. He'd said he couldn't 'save her'. When she'd asked him to explain he'd clammed up, changed the subject saying that he shouldn't have been there anyway and there was nothing to be gained by discussing it.

The sound of a cock crowing she found reassuring. Dawn was near. The silence of the night had caused her to fear she'd lost her hearing. The sound of her own voice and now that of the noisy cockerel meant not only was she not deaf but somewhere beyond this place life was going on normally. Perhaps he would decide to release her. Maybe she could persuade him. If he came back . . . at all . . . she would have a chance.

Silence fell again. Her throat was so dry the little saliva she had was hard to swallow. Hunger wasn't a problem. She wanted to pee now, but she would try to hang on.

When he swung open the garage doors there might be a second when he was off guard, when his arms were raised. Could she manage to prolong that moment?

Time passed. She *had to* pee, she couldn't wait. She used the plastic bucket and thought about throwing it over him but unless he was speaking at the time she couldn't be sure of her aim. If she got out he'd be right behind her and running blind wasn't something she'd ever tried. Hanging back away from the door might be an option. He would have to come and get her and she knew the garage layout now. She even contemplated using Barney's body as a weapon: coming out of her prison like a mad woman swinging the corpse wildly, hoping he would be taken by surprise.

When he did make his move it was she who was taken by surprise. There was the noise of a key clicking, then the metallic clang as he raised the door. Then nothing. Just cold air and silence. She stood in an agony of indecision. She strained to hear him breathing but couldn't, yet she knew he was there. Waiting like a scorpion for the strike.

'Why are you doing this?' she asked, trying not to screech hysterically.

'This place is only temporary.' He chuckled. 'I'm going to prepare a place for you.'

He was standing close to her. So close, she could smell his cleanliness. He smelt of aftershave and mouthwash. His being so clean felt like an added insult. She was cold, thirsty and she felt filthy.

He touched her arm. 'Don't be afraid,' he murmured. 'I've brought you a flask of tea and some hot toast.' He took her hands and placed the flask in one and a package in the other. 'I'm putting some blankets on the mattress.' He paused. 'What do you say?'

For a second or two she didn't understand. 'Thank you.' Her voice seemed a pathetic whisper.

'Good girl. I'm going out, but I'll be back in a few hours and then I'll introduce you to your new home.' She sensed him stepping aside but he was quick and by the time she realised he was picking up Barney's body, the door was clanging shut. Then came the click of the key. She waited for the sound of his footsteps but she could hear nothing. Moments later she heard a van drive away. The engine noise totally different to the soft purr of the BMW.

So much for putting up a fight, but at least starving her to death wasn't on his insane agenda. But what the hell was?

She wrapped herself in the blankets, drank the hot sweet tea and ate the buttery toast and thought it was probably, even in the circumstances, the best meal she had ever eaten. Then she lay down on the mattress and fell asleep, a sleep punctuated with dreams of knives and rape and murder.

A hand on her shoulder woke her and he said excitedly, 'Come on, come on, my darling. Dog's dead, dog's buried. Rest in peace. Forget it. You're with me now.' He was pulling her to her feet, pushing her forward. She felt giddy and sick, so giddy and sick that she wondered if her tea had been poisoned.

Soon she was in a house, though the sudden warmth and household smells were not reassuring. He was rushing her upstairs, still excited, manic, calling her darling. At the top of the stairs he opened a door. She knew immediately it was the bathroom. It smelt of damp towels and bubble bath. 'I've run the bath for you, darling,' he said as he helped take off her coat. 'Nice and hot and I'm going to play the gent and wait outside for you.'

He continued to try to undress her. 'I can manage, thank you,' she said, amazed at how she could sound so normal. He stopped touching her.

'You needn't be afraid of me,' he said. 'You see, I'm special and we're going to be together till the end of time. So you should be happy. You need me, you really need me.'

It took her several seconds to manage a murmured, 'Yes, H.'

Like the meal, the bath, in these worst of circumstances, was the best she'd ever had. She'd heard the door click shut and for several moments the sensual delight of the hot water on her cold feet kept out the fear to some degree. She felt around for the soap and then soaped her body slowly. She wasn't going to rush unless he made her. She was trying to locate the soap dish when her hand found a small object.

Plastic with rounded contours. She recognised it at once – a razor – a woman's razor. The realisation that another woman had been in this bath most probably in the same situation was nearly as great a shock as finding Barney's body. That the woman was Sara Bolten seemed most likely. Any man who was capable of killing an amiable dog could kill a woman, of that fact Alexis had no doubt.

She jumped up from the bath and with arms outstretched managed to find the lavatory. Kneeling on the floor she clutched her stomach while bile and saliva filled her mouth. Once she'd finished vomiting, she felt exhausted but it had relieved the pain in her stomach.

He came in then, dried her wet body and slipped her into a towelling robe, all the time murmuring endearments. She didn't attempt to help herself or struggle. She sensed helpless passivity would keep him calm, but how long could she keep it up? How long before she became panicky and hysterical?

'This is our beginning, my angel. Our own glorious time.'

Thirty-One

Rydell and Denni passed the hour's wait in a cafe. Shoppers struggled in gloved and scarved with harassed expressions and weighed down with Christmas presents and bulging plastic bags of food.

'I haven't given Christmas a thought yet,' said Denni, as she felt the first twinges of pre-Christmas panic.

'I rarely do,' said Rydell. 'Last year I worked. I didn't have to, I just didn't have anywhere else to go.'

'And this year?'

'No change. But if we haven't found him, I won't be in the mood for sitting around eating and drinking.'

'Don't you have any family?'

'One sister. She does invite me for Christmas dinner but her husband's pontifications on life depress me and their house is a tip—' he broke off realising he might say too much about his obsession.

'It's only a week away,' murmured Denni, 'and then it's the new millennium. I suppose I should have made plans for that too, but I haven't yet.'

Rydell stared at her. 'That's *it*! That's what he's waiting for. His own personal Armageddon. He took Sara, then Alexis. He's planning his own end-of-the-world scenario.'

'What about Maria?'

'Maybe she got difficult, tried to escape – who knows?'

'It's only guesswork though, isn't it?'

Rydell smiled. 'A hunch by any other name.'

'If it's hunches you're after,' said Denni, 'I've got a

231

couple. First, our murderer, like Woods, didn't realise Maria was a prostitute. When he found out, she had to die. Second, I think Stephanie's rapist is the same man who raped Maria here in London. It would have given him a real buzz not to be recognised by her. Even more of a buzz when he found out she was pregnant and thought he was responsible.'

Rydell didn't look that convinced. 'Woods thought he had a slight Scots accent but Stephanie didn't seem to notice that, did she?'

'No,' agreed Denni. 'But she's very young and for God's sake, she was being raped at the time.'

Rydell looked at his watch. The cafe was emptying now, tables being cleared, the last shoppers wearily making their way home. 'Come on, Denni, let's go and look at the face of our murderer.'

Adrian Woods was waiting for them in his empty shop. 'I haven't quite captured him somehow,' he said dejectedly.

'Neither have we,' said Rydell. 'Like us, you can only do your best.'

Woods handed the charcoal drawing to Rydell, who stared at it for a few seconds before handing it over to Denni. It was an average sort of face – unremarkable – except for the eyelashes. Rydell seemed to be having trouble responding.

Eventually Denni asked, 'What height would you say this man was?'

Woods didn't hesitate. 'About five ten like me.'

'Build?'

'Quite muscular.'

'Is there anything else about him you noticed?'

Woods thought for a moment. 'He didn't have an artist's hands, if you know what I mean.'

'Would you explain that?' said Rydell.

'They were squarish – peasant's hands.'

'How old did you say he was?'

'I didn't – early forties I would think. Little flecks of grey in his hair. There's something else you didn't ask.'

Rydell noticed the implied criticism. 'What was that?'

'You didn't ask what he bought.'

'I'm asking now.'

'He bought oil paints but mostly it was watercolours and our best sable brushes. And once he bought some very expensive vellum notepaper.'

'Could you show us?'

Woods searched the shelves and returned with a sample sheet and envelope.

Rydell held the notepaper and fingered it thoughtfully. 'I'd like to take this with us.'

Woods nodded. 'I hope I've been of help.'

Denni shook his hand warmly. 'You've been a great help. There is just one more question – did he ever buy any turps?'

'I'm apt to remember only the big purchases but, yes, I'm fairly sure he did. Not everyone sells turps these days, white spirit is more common. Household paint is often water based, you see.'

'So he did buy turps?'

Adrian Woods nodded firmly. 'Yes.'

Ram planned to avoid DCI Fenton but he'd just turned into the main corridor when Fenton left his office and they collided. 'What the fuck are the NHS playing at letting you out so soon? You can't even walk straight.'

Ram righted himself, shrugged nonchalantly and stayed silent, not wanting a bollocking for discharging himself. 'Oh, well,' said Fenton. 'Take it easy. Read a few reports, catch up with what's going on. There's a major search under way and sod all progress so far.'

At his desk in a now staff-free zone, Ram logged on to his computer and then began sifting through written reports. One was of interest, a report on an informal interview with Vernon Greenly which mentioned his being a patient at Four Fields Psychiatric Hospital. In his search for possible arsonists he'd contacted that particular hospital. Arsonists, he'd found made very unpopular patients, not surprisingly, and many were sent either to prison or to Broadmoor. Which of course provided a pretty watertight alibi.

Ram sucked a humbug slowly and thoughtfully. He knew he was only going over old ground. The murderer must have found out about the barn from somewhere or from someone. Unless of course he lived so close to it he couldn't fail to have known of its existence. Somewhere along the line he knew there was a connection. Either another barn or another place.

At four p.m. it was dark, and he sat in the canteen and watched the search party drifting back. He didn't need to ask if they'd had a result. They queued in silent dejection for tea and sandwiches and one or two drifted over to him to share tales of brass-monkey cold and wasted time.

By six, Ram had a headache and he knew his concentration was poor. He drove to the guesthouse threw his belongings into a selection of bags, paid his bill and left. He'd never been to Denni's place and somehow he didn't expect it to be so feminine or so tidy. It was all soft muted colours, lamps and candles and lacy cushions. He'd taken his bags upstairs to the spare room and had opened the hall cupboard to hang up his coat. He stood back in amazement. The cupboard was crammed with books, hundreds of them, mostly novels. He'd only read novels at school when he was forced to. He shook his head thoughtfully and closed the cupboard door. He would have to say something to her. He realised he didn't know Denni at all, she had always seemed so sensible. Did she need a life or what!

Seeing her house lights on it took Denni a few seconds to recall that she had a new lodger. Ram lay sprawled asleep on the sofa fully dressed, shoes and coat beside him and sweet wrappings on her coffee table. She filled a kettle to make tea hoping that would wake him, but he didn't stir. She felt disappointed he hadn't woken up yet. She'd slept in the car and now she was wide awake and wanting to talk. Even after she'd had a bath he still showed no sign of waking, and in the end she decided to leave him covered with a blanket. The talk would have to wait.

She lay restless in the dark and turned over and over in bed like a chicken on a spit. Thoughts of Christmas only led to memories of last Christmas which she'd spent with Alexis. Denni had helped with cooking and they'd invited various waifs and strays, and Alexis had said that it was her best Christmas ever – sighted or blind.

This year the festivities might have to be deferred. She told herself a one-stop shop at Marks and Spencer's on Christmas Eve would be more than enough for what would probably be a working holiday. And a miserable one.

She still wasn't asleep at two when the phone rang. It was Rydell. 'It's not good news.'

Denni sat on the edge of the bed and braced herself.

'We've had a report of a woman's naked body tied to a tree about ten miles out of Harrowford. An anonymous caller, either drunk or shocked, phoned from a mobile. I'll pick you up in ten minutes.'

Denni pushed the horrifying thought away that it might be Alexis. She quickly dressed in boots, jeans and two jumpers, and was about to slip on her jacket when Ram woke.

'What's going on?' he asked, his voice still slurred with sleep. When she explained, he roused himself and sat rubbing his face and began fumbling in his pocket for a stray humbug or two.

'You're an addict,' said Denni.

'So are you.'

'What do you mean?' she asked suspiciously.

'I wasn't prying, just attempting to hang my coat up in your cupboard upstairs.'

'I like reading,' she said.

'There's no need to blush, Denni.'

'Sod you, Ram, I'm not blushing. If you tell anyone, anyone at all I'll –'

'Take away my humbugs.' He smiled and put an arm around her. 'I'll guard your guilty secret with my life. And that's a Hindu promise.' Then he added, 'You should be out socialising, Denni, not tucked up in bed with a book.'

'I know. My trouble is I'm looking for a hero.'

Ram wagged a finger. 'You won't find one between the pages of a book.'

'I do know that. But with my men I can't get hurt, pregnant, HIV or disillusioned with smelly socks and snoring.'

'I'll have to counsel you some time,' said Ram with a grin. 'You could become a very sad person.'

They heard the car draw up, grabbed their coats and hurried to Rydell's car. Apart from Rydell's brief rhetorical, 'You two OK?' they remained silent in the car. After a few miles it began to rain and the silence grew miserable and oppressive. Eventually Rydell said, 'It's along here.' He continued to drive along the unlit narrow lane spiky with overhanging bushes and bumpy with rain-filled potholes. Occasionally the lane widened a little to allow space for cars to pass, and then abruptly they could drive no further. The road had been closed off by yellow and black ribbon and a uniformed constable stood guard.

'The doc's on his way, sir,' the constable informed Rydell.

'SOCOs arrived yet?'

The young, wet constable shook his head.

'Get out of the rain,' said Rydell. 'It's not exactly Marble Arch, only police personnel are fool enough to be out here at this time of night.'

'And the bloke that found her, sir.'

'Where is he?'

'Sitting in the first car – he lives a bit further down the lane.'

'I'll see him when I've seen the body.'

Denni and Ram followed Rydell in single file beside the

parked police car. About thirty yards from the road three uniformed officers were struggling with plastic sheeting and portable lights. At first glance the body looked like a shop-window mannequin, her white skin stark against the dark tree. There was the same purple rope forming a noose around the neck and she was naked. Her legs were partially burnt. The faggots of newspaper surrounding her in a circle had been lit but were now black and crushed. Her head was down, wet hair clung round her face and the rain hitting her face seemed to mock her death. The rain was active and seemed alive, but Sara Bolten was no more.

He sat watching the proceedings. He felt excited, elated, but to them he had to be the poor shocked businessman, the good landlord returning home late from renovating one of his properties. He'd noticed the woman detective looking at him closely but he was ordinary-looking. He was only special on the inside.

He'd lit the fire and watched the flames for a while and then it had begun to rain so he'd stamped on the faggots and then just stood there, watching her. Dead women were so beautiful, so quiet. Fucking her after death had been an experience he'd never forget. He supposed he would have described it as a challenge. Life meets death. Fucking a corpse was the second time he'd had a near-death experience. He wanted to laugh, but he had to maintain a solid exterior. In just over a week he would be dead too. They would catch him eventually but it would be too late. Death beckoned him and Alexis. Death beckoned everyone but he wanted to go out in style. His fire angels would be by his side, his baby angel in his arms. Strong and invincible, ready for the glorious afterlife.

The initial interview while he had been sitting in his car had been brief: name, address, occupation. He told them he owned property and they'd been impressed. The fat Asian detective was definitely interested in renting from him. Ironic he thought that they didn't suspect him at all. Of course he was too clever for them. He knew about body language and not blinking too much or touching your nose. Psychiatrists were helpful people. They sussed when you were not quite telling the truth so you learned to be more careful the next time. A little hesitation was OK. It was natural to forget things.

The inspector said he would be in touch. They always said that. No originality. He supposed they would go back to the station and check him out on criminal records. Check that he was who he said he was. Check his car registration. But they'd find nothing. The police, not being very bright and being prejudiced, would expect their main man to be stupid. An unthinking maniac. Rough and ready. Twitching with staring eyes. But when the time came he would go down in history not only as intelligent but also as compassionate. He was leaving his money and properties to good causes. He hadn't quite decided which ones, but he thought it would be a nice touch if he left some to the fire service.

He offered to appear at the police station in the morning if they wanted a formal statement and they seemed grateful for his help. Of course he had been more than helpful. He'd told them about the two men he'd seen driving off in a white van. The number plate had been muddy and at first he hadn't been suspicious. He thought they had just stopped for a pee. It was only then that he'd caught sight of the body. One was a tall black man, the other was shorter, white, middle-aged and wearing glasses. Would he be able to identify them again? Of course, Inspector. I'm sure I could pick them out in a line-up or from mug shots. I got a good view of them in my headlights.

The laughter threatened to spill out. Every poor black man from Harrowford to Birmingham would be stopped on suss. That alone could keep them busy for a week. He was home and dry. His reunion was at hand. A place had been prepared for him and soon they would be together. His *own harem. His world, his universe. All his to command. Never again to be weak and helpless. In the next world his strength would be undeniable, unchallenged. He would never fail again.*

Thirty-Two

R ydell had suggested they returned home to sleep for a few hours. He hadn't slept properly in days. He hadn't been running recently, which didn't help, but mostly his inability to sleep was because he felt consumed with the case, and feeling that way he feared that one day when he was running he would just keep on going.

When his head had hit the pillow he'd slept as though bludgeoned, but it had only lasted for less than three hours. When he woke, he lay flat on his back with his eyes closed to prevent him worrying yet again about the crack in the ceiling.

The witness Hamish Harland's account of two men had thrown him. Two men were of course a possibility, but he wasn't convinced, and Harland himself fitted the description Woods had supplied. He had cobalt blue eyes and noticeable eyelashes. It could be mere coincidence, or, of course, he could be merely an art shop customer and nothing more. On the other hand . . .

In the kitchen Rydell made coffee and tried not to see any dust or fingermarks real or imaginary, but eventually he succumbed to disinfecting the kitchen surfaces. There's no bloody law against it, he told himself as he worked, but he still felt as guilty as a man trying to hide a porn habit. He knew he was obsessional but the rituals calmed him. He'd always had the tendency, but divorce, like age, had made him more so. He found it embarrassing, especially as more women than men were obsessed with cleaning and

240

the abolition of germs. He knew some of the force looked at him sideways, puzzled. There was no woman in his life and they had never seen him womanising or mentioning bums or boobs. He suspected they thought he was gay and that irritated him. He just wasn't ready for a relationship yet. Meeting Alexis had sparked something in him – he wasn't sure what, but he couldn't let it get in the way of finding her, dead or alive.

Sara's post-mortem was due to begin early afternoon and he would have to pay David Bolten another visit. This time there was no doubt, the formal identification would be mere rubber stamping for the CID, but for her family and her son it was part of a long and protracted tragedy – which again he couldn't afford to dwell on.

At nine he rang Denni's home but there was no answer. He left a message saying he wanted her and Ram to visit Four Fields Hospital again and not to return without more information.

Then he rang Hamish Harland and asked him to come to Harrowford station to make an informal statement.

Harland turned up promptly wearing jeans and an Aran sweater. 'I'm on my way to sort out a tenant, Inspector. But I'm more than happy to be of help.'

Rydell took him to an interview room, left the door open and told him to wait. Harland irritated him; perhaps it was his air of supreme confidence or his cocky cheerfulness. Either way he wanted him to be a little less in control. Being Sunday the place was practically deserted and Rydell hoped to find a constable free to sit in with him. He had almost given up hope when Denni rounded the corner.

'Didn't you get my message?'

She looked mystified. 'We came in early.'

'I've got the witness Harland in to give us a statement. Come and join us.'

Harland, still relaxed, smiled at Denni. She leant over and put a notepad and pen in front of him. 'Can we

offer you anything, Mr Harland – tea, coffee, a cigarette?'

He shook his head. 'All bad habits,' he said with another
smile.

'Tell me again why you were in the area at that time of
the morning,' said Rydell.

There was a momentary pause. 'I was on my way home.
I'd been to a tenant's earlier in the evening. Only a blocked
drain and a dripping tap, but they make such a fuss. They
rang me about ten o'clock. I finished there about eleven
thirty and then I went to one of my empty properties and
did some decorating. I was in town and I live alone and one
of your colleagues wants to move in soon, so it seemed a
good time.'

'Are you a plumber?' asked Rydell.

Harland shook his head. 'No. I'm just a good all-rounder.
I can do most things.'

I bet you can, you bastard, thought Rydell as he nodded
at Denni to take over.

'I'm surprised you're not married, Mr Harland,' she said,
'you being so handy with a spanner and a plunger.'

He didn't pause, he just grinned before saying, 'I like
women. I was in love once but destiny wasn't on our
side.'

'You believe in destiny?'

'Of course. I think it rules our lives.'

'In what way?'

'I believe a divine being ultimately guides us all.'

'To where?'

'A better place.' He smiled at her slyly and Denni knew
in that moment that this was the one. She sensed rather
than *knew* he was insane. She guessed he had spoken to
psychiatrists before. He was used to answering questions
and didn't need to know if they were relevant. He gave
answers *he* thought were appropriate. Truth didn't matter.

'Where were you born, Mr Harland?'

'I was born in Scotland but we moved to England when I was fourteen.'

'We?' she queried.

'My mother and I.'

'Where did you live?'

'London for a while, then Manchester.'

'Why did you move here?'

'My mother moved abroad, leaving me a house and some money. Housing was cheap here and so I decided to stay.'

'When was that?'

'More than twenty years ago.'

'Have you ever been to Artist's World in Palmers Green?'

He showed no surprise at the change of tack. 'Several times. I buy my brushes there.'

'Did you know Maria Seaton?'

'There was a customer there I spoke to called Maria.'

'Why didn't you come forward when she was found dead?'

'I didn't know it was her. The Maria I knew was an art student.'

'What about Sara Bolten?'

'I'd met her twice.'

'In what connection?'

'I did a portrait of her son.'

'Alexis Openshaw. Do you know her too?'

He nodded calmly, unconcerned. 'I did a portrait of her dog. A brave lady. I was very sorry to hear she was missing.' Before Denni could ask another question he added, 'A constable did come asking questions and he was satisfied with my answers.'

'Oh, good,' said Denni with a forced smile and a glance in Rydell's direction.

On cue, Rydell asked, 'Do you have a cellar?'

'Two of my houses have cellars.'

'Would you mind if we check them out?'

Harland shook his head. 'Not at all. Are you interested

in attics? I have an attic in my own house and two attics in my properties. All converted by yours truly.'

'Your talents know no bounds, Mr Harland.'

'I'm a pretty good cook too.'

'Of course you are,' said Rydell. 'Tell me about last night once again.'

His repeated account didn't deviate from the previous one. 'Write it down now,' said Rydell. 'Just as you've told us.'

Harland had a scrawly handwriting style difficult to read, but this time he mentioned the darkness of the sky and the low clouds. Odd but not incriminating.

'Could you hang on here with the Sergeant, Mr Harland? I need to speak to my senior officer.'

Harland nodded and grinned again at Denni.

Finding a more senior officer was impossible on Sunday so Rydell rang Fenton at home.

'Has he got a record?' asked Fenton.

'No, nothing on CRO.'

'What evidence have you got?'

'Nothing at the moment. But he's very odd.'

'For God's sake, man,' boomed Fenton. 'If we arrested every odd bugger who came our way there would be more out than in. Let him go, see if you can get a dekko at his home.'

'What about surveillance?'

'What about it?'

'Can we put him under surveillance?'

'For being an oddball?'

'No. For being the person we suspect of two murders and abduction.'

'If he's the one there must be evidence – find it. We don't have the manpower for people to sit on their arses in cars.'

Rydell gritted his teeth. Fenton always had the last word. This time his last words were a bit more hopeful. 'Look, Rydell, if you're convinced he is our man then use whatever means you want to get the evidence. As long as you don't do a plastic bag over the head job, I don't want to know. I haven't said this so if your oddball gets your balls squashed don't blame me.' He gave a raucous laugh down the phone just before replacing the receiver.

Rydell slipped back into the interview room as Denni was asking Harland about Scotland. 'Aye, I can slip back into the accent,' he was saying, 'but I came from near Edinburgh, where they roll their "r"s and sound posher than Glaswegians.'

'I've heard there's some good fishing up there.'

He nodded. 'The best. I go back occasionally just for the fishing.'

Denni flashed Rydell a knowing glance.

'You can go now, Mr Harland,' said Rydell briskly, 'but I would like the addresses of your properties before you go. And your permission to have a look at them.'

'No problem, Inspector, I've got nothing to hide.' He proffered a hand to Rydell who pretended not to notice.

When he'd gone they went back to their office and Rydell stared out of the window and watched Harland drive away in his silver BMW. 'He's such a confident bastard or a bloody good actor, perhaps he isn't the one.'

'He could be a manic depressive,' said Denni.

'If that's depressed I want some.'

'He's not depressed now, but he seemed manic to me although he was controlling it well.'

'So explain it to me.'

Denni began tidying her desk. 'The depressive part of the illness can lead to suicide, and during a manic phase the sufferer will be excited, possibly with delusions of grandeur.'

'What's the treatment?'

'Lithium works well.'

'We could contact his doctor.'

'He or she might not be willing to give us any information if we haven't got any real evidence.'

'I'm sure on the doctor front you'd be able to find out.'

Denni wasn't so sure and until Monday morning wouldn't be able to try. 'I did notice something about him, Guv.'

'What?'

'He smelt of baby powder.'

'Oh, God,' murmured Rydell.

Ram walked in then looking pleased with a big grin on his face. 'We're all ears,' said Rydell.

'I rang Four Fields. They have a few private wards. Checked out a few names and two came up. Guess who?'

'Vernon Greenly and Hamish Harland,' suggested Denni.

Ram smiled. 'Yes, but Hamish wasn't a patient. He worked there as a casual art therapist. So casual they found out his qualifications were false. They sacked him but not before he'd given several art classes and one of the pupils was –'

'Vernon Greenly,' supplied Denni.

'Correct. Go to the top of the class.'

Rydell muttered something about Greenly's empty cellar and all roads leading back to him and then said wearily, 'So it means yet another visit to our friend Greenly.'

He was singing as he drove home. He had a good voice – she *always said so. No one else had noticed. His mother certainly hadn't but she was always too busy pandering to the men in her life. He was her son and he* should have been the man in *her life. Instead he was always 'he' or 'him'. 'He'll do it,' they used to say or, 'Leave him be,' or, 'You spoil him.' Occasionally he was given a name – 'little bastard' or 'lying bastard'. He'd been a little sod but he'd found satisfaction in a bit of vandalism or the setting of fires. He liked worrying his mother, it meant she took notice of him. Then* she *had come into his life. Samantha. Living next door. Two years older than him, but she looked younger. She'd been beautiful on the outside and the inside. And that year he'd been happy. They walked home from school together, did their homework together in her front room. His mother always called him Hamish and welcomed him into their home. Even her father was pleasant to him. That year he'd worked well at school and stopped roaming the streets at night. And then . . . Don't think about that, he told himself. One more week and they would be together again. The police were suspicious. Could he hold out for another week? He could if he disappeared or he might have to make a sacrifice. He laughed out loud. Why the hell would he need a BMW in the next life? In the Elysian Fields he wouldn't need a fucking car.*

Thirty-Three

'It's the frigging pigs,' shouted Liam having heard the car and peeked through the curtains.

'I can hear you. There's no need to shout, I'm only in the kitchen.' Vernon took off his orange with green herbs plastic apron and hung it on the back of the kitchen door. He looked at his watch, he was roasting lamb and he didn't want to overcook it.

Rydell and his busty sidekick didn't seem surprised to see Liam. The sergeant took an interest in the half-decorated Christmas tree in the corner of the room, lights still dangling but with a silver fairy placed on top. 'It'll look really nice when it's finished,' she said.

Liam smiled, pleased. 'Yeah. I'm quite looking forward to Christmas this year, Vernon says—'

'The sergeant doesn't want to hear about that,' interrupted Greenly. 'What can I do for you officers?'

'Tell us about your time at Four Fields Hospital,' said Rydell as he perched on the arm of a brand-new sofa.

Greenly shrugged and looked surprised. 'What is there to tell? I was in for six weeks as a private patient. My mother paid, she was a snob, she thought private psychiatric treatment had more status than mere NHS.'

'Did you have any therapy?'

'What's all this about? It was five years ago. I was just severely depressed. I wasn't sectioned.'

'Just answer the questions or the lamb I can smell cooking will be burnt to a crisp.'

Greenly sighed and folded his arms defensively. 'I had anti-depressants and some group therapy, that's all.'

'Art therapy?'

'Yes – three or four sessions.'

'Who was the tutor?'

There was a pause. 'Hamish something or other. I can't remember.'

'I think you do,' said Rydell slowly. 'Was he another customer of yours? He did after all paint the picture of Rusty hanging in the hall.'

Greenly sat down heavily as though defeated. 'I admit I've had a few customers over the years. I've never sold to kids though. I do have some principles.'

'The dealing is not my concern,' snapped Rydell. 'I'm interested in Hamish Harland and what you either painted for him in those sessions or told him about.'

Greenly seemed genuinely dumbfounded. But eventually said, 'The barn at Haddon's Farm.'

'You painted that?'

'He told us to paint something that was significant to us so I painted the barn.'

'Why?'

'I used to meet someone there.'

'Who?'

Greenly looked uncomfortable now and he glanced at Liam as if to confirm he had no choice, then his eyes returned to Rydell. 'A young lad. He needed a friend and I was that friend.'

In the recesses of his mind Rydell tried to remember what Ram had found out about the local farms. Nothing came, so he said, 'Why Haddon's Farm?'

'The barn was hardly used and we . . . smoked cannabis and he told me about his dad and the abuse. Physical not sexual.'

'How old was he?'

'Fifteen.'

'So obviously nothing improper happened.' The sarcasm wasn't lost on Greenly.

'I felt sorry for him and I was fond of him, but nothing else.'

'Would he say the same?'

'Of course.'

'Regular little do-gooder, aren't you?'

'It was a long time ago.'

'How long?'

'Fifteen years.'

'Let's get back to the present,' said Rydell. 'Are you friendly with Hamish Harland?'

Greenly shook his head. 'At first he seemed OK, but he had some peculiar ideas.'

'About what?'

'Most things – religion, women. He seemed fixated by the cleansing power of fire, witches and whores and the end of the world. He should have been the patient.'

'And it never crossed your mind that he could have been responsible for the murder and the fire?'

Greenly's expression gave him away. It *had* never crossed his mind. 'I'd forgotten all about him. He was . . . strange, but he never seemed violent. I thought he was a dreamer.'

'Have you ever been to his house?'

'No. I last saw him about four years ago. He came here to paint Rusty. He didn't say much, just got on with the job. And yes, before you ask – he did buy some cannabis.'

'Where is Rusty?' asked Denni.

'Asleep. He's growing old.'

Rydell turned his attention then to Liam King who sat twiddling the laces on a brand new pair of Nike trainers.

'Liam, would you say you are good at doing nothing?'

His young face registered only a little puzzlement. 'Yeah. Got an "A" in dossing about.'

'Can you drive?'

'Yeah.'

'Licence?'

'No.'

'Forget it.'

'I thought you were going to offer me a job.'

'Learn to drive, you might get one.'

'Bollocks.'

Denni managed to keep her curiosity under control until they were driving away.

'What was that all about, Guv?'

'I thought I might use him for a bit of surveillance, but I changed my mind.'

Denni laughed. 'That's a relief. I know the force is hard up but we're not that desperate.'

'Do you want to find your friend or not? And anyway, does this sort of surveillance need a trained cop?'

Denni shrugged. 'No, but it needs someone slightly more intelligent than a mothball.'

'I bet you've never even seen a mothball.'

'I've heard of them.'

'I'll get Ram to do it. He could do with a rest.'

'What do you hope to achieve anyway?'

'Once Harland's on the move in that BMW he can be followed easily enough. And we could do a little unconventional entering of premises.'

Denni felt uneasy about the whole thing but she didn't have much choice and finding Alexis was their aim, how they achieved it was Rydell's responsibility.

Early the next morning they drove to Harland's house. The murder spot in the lane was no longer closed off, but the sheeting was still in place and a few uniformed men remained to search the area. The lane itself had a gloomy, claustrophobic feel especially when there were grey clouds and feeble sunlight. She was relieved when the lane ended and widened into the small hamlet known as Lower End. There were two small terraced cottages, two up two down,

built in 1864, according to the plaque above one. About fifty
yards away stood Forget-me-not Cottage. A conversion of
three cottages into one. White stable doors, ivy resolutely
creeping up the walls, stark white nets at the window. In
one corner of a bedroom window a black and white cat sat
surveying his or her kingdom.

Harland opened the top half of the stable door and let
them in. He seemed pleased to see them. 'We were in the
area,' said Rydell. 'Thought we'd drop in on your rural
paradise.'

'It's nice to have visitors. I like showing off my handiwork. I'll give you a guided tour if you like.'

Denni couldn't help herself. She loved the place. The low
beams and shiny antique furniture were her idea of heaven.
In the main living room a huge fireplace featured a roaring
log fire and on the dining table a tall cut glass vase held a
dozen red roses. A striped silver chaise longue had been
placed by the far window and two sumptuous armchairs in
maroon leather gave the room her idea of classic comfort.

There were no doors that could lead to a cellar and the
long attic room upstairs contained a telescope, a computer,
an easel and paint brushes stored in a wine rack. On a
freestanding black shelving unit, paper and boxes of paint
were stored in descending size order. Harland was obviously
a very tidy man, organised and methodical. But somehow it
gave Denni the impression that his artwork had ceased. As
if he'd organised everything to the point of departure, there
was no work in progress and no work on display.

Rydell gave her a quick nod towards the door. 'I saw a
cat in one of the bedrooms,' she said to Harland. She was
beginning to feel more and more like a prospective buyer.

'Only a pretend cat,' he said. 'Much less trouble.'

Denni asked to use the bathroom and Harland, smiling,
indicated the door. Once inside she opened the bathroom
medicine cabinet. There was fungicidal foot powder, aspirin,
a bottle of indigestion mixture and a bottle of Phenergan. She

was about to close the cabinet when she glimpsed something behind the foot powder. A Lady Shave razor. She searched her pocket for a pair of rubber gloves, found one only, slipped it on and picked up the razor, then turned the glove inside out so that it enclosed her find.

Downstairs Harland was still playing the good and cheerful host and offered them coffee.

Rydell was about to decline when Denni winked at him. 'Yes, thank you,' he said. 'Coffee would be good.' Denni followed Harland into the kitchen and watched him grinding fresh coffee beans. His back was towards her and as she glanced around she noticed, amongst a pile of opened correspondence, a business card edged in green, the word 'Car' visible. Warily watching his back, she pocketed the card. 'It's such a lovely cottage,' she said when the noise of the grinder stopped. 'Are you a man who has a girlfriend to stay occasionally?'

He smiled, but his eyes didn't reflect the smile on his lips. His pupils had dilated and she recoiled slightly when she realised it was lust she saw in his eyes. 'I would,' he said, 'if I knew a woman like you.' She backed towards the sink, but he wasn't a man who could read signals and he came closer so that she could actually smell his aftershave. 'Does your illness,' she blurted out, 'make life difficult for you?'

'What's that supposed to mean?'

'Didn't you tell me you suffered from depression?'

'I don't remember.' He backed away slightly. The smile had gone now, the lust-light fast dimming.

'It must have been someone else,' she said quickly. 'I meet so many people these days who are depressed.'

He visibly relaxed. 'I suppose you'll find out sooner or later. I do see a psychiatrist privately in London. He prescribes anti-depressants when I need them.'

'They must work, because you don't seem depressed now.'

'I don't need them any more. I'm happy, I'm successful. I have everything I want.'

'You're very lucky.'

His mouth tightened. 'Luck has nothing to do with it. I've worked very hard for what I've achieved. You have to be a special kind of person to do what I've done.'

Denni returned to the living room and suddenly she felt sick at the thought of drinking his coffee. She glanced at her watch and feigned surprise. 'I didn't know it was that time. We have to go – an urgent meeting with our bosses.'

'That's a shame,' Harland said. 'Just as I was getting to know you.'

Rydell immediately took her cue. 'Damn – I'd forgotten.' He paused. 'By the way, I believe one of your properties is empty, we'll need the keys to that.'

Without hesitation Harland reached into his pocket and produced a set of keys. Rydell's heart sank. He knew then that their visits would yield nothing. Harland was so bloody cocksure. And perhaps more to the point he hadn't even mentioned finding the dead woman tied to a tree. The dead woman he was supposed to have found only a few hours before.

Thirty-Four

'Is he watching us?' asked Rydell as they sat in the car. Denni turned her head slightly, trying to appear casual. 'He's bloody waving.'

'Give him a royal wave back then.'

'Two fingers would make me feel better.'

Rydell drove a hundred yards or so and then stopped. 'I think we'll visit his neighbours and see if they've heard anything.'

'I found this,' said Denni, producing the plastic card. 'It's a car valeting service.'

'Get it checked out as soon as you can.'

Serious banging on the door yielded no response but Denni peered through the murky front window and saw an old man wearing a cap and dressing gown sitting by a coal fire. Eventually he spotted her and using a Zimmer frame managed to answer the door. Answering questions was a different matter. He was profoundly deaf and seemed confused, but with a mixture of amateur sign language and lip reading they finally got a response. ''Im with the big car you mean?'

They nodded expectantly. 'Don't know 'im. 'E waves at me when he sees me.'

Next door they didn't fare much better. A Mrs Freda Clark told them she was ninety-two and Mr Harland was a wonderful neighbour.

On their way to check out Harland's properties Denni told him about the lady shaver. 'You're a star, Denni,' he said, with a huge smile. '*If* – and it's a big if – Sara Bolten's prints are on it we can go in straight away – battering rams, burly plods, the works.' Then he added, 'Even a court order.'

'So the Sunday nap is off?'

'Certainly is,' said Rydell. 'It's check out his empire then back to the office, get this to the lab, wait for the results of the post-mortem and we could be in luck.'

The Harland properties were squeaky clean, he was a 'landlord in a million' and the two cellars were both empty and unused. In the third house an attic provided a room for two students who thought Harland a little obsessed with fire precautions. All his tenants had to be non-smokers.

Rydell left Denni in the canteen with coffee and a toasted teacake as a reward but was back in minutes with a face like thunder. It was a few moments before he'd calmed down enough to say, 'Nothing's happening till tomorrow. A skeleton staff in the lab and the pathologist can't complete until tomorrow due to pressure of work.'

Denni got him a coffee and a wrapped slab of fruitcake because he never ate unwrapped cakes for some reason and then asked, 'Where's Ram?'

'Gone home, he's not feeling so good.'

'I'd better check he's OK.'

'You do that. See if he's up to a bit of surveillance on Forget-me-not Cottage. If not, I'll find someone else.'

It was dark and beginning to rain as she drove home and seeing her lights on and the curtains drawn gave her that coming-home-from-school feeling knowing someone was in and the place would be warm and the kettle might be on. It wasn't.

Ram was sitting on the sofa holding his head. He muttered one word, 'Headache.'

'Have you taken anything?'

'No. I usually just suffer.'

Denni gave him two painkillers and after about half an hour he felt better and suggested he cook supper.

'Great,' she said. 'I've got two eggs, some Brie, a cabbage that's so old it's got dementia and four shrivelled mushrooms.'

'No problem.'

'You mean you can create a meal from that?'

'No. I'll order a takeaway.'

While they were waiting, Denni told him about Rydell's request. Ram frowned. 'I'll do it if the pills and the curry buck me up.'

'He could find someone else. I don't think you're well enough.'

'I'm as strong as an ox.'

They fell silent for a while. 'Rydell's a good boss,' murmured Denni. 'We don't want to lose him.'

'Why would we lose him?' asked Ram.

'If this investigation doesn't pan out Fenton would do his best to get Rydell transferred.'

'Can't let that happen,' said Ram. Then out of the blue he asked: 'Do you think he's fallen for Alexis?'

Denni laughed. 'He's only met her twice. He seemed more impressed with her tidy flat than her.'

'Could have been love at first sight?'

'What for, her flat?'

'I'm serious,' said Ram. 'It might make him careless if he fancies her.'

Denni wasn't convinced. 'He's not the passionate type.'

'Still waters and all that.'

'I just hope—' She broke off as her front door bell rang. Their curry had arrived.

Ram ate quickly and within half an hour was ready to leave.

'You don't think Harland will panic, do you?' she asked.

'Does he strike you as someone who would?'

'No. But what puzzles me is why his arson attempts on the bodies were so – inefficient.'

Ram nodded in agreement and began putting on his coat.

'Either coincidence or maybe he didn't really want them to burn.'

'A subconscious thing?'

'Yeah. Could be.'

'Our only real hope is for Sara or Maria's fingerprints to be on that razor. At least then we'll get a court order to search his house properly.'

'Where the hell would he be keeping her?' asked Ram.

'There's a garage,' she suggested. 'And a shed in the garden.'

Ram wasn't convinced. 'I think he's been keeping them prisoner somewhere else entirely. He needs keeping under surveillance and following until he's forced to make a move.'

Denni looked so despondent that he added, 'I'll have a nose round the garden and the garage while I'm there.'

'Take care, won't you.'

'One beating a year is all I can cope with.'

Did they really think he was that stupid he didn't know he was being watched and was in fact their main man? He had two options: one was to create a diversion, find a man similar to himself in build and colouring, pick him up in the van, kill him, then set fire to the van. Identifying the body would take some time and in the meantime he could disappear. He could stay in the cellar until the magic time. That option had its risks though, if they came to search the house they might find the cellar.

The second option was not to wait. The conflagration could happen tomorrow, today even, within the hour. He'd been ready for thirty years, what difference did a few days make?

They were all going to fly, flames licking at their heels, the three of them together. But where would they fly from? He had thought this house would be perfect but he'd changed his mind, the house just wasn't high enough. Like 'quality

*assurance' he wanted 'death assurance', and at the moment
the fat Indian in the lay-by was getting in his way.*

Denni couldn't settle once Ram had left, now seemed as
good a time as any to check out the car valeting service.
She searched her pockets, finding it eventually, caught in
the lining of her pocket. Being Sunday, she rang to check
that service was available. It was, but it closed within half
an hour. Last service was in fifteen minutes. She threw on
her coat and drove as fast as she dared.

A young lad in a smart green uniform directed her to a
cubbyhole waiting room and a coffee machine. 'Have you
worked here long?' she asked

'A few months. I do a good job.' He sounded defensive.

'I'm sure you do,' she said. 'I got your card from a man
with a silver BMW.' She reeled off the registration number.
'I thought you might know the owner.'

He gave a slight smirk. 'We have a few BMWs in –
silver's this year's colour.'

'The owner's in his forties, tallish, dark hair, very blue
eyes.'

'I don't notice their eyes.'

'What do you notice?'

'I notice a big tip and he gives a good tip.'

'So you do remember him?'

'Yeah. He's brought his car and his van here a few times.
He's very fussy. Really checks his vehicle out. If he finds
a speck he wants it done again.'

Denni put on her most serious expression. 'This is
important –?'

'Ian.'

'This is a police matter, Ian. Did you ever find anything
unusual in the car or the van?'

He looked only slightly surprised, pushed his peak cap
back and scratched his head as though remembering was

an effort. 'Last time – that was about a week or so ago – I found a load of dog hairs in the back of his van.'

'Did you say anything to him?'

'You must be joking. We're not allowed to make any comments to the customers.'

'Fair enough. Do a good job on my car and I'll make your day. Especially if you can remember the van's registration number.'

'We do keep records,' he said. 'But I remember it anyway.'

She jotted down the number.

'And I remember something else too,' he said. 'But I don't know if it's important.'

'I'll tell you if it's important or not.'

'He always buys his paraffin here. Bought a load last time.'

Denni smiled and mouthed him a kiss. 'That, Ian, *is* important.'

He crushed the sleeping tablets between two spoons, made the tea and tasted it. Slightly bitter but he added two teaspoons of sugar and re-tasted it. Now it was OK. He placed a pile of chocolate biscuits on a plate and walked to the fat man's car. 'Thought you might like some tea.' He did of course. Yes, he did take sugar. And the biscuits were his favourites. The man was a twice-over pig.

He left him then, knowing that in about half an hour the fat pig wouldn't be able to keep his eyes open. In a car he probably wouldn't sleep for more than two hours. Two hours would be enough.

He had to rouse Alexis first. He'd overdosed her a bit. Fucking her the night before had been like fucking a corpse. He laughed. Actually fucking a corpse had been better. Much better. More spiritual somehow. Now she'd let him fuck her, he didn't feel quite the same way about her. She wasn't pure anymore but fire would make her pure again. Purity was hard to find. He'd found it once and only death could reclaim it. Scared? Was he scared? Not any more. He wasn't going alone. And the little brown fat man would never even know he'd left the house. Silly bastards had left it too late. He'd outwitted them all. History would remember him.

Thirty-Five

*N*ow *he'd given it some thought he knew he had no time to waste. Darkness lay all around him like a comforting cloak. He would make his own dawn. Sedating the cop had been easy enough but he could wake at any time. He was strong but he couldn't drag him that far. He picked up the baseball bat he kept under his bed and went to the garden shed. He could manage him in a wheelbarrow.*

When the car door opened the pig had stirred a bit so he'd walloped his skull twice, once above the eye and he had bled just like a stuck pig. He drained the petrol tank so that if anyone came looking for the pig he would simply say he'd realised he was out of petrol and had gone off to find a petrol station. He managed to get him in the wheelbarrow easily enough. He wasn't sure if he was dead or not, but no matter, he gagged his mouth and tied his hands, threw a blanket over him and locked the shed door.

It was beginning to grow dark. Not long now. The paraffin was in the van. Now he would sit and make the faggots of newspaper for their funeral pyre. Fun-er-al. That was a strange word. The burial of the dead started with the word fun. A fune-ral would have been more appropriate.

At six thirty that evening Denni rang Ram's mobile. There was no reply so she left a message. By seven she was beginning to get concerned. She drove to the station and found Rydell busy reading the PM report. He was not in a good mood.

'Ram's not answering his phone, Guv,' she said. 'I'm going to drive out there to check on him.'

He hardly raised his head. 'If he wasn't fit he shouldn't have come back to work.'

'I'll tell him that, shall I?'

'You do that. Be back as quick as you can. We could be raiding Harland's place in the early hours. So don't be seen.'

'By the way I checked out that valet car place,' she said, one hand on the door. 'The lad there remembers him and said he found dog hairs in the back of his van. And he bought paraffin there.

Rydell smiled at last and gave her the thumbs up.

She drove straight to Lower End. The car in the lay-by was without lights but covered in a fine layer of frost. There was no sign of Ram Patel. She opened the car door thinking he may have left a note. There was a message. Only it was in blood: on the dashboard, on the seat, pinpricks of blood on the driver's window. Coagulating blood. She looked towards Forget-me-not Cottage. The lights were on and the curtains were drawn. She didn't think, she ran to the cottage and banged heavily on the door. There was no answer. She ran around to the back of the cottage. The garage door was open. The BMW was there, but not the van.

She rang Rydell on her mobile phone giving him a quick but garbled account. 'Just stay with your car, Denni,' said Rydell. 'I'll be with you in ten minutes or so. If I find you anywhere but in your car, I'll –'

'I get your drift, Guv.'

She felt better at hearing Rydell's calm voice, but now she was trembling and shivering at the same time. Whatever he said she was too hyped-up to sit down. She had her torch in her hand and she began looking for more bloodstains. She didn't have far to look, there was a thin trail leading to a shed at the bottom of the walled garden.

The shed door was padlocked. The tiny window curtained.

She tried kicking the door but nothing happened. With the torch she smashed the window and ripped the curtain out. In the beam of her torch she saw first the wheelbarrow, then Ram's feet. His head was covered, the blanket over his face dark with blood.

She rang the ambulance service. 'I want paramedics or the air ambulance.' Her voice didn't belong to her, it was demanding and high pitched.

'Just stay calm,' said a voice, 'we'll be there as soon as we can. Is the patient's airway clear?'

'I don't bloody know. I can't get to him. I can't see his face. For Christ's sake, he could be dead.'

'Just stay talking to me. Help will soon be there.'

'I can't wait,' she said shoving the mobile phone in her pocket. She ran to her car and drove it alongside the garage towards the corner of the garden shed. With careful revving she thought just one touch would be all it needed. She was wrong, it needed two rams for Ram but finally the wood cracked and split and the corner of the shed caved in. The wheelbarrow was only inches from the car. Throwing back the blanket from his face it was a renewed shock to see more blood than face. She tore off the gag, felt for his neck pulse, then wiped the blood from his mouth with a corner of the blanket. She wasn't sure at that moment if he was alive or dead; whichever he was, she couldn't do mouth to mouth with him in a wheelbarrow.

Hesitating, she had to plan how to get him on the floor without causing more trauma to his head and neck. There was only one way. She held his head and shoulders and dragged him down onto herself. She kicked the wheelbarrow away with her right foot. He made no sound, his body half covered hers. Winded, she managed to ease herself from under him. Gasping, she slipped off her jacket and placed it under his head. Then ignoring the bloody mess of his face she watched his chest rise and fall weakly. And then stop. She started CPR immediately. Robot-like, not thinking, just doing.

Everyone seemed to arrive at once. Paramedics moved her firmly out of the way and began intubating him, putting up an intravenous infusion, placing a collar around his neck, a dressing to his head wound.

'He's stable,' said one of the paramedics after a few minutes. 'Let's get going.'

Denni sat down on her haunches feeling totally drained. She heard Rydell giving orders.

'Take the place apart. Floorboards – the lot. Get on with it.'

She stood up, about to follow, still robot-like but now a robot with no knees. 'Not you, Denni. Stay where you are. Take a few deep breaths.' Deep breaths were the last thing she needed. A slug of brandy would have worked better. She vaguely heard the sounds of doors being battered.

After a while Rydell took her arm, walked her through Harland's back door and sat her down in the kitchen and someone produced hot sweet tea. After a few minutes she began to feel relatively normal.

'Found it, Guv,' shouted someone excitedly. An armchair had been moved and the Persian rug underneath lifted to reveal a trap door. One of the uniformed men went down first and came up quickly. 'Looks like a woman and a baby have been held down there.'

Rydell was already ringing the SOCOs. Then he rang traffic and gave the van details. 'I want the bastard stopped. If necessary get a helicopter out.'

Once the cellar had been found and searched a dull numbness seemed to settle over everyone. There was nothing to do but wait. Denni felt exhausted and only negative thoughts entered her head. Ram probably wouldn't make it and if Harland wasn't spotted by a patrol car that was it – there was no hope for Alexis or the baby. Denni was convinced that Harland had decided that tonight was his own personal millennium. The death knell of almost two thousand years 'celebrated' by bizarre murder and probably suicide.

'I can guess what you're thinking, Denni,' said Rydell. 'But Harland could still be holding out for New Year. We've still got time.'

'Yes, Guv,' she said dully, unconvinced.

Rydell drove her back to Harrowford and suggested he took her home.

'No thanks,' she said with a weak smile. 'Being on my own is the last thing I want but I would like to sit with Ram because I think –' tears choked her voice, 'I think he might die.'

'He's strong, he'll make it.' There was no conviction in his voice.

'I'd like to see him.'

'No problem.'

At the hospital's A&E department they were told Ram was in theatre having a blood clot removed from his brain, after which he would be in intensive care, probably on a life-support machine.

They waited in a side room but after a few minutes Rydell began to look ashen and twiddled with his tie as though he were being choked.

'I should get back to the station if I were you, Guv,' Denni said. 'There may be some news.'

Denni could see his relief and he was on his feet and at the door in seconds. 'I'll keep you posted,' he said, and then he was gone.

'Fingerprint report on your desk,' said DCI Fenton as he emerged from his office. 'Only a partial. How's DS Patel?'

'Having surgery.'

'Bloody shame. Good bloke. We've got to get this bastard.'

Rydell didn't answer. It was too late now. He was out there – free. And now Rydell was beginning to blame himself. He muttered to Fenton, 'I'll stay at my desk however long it takes.' Fenton stared at him for a moment. 'We'll have a drink when this is all over. You look as if you could do with one.'

On Rydell's desk were the PM report on Sara Bolten and the report of a useless partial fingerprint. The post-mortem showed similar characteristics to the findings on Maria's body. Except there was a slight reversal this time – a full stomach, a bath, death by drowning and then sex.

The blood reports for drugs, alcohol and so on would follow. Also on his desk were the reports on Scottish fires that Ram had been working on: pages and pages going back to the 1950s. They knew that Harland had lived outside Edinburgh.

But so far there was no other information on his early background. He may have moved frequently. It was worth checking every fire in and around Edinburgh. He scanned the details of chip-pan fires, kids playing with matches, fires from unprotected open fires, electrical fires, when it occurred to him – the key word was *victim* not arsonist. He concentrated then on those fires where someone had died or had been badly injured.

He carried on reading and knew that he if sat long enough the answer was there. He sighed wearily, at this stage of the investigation details were more likely to be of academic interest only. They would find Harland but probably too late for Alexis and the baby. His only consolation at that moment was the old saying that knowledge equals power. He tried to believe it.

Denni sat by Ram's bed in intensive care. Machines and tubes had taken him over like some alien force. His usual coffee-coloured skin had now taken on a greyish hue and it seemed so bloody unfair to be the fall guy not once but twice. She held his hand and talked to him as if he could hear her, but after two hours she began to feel claustrophobic and tearful. She certainly didn't want to go home and sit alone with her morbid thoughts. What she really wanted was to get drunk and be totally out of it. Just before leaving she kissed his hand and whispered in his ear the only Gujarati prayer she knew. A prayer for a friend:

Bagwaan Hu tamari passe bikh magoo chu
Ka tame mara dosht ne jaldi saroo ka ri duo.

Then she added, 'Sorry about the pronunciation, Ram, but it's the best I can do.'

Outside it was cold with a wind that struck her face sharp as a whiplash. She didn't care and after the initial shock she walked fast towards Harrowford nick.

Rydell looked up as she walked in. 'You could do with a drink,' he said. 'We'll have one later. Just look at this first.'

He handed her a single sheet of paper and there it was – a fire report dated 1969. Harland's name a mere footnote.

At the multi-storey car park, Dick Read and Alan Coutts came on duty at ten p.m. 'Quiet as the grave,' said one of the outgoing security men. 'Is it cold outside?' asked the other.

'Bloody perishing,' said Dick taking off his sheepskin coat and draping it behind his chair in case he needed it in the early hours.

They settled back in their chairs, the soft purr of the CCTV screens the only sound in the room. Their eyes flicked backwards and forwards from town centre screen to the twenty-four-hour multi-storey car park. It *was* as quiet as the grave. The pubs and clubs hadn't closed yet and that was when trouble usually started.

'Time for a brew,' said Alan. The corner of the room boasted an electric kettle and a sink. They brought their own mugs in for tea. Alan produced hot strong sweet tea and they sat, hands cupped round the mugs, gazing at the various screens.

Just after eleven taxis became active picking up people from various venues. A small scuffle broke out outside the Black Bear pub, but a girl intervened and after a few moments of fist raising and a bit of pushing and shoving the girl won.

'These young girls today are worse than the boys,' commented Dick.

'You're right.' Alan paused as he saw a blue van park at the top of the multi-storey. 'That's funny,' he said, peering doggedly at the screen.

'What is?'

'No one's getting out.'

'Could be having a kip.'

'I'll keep an eye on it.'

Dick laughed. 'That's all we ever do.'

A little later scuffles began to break out outside another pub but a patrol car was in the area and it was soon broken up.

'At last a bit of movement from that van,' said Alan. 'A bloke's just got out.'

'I bet his wife's given him the elbow for the night.'

'Yeah, maybe. Check the registration number, see – what the fuck . . . ?'

'Christ! Is that what I think it is?'

'It's either petrol or paraffin. Check the registration. Get the police and the fire service.'

Alan watched in horrified silence as the man helped a woman from the back of the van and then propped her against the parapet. Not only did she seem drunk or doped but also she kept putting her arms up and flailing them around as if she couldn't see and was terrified. Her mouth was gagged with black tape. It was only then he noticed that she had a rope round her neck.

'Police are on their way,' said Dick. 'They've been looking for that van.'

'They could be too bloody late – what's he doing now?'

The man had returned to the van briefly and now returned carrying a bundle, which he handed to the woman. Alan zoomed in on the scene. The 'bundle' he could now clearly see was, in fact, a baby. The woman was pulling away and seemed to be wordlessly pleading with him by offering him back the baby. He ignored her and began placing rolled-up newspaper all round the woman and child. She began kicking out, unseeing, the random kicks sending the newspaper faggots up in the air. The wind whipped at her long dark hair and the man's hand shot out and grabbed the rope, yanking her to him.

'Oh, God,' said Alan. 'This is the worst thing I've ever seen.'

Dick's voice emerged as an excited croak. 'He's trying to get her coat off now.'

He managed to get her arm out of one sleeve, but with her other arm she held the baby. There was a glimpse of a white dress under the coat. Suddenly he took the baby from her, at the same time hitting her backhanded. The blow to her face made her stagger, then she fell to the ground. The man returned to the van with the baby and as he did so the woman began trying to crawl away on all fours.

The security men were so engrossed in the scene they didn't hear the sirens. The woman continued to crawl. When the man reappeared he had the baby on his back in a sling so that his hands were free. He hauled the woman to her feet, roughly removed her other arm from her coat and began dragging her to the parapet and then along to the stone column at the corner. Once she was standing Alan could see the dress properly. It was a nightdress.

It was then that Alan spotted the armed police. Two were crouching at the side wall of the lift. Another two were hiding by the exit stairs. The woman was still struggling and kicking at her captor's legs, although she mostly missed. He grabbed the rope around her neck and tried to haul her up onto the parapet. He gave up after a few seconds and grabbed one of the plastic containers and threw the contents over her. She staggered slightly but her feet still kicked out, hitting nothing.

Then the man turned towards the camera and smiled a slow knowing smile.

Dick's mouth dropped open. 'Fucking hell, he's as mad as –' he couldn't find the words.

'Cunning bastard knows where the cameras are though, doesn't he?' said Alan.

'I'll do it,' said Denni. 'It's no problem.'

'I'm not happy about it,' said Rydell, knowing that this was no time for a debate. 'But I'll be right behind you.'

The blue van was the only vehicle on the top floor. At that moment Denni thought about no one but Harland. She had to give him all her attention. A wrong word from her – just get on with it, she told herself.

'Hamish. Stand still,' she called out through a megaphone. 'I want to talk to you.'

He seemed startled for a moment but he picked up the paraffin container and began dousing himself, pouring so much down his front that it formed a pool at his feet.

'Hamish. Don't move,' Denni said. 'We know about Samantha.'

He stopped then, not turning round. Listening, as if the voice were in his head and not real.

'I know she died,' Denni continued, 'why don't you tell me about it?'

He nodded slightly and fumbled in his pocket, his hand emerging with a lighter. He held it up high above his head – smiling.

'Hamish, this isn't what Samantha wants,' said Denni. 'Let me come closer and talk to you properly.'

'How do you know about Samantha, you bitch? And stay where you are.'

He was ignoring her movements and still trying to secure a struggling Alexis. Denni inched her way forward, she knew Rydell was nearby and that the marksmen were in position but with a baby on Harland's back they were unlikely to shoot unless there really was no choice.

Denni put down the megaphone and walked towards him. He turned sharply from Alexis when he heard her footsteps. 'I told you to stay where you were. I've got an appointment to keep. What do you want – money? I've got money.'

'You're not thinking straight Hamish. You want to join Samantha and die like she did. Is that it?'

'It's destiny. You can't argue with destiny.'

'Is that what Samantha wants? Why would she want another woman and another woman's baby?'

'It's what I want.'

'You're being very selfish. Were you fond of Samantha?'

'Fond? Fond? You stupid bitch.' He picked up another container of paraffin and came towards her menacingly. Out of the corner of her eye, Denni saw Alexis frantically trying to escape from the rope which now bound her to the pillar. Then suddenly the baby began to cry, loudly. It seemed to agitate Harland.

'Give the baby to Alexis,' she said.

He laughed. 'It's my baby. I'll keep it. Do you think I'm stupid? They want to shoot me.'

'I don't want you to get shot, Hamish. You're ill, you've stopped taking your medication.'

'Are you saying I'm mad?'

The baby continued to cry loudly.

'No,' said Denni.

He laughed again. 'Wrong answer, you stupid bitch. Of course I'm fucking mad. But this is *me* now, not a drugged-up zombie. I'm myself and we're on our way.'

'To where?'

'Does it matter? A better world than this.'

'The baby hasn't had a chance in this world. And Alexis, surely her blindness –'

'In the next world she'll see. She'll be grateful.'

'Do you think Samantha will be waiting for you?'

'I've told you already.'

'But will she want another man's baby?'

'She's mine.'

'No she isn't, Hamish. You thought raping Maria caused her to get pregnant. But she was already pregnant.'

'You lying whore . . . you frustrated old cow you . . .' He lunged towards her, the lighter clenched in his fist. She ducked quickly, sidestepping him. A blow caught her on the side of her chin making her stagger. Her hand found the nightstick in her pocket, she clenched it tight and then with her arm in a wide arc brought the nightstick down hard on his wrist. She heard the bone crack, heard his howl of pain heard the lighter skitter across the concrete.

Then the place erupted into a dizzy frenzy of running footsteps, white foam, weak knees, a sick feeling, head whirring. Then came voices and commands, the sound of Alexis's relieved gasps and sobs and through it all, the baby still screamed.

Finally Rydell was leading her away, a blanket around her. 'Is it over?' she asked, totally disorientated.

'I'm proud of you, Denni,' he said.

'Is Alexis OK?'

'She's going to hospital and so are you. That was quite a punch you took.'

She wanted to argue but suddenly she was too tired. She had thought she'd be jubilant once he was caught, somehow she wasn't. She was totally drained. It hadn't gone as she'd planned. She'd made him more manic rather than less.

'I've lost my touch,' she said.

'Shit hot with a nightstick though,' said Rydell.

273

Thirty-Six

*T*he duty psychiatrist was young, he looked about twenty-
two and had a round bland face and half-glasses.

'Hello, Hamish,' he said, smiling as if he were an old pal.
A uniformed police officer stood guard outside the door.

'Hello, Doc.'

'How are you feeling, Hamish?'

'Disappointed. And you?'

He stared at the doctor who shuffled his notes. Eventually
he came up with, 'How long have you suffered with manic
depression?'

He smiled to himself. This bloke was definitely a novice.
He was begging to be tied up in knots.

'Well, Doc, let me think back . . . Since they told me I was
a manic-depressive when I was sixteen, I've been a martyr
to it ever since.'

The doctor ignored his little joke.

'Have you always been non-compliant?'

Non-compliance was psychobabble for not taking the
pills. So he nodded. 'On and off, Doc.'

'Why don't you take the lithium?'

'See this,' he said, showing him his newly plastered arm.
'The plaster of Paris immobilises the bones. Lithium does
the same thing with my brain. My thoughts can't move on
that shit.'

'How does it affect you when you stop taking it?'

'I feel as if I'm going mad and then I get there.'

'So you think you are mad?'

274

'I don't think I am. I know I am. And you know I am.'

The doctor scrawled a few more notes. *'You sound untroubled by the idea.'*

He stared steadily at the half-glasses. *'I suppose you'd say Hitler was mad.'*

'I would say he had a personality disorder.'

He laughed. *'Let me put it this way, Doc. Society, the establishment, health gurus, whatever those words mean, Hitler's beliefs and attitudes were similar.'*

'Would you like to explain what you mean by that?'

The little prat would need it spelling out. *'Hitler wanted everyone to be the same: Aryan, heterosexual, of fixed abode, non-smoking and preferably vegetarian. But of course he had "a personality disorder". How come millions of sane Germans didn't seem to notice or maybe they just didn't care.'*

'So what's your point, Hamish?'

'My point is I'd rather be mad than sheep-like. You see, the average human sheep doesn't have . . . beliefs. The insane have beliefs – maybe they think they're God, or that voices speak to them from the television or that there are voices in their head or even that they've died. But at least they have *beliefs. They don't accept all the bullshit fed to them via the media, they do at least make up their own bullshit. Unless, of course, some medic decides those particular beliefs don't suit.'*

The doctor looked a bit uncomfortable. *'It's our duty to protect those who are mentally ill from harming themselves.'*

'More bullshit. Who gives a toss? One more lunatic topping themselves. Cheap and efficient.'

'We have to—'

'Let me finish it for you, Doc. You feel you have a duty to protect the innocent. God doesn't protect the innocent, so why do you think you can do any better? Mad or bad, that's the question. The answer is the mad can be bad and the bad can be mad. Being mad is an excuse.'

275

'So you think your mental condition excuses rape and murder.'

'I didn't say that. My manic highs give me flights of fancy I enjoy. That's the bottom line, Doc.'

'Tell me about Samantha.'

Did half-glasses think he'd stumble on that one? 'Samantha's dead, but she's waiting for me.'

'Where?'

He laughed. 'She's not on Sauchiehall Street.'

'Where then?'

'Your guess is as good as mine.'

'You were really upset by her death?'

'Yes. Of course I bloody was. I tried to save her . . . but I don't want to talk about it – not to you or the police. I don't see the point. You wouldn't understand. Her dying didn't make me mad or bad. It depressed me. It ruined my life, but even if she'd lived I might still have been as I am now. When I'm really low I think I might have killed her anyhow. The dead can't betray you, or grow older, or change, or stop loving you. She died in a state of grace. A young virgin who loved me. There is only one answer, Doc, and that's death.'

He refused to say anymore and young half-glasses began looking at his watch. Interview terminated. More to follow.

Rydell tried to insist that Denni took time off but since two of her friends were in the same hospital her time off took the form of sitting at bedsides. Ram was still in intensive care on life support, his recovery still in doubt, but at least his vital sighs were stable. Alexis was in a six-bedded unit under sedation but was generally in good condition. The baby lay fat and contented in the children's ward and would soon be found foster parents.

On the second day of her vigil Rydell came in and said, 'I want you back in the office. I need you there to help with writing reports and interviewing Harland.'

She knew he was lying. He could easily manage without her. The case against Harland was watertight. She would have preferred to stay at the hospital partly because she didn't want to see Harland ever again. Perhaps Rydell guessed and thought she was losing her nerve.

In the event, he was sent to a secure psychiatric unit pending further psychiatric assessment. She wished she could feel sorry for him, but she didn't. She felt angry. She wanted to hurt him, wanted to smash *his* head with a baseball bat but she admitted that to no one, least of all to Rydell.

The afternoon of her first day back she went to see Stephanie. She'd just come in from school and she looked worried when she saw Denni. 'It's good news, Stephanie. We've got him. He'll never bother you again. And you won't have to go to court.'

Her young face became wreathed in smiles and she rushed towards Denni. They hugged each other, clinging together, hardly noticing the change from smiles to tears, neither really understanding why they were both crying.

That evening at the hospital Alexis was drowsy but beginning to surface. Her lips were dry and cracked, her face ashen, her neck was ringed with bruising and she clung to Denni's hand as if it were a lifeline. Denni sat without speaking for some time, trying to find the right words and failing. In the end she fell back on, 'How are you feeling?'

Alexis sighed, and then answered in a husky croak. 'I'm not sure. Spaced out. I've been dreaming.'

'What about?' asked Denni, not really wanting to hear about suffering and fear.

'About finding poor Barney's body—' she broke off. Then in a whisper she added, 'He raped me.'

Denni hadn't known for sure but she'd guessed. At that moment she was glad her friend couldn't see her face and the tears welling up. 'The worst part,' continued Alexis, her voice so quiet that Denni had to lean close. 'The worst part . . . after finding Barney, was going down that ladder into the cellar. It was like going into hell . . .' she broke off, silent tears sliding down her cheeks.

When Denni thought Alexis was asleep she got up to leave, but Alexis grabbed her wrist. 'He told me there were others – not just Maria and Sara – buried.'

Denni swallowed hard. So the arrest of Harland wasn't the end. She was about to ask more questions when Rydell walked in. Denni wasn't sure if she should stay or go, but Rydell said, 'Grab a coffee. I'll meet you in reception.'

She turned at the ward door to see Alexis managing a wan smile and Rydell holding her hand. He too was smiling.

The lithium was beginning to kick in. The memories came back with it. Memories of helping Samantha decorate the tree. They were as excited as five-year-olds. They'd spent the evening wrapping presents. He didn't have a tree at home. His mother couldn't be bothered. The lights were still working from the year before and they'd had candles too. She lit three and placed them on the mantelpiece. When he left he told her to be careful. Her mum and dad were out and she was alone in the house. He'd gone home to bed then. They were watching television cuddling up on the sofa, his mother and her current man. They didn't even notice he had come in.

He'd gone to sleep straight away, thinking about Christmas and the tree and her. He'd woken later, he didn't know the exact time, to the sound of glass breaking and Samantha screaming. Terrible, terrible screams. He'd run outside. The ground floor of Samantha's house was fully ablaze. He'd tried to run inside but someone had held him back. The choking smoke was everywhere. Then suddenly he saw her face at the window. She was screaming for help and he was screaming back – 'Break the windows! Jump! Jump!' She broke the window with a chair. 'Jump! Jump!' he kept shouting. And then she did. Her white nightie was white like a wedding dress but with orange flames licking at her legs. She seemed to float down, just like an angel. He was there with his arms outstretched waiting to save her. But he missed. He fell and was knocked out by the bottom of the stone birdbath. A fractured skull, they told him later.

When he came round, he kept asking for her but the nurses said they didn't know where she was. His mother told him in the end, bluntly, 'Sorry, son. She's dead.'

'I tried to save her,' he'd said over and over again until she told him to shut up and pull himself together.

He wasn't allowed to go to the funeral and he never saw her parents again. They left the area straight away.

He read, incredulous, the report in the paper.

TRAGIC DEATH OF TEENAGER

Samantha Anderson, aged fifteen, died of burns and smoke inhalation in what the fire brigade described as an 'inferno'. The house took only minutes to burn down. Samantha was alone in the house at the time and the fire was suspected to have been caused by candles setting fire to the Christmas tree.

A young neighbour, Hamish Harland, aged twelve, collapsed at the scene and was knocked unconscious. He is making a good recovery in hospital.

He asked his mother why the newspaper had got it wrong? Why hadn't they mentioned that he'd tried to save her, that she'd jumped? 'I was there,' his mother said. 'She didn't jump. The smoke got to her. You're imagining things.'

At first he hadn't believed her but other neighbours who saw the fire said the same thing.

He'd realised then how powerful his mind was. How special that made him. Later on, doctors would tell him he had a mental illness. But in his madness lay his solace. Always had been. Always would be. World without end. Amen.